BLOOD TIES

Also by the same author

Our Vinnie
My Uncle Charlie
My Mam Shirley

JULIE SHAW

BLOOD TIES

FAMILY IS NOT ALWAYS
A PLACE OF SAFETY

Certain details in this story, including names, places and dates,
have been changed to protect the family's privacy.

HarperElement
An imprint of HarperCollins*Publishers*
1 London Bridge Street
London SE1 9GF

www.harpercollins.co.uk

First published by HarperElement 2016

1 3 5 7 9 10 8 6 4 2

A catalogue record of this book is
available from the British Library

ISBN 978-0-00-814291-9

Printed and bound in Great Britain by
Clays Ltd, St Ives plc

MIX
Paper from
responsible sources
FSC
www.fsc.org   **FSC™ C007454**

Family is everything. It is the be all and end all, and I have the very best. My husband, my kids, my parents, siblings and all the rest of the clan, I love them all so much. However, the bond between a mum and her daughter is very special. The cord that once bound daughter to mum before birth never really breaks. No matter how far apart they might be, that invisible tether just gets stronger and I'd like to dedicate this book to my beautiful, brave cousin, Tanya Jagger, who is currently fighting the battle of her life, and her equally brave mam, Pauline Jagger, who has endured far more than she could ever deserve.

My Girl

My darling daughter, don't you grieve.
I have not really gone,
It's hard right now, but please believe,
I've been here all along.

I've watched with pride, how much
you've grown,
I've shared your smiles and laughter,
I've felt your pain when you've been alone,
Praying for your happy ever after.

I thought I had more time with you,
Hoped we'd never be apart,
You make me proud, you really do,
I love you, my sweetheart.

Chapter I

Bradford, August 1965

Kathleen was used to being invisible. In fact, she liked it that way, because when people didn't see you, they couldn't hurt you. It never lasted, though; it didn't matter that she was curled up tightly on the couch, saying nothing; she knew it would only be a matter of time before her stepmother noticed her anyway.

Irene was screaming at Kathleen's dad when it happened. 'And what are you frigging staring at, you nosy little get?' she yelled at Kathleen, her fat bosom heaving as she puffed herself up and pointed. 'I bet you're bleeding loving this, aren't you? *Him*!' She jabbed a finger towards her husband. 'Picking on my poor Darren again!'

Kathleen hung her head, letting her hair provide a safety curtain, wondering how anyone could 'love' such a scene. Irene was now jabbing her finger into Kathleen's dad's side, and that was definitely a bad sign – it meant her stepmum was after a fight. The question wasn't really a question, and she knew better than to try to answer anyway. She was just another target at which Irene could vent her anger. She drew in her breath – another reflex – and silently prayed that her dad would step in and take the attention back away from her.

John's tone always grew quieter the more Irene's increased in volume. Sometimes Kathleen thought this might be a good way to calm things down. At other times, she just wished he'd shout back louder. 'Can't you see what he's doing, love?' her father now said quietly. 'It seems that everyone and his horse knows what's going on but you. The lad's got gambling fever, Irene!' he added, with just a slight edge of exasperation. 'He can't possibly lose his wages *every* frigging Friday, can he? Every frigging week? Love, come *on*.'

Kathleen's eyes widened in disbelief. Was he spoiling for a fight as much as she was? Yes, she was happy her dad had deflected Irene's attention back to him again, but accusing her stepbrother of having gambling fever was going to rile Irene even more. She wished she could slip away, hole up in her bedroom – well, if bloody Monica wasn't in there, anyway – but her way was blocked and, besides, she knew all too well that if she moved, she'd just become the target of Irene's fury once again. She needed precious little encouragement to yell at her at the best of times.

Kathleen watched her stepmother puff herself up even further, like a balloon that was in danger of being blown up too much. 'Gambling fever? Gambling *fever*!'

she screamed, predictably, her bust now almost bursting through her blouse. It was made of red satin, an even brighter shade than her hair, and was much too small for her; almost everything she liked to wear was. She lunged at her husband now, both fists hammering at his chest, and Kathleen was struck by what a ridiculous sight she looked, because her dad was a full ten inches taller. 'You miserable twat!' she yelled. 'My poor boy gets robbed on his way home from work again – *again*! And do you have any sympathy? No, you do not! Be a different story if it was little miss prig over there, wouldn't it? But, no – all you can do is call him a frigging liar! How dare you! You better shut your trap, John Adamson, or I swear, I'll shut it for you. So help me, I will!'

Kathleen tried hard to see the humour. To hang on to the ridiculous image of her stepmother as a balloon that, once upon a time – how long ago was that? – would have at least made the shouting more bearable. But she'd lost the knack. Now it was all she could do to hold back the tears. All she wanted to do now was to simply open her mouth and scream. She was sick of it. Sick to death of it. Sick of the wretched, repetitive drudge of it. Sick of every day seeming to hold the stomach-churning potential for upset and violence and bile. Sick of living above a pub, wishing she could go back to being in school again. Wishing she could go anywhere – anywhere to escape this horrible place. She was sick of her entire life seeming now to revolve around it; the monotonous grind of working all hours in a job she could not detest more.

Most of all, though, Kathleen was sick of the family she'd inherited when her father, having taken over as landlord at the Dog and Duck had attracted – and married – this cow of a woman. That had been a day to remember – the day she'd *always* remember, as being the one where her old life had come to an end. The day she'd been gifted not just a wicked stepmother worthy of any gruesome fairy tale, but an ugly stepsister (ugly on the inside even if she wasn't on the outside) and a stepbrother who, though he could occasionally be kind to her, was – as was so often the way with Darren lately – the root cause of her current misery.

Irene was an idiot. A stupid woman who couldn't see past her own nose. Not when it came to her precious son. And since Darren himself was the one who understood that the best, he never wasted an opportunity to exploit it. He didn't pull any punches about it, either. So much so that all the regulars in the Dog and Duck knew the truth of what was happening, and how Darren was taking the piss out of Irene. But, oh, how she wished her dad hadn't just said what he'd said. Not just because it set Irene off on one of her rages but because everyone downstairs in the pub would be able to hear it – and knowing Mary, the other barmaid, they'd be able to hear it all too well, because she'd probably turn the music down so that everybody could have a laugh.

Worse still, though, was that this could go on for hours yet. Once Irene was off on one, she didn't have an off button. Kathleen glanced at her watch. She really needed to leave them to it. She was due on the bar again in an hour and she'd yet to even have her bath. She shifted her legs a little, which had stuck to the stupid plastic cover Irene insisted on keeping on her stupid settee. *Why the fuck she insists on covering this piece of shit up, I'll never know*, she thought as she painfully extracted the back of her thighs from it. Happily, Irene was too busy shouting at her dad and punching him in the chest to notice, so she was able to stand up and slip past the pair of them to the door.

Well almost. She'd not quite reached it when she felt a sharp tug on her pullover. 'Go on, you ugly little bastard,' Irene spat. 'This is all your fucking fault!'

How the fuck is any of this my fault? Kathleen thought. She remained silent, though, knowing better than to voice something so inflammatory. Instead, she found herself cringing slightly, as she so often did, in anticipation of the usual crack around the head. But it seemed Irene hadn't finished ranting yet.

'If *he* didn't have you to support,' she railed, almost as if she'd known what Kathleen was thinking, 'we wouldn't be in this sorry position in the first place! Fucking leeching off us all the time, never out of our frigging sight, then maybe your *father* wouldn't begrudge my frigging kids a bit of something when they need it!'

5

'Irene!' John shouted finally. 'For God's sake, let the girl go. She's got to get ready for work, hasn't she? And there's no point giving her a bollocking, is there?'

With Irene letting go of her, so she could return to the assault on her husband, Kathleen took the opportunity to slip out of the door. And she would have legged it, had she not almost fallen arse over tit over Darren himself, who'd clearly been squatting down, earwigging at the keyhole. He was twenty. A grown man. But he looked like a ten-year-old, sneaking around, looking like the shifty sod that he was.

He stood up. And then he grinned at her. 'Steady on, kidda,' he whispered. 'You'll do yourself an injury.' He gave Kathleen a friendly slap on the back. 'Everything alright in there?'

Kathleen didn't even reward him with a dirty look. 'You know damn well it isn't, Darren,' she hissed. 'Have you gambled all your wages away again?'

'Tut, tut, tut, our young 'un,' Darren said, managing to mock her even as he'd caused so much shit. 'I was robbed on me way home again. Two black 'uns it was. Big as houses and bold as brass, the pair of them. It's called "demanding with menaces", it is. Should be a law against it, shouldn't there?'

'And I suppose she's subbing you all week again to make up for it, is she?' Kathleen demanded, shaking her head. She stabbed a finger towards the living-room door. 'You cause all this shit, Darren. *You*. So how is it

6

fair that it's me that's on the end of it all the time? I'm the one who has to work here, remember? You're off doing your job, and Monica's off doing hers. And *I'm* the one who has to deal with all the *shit* you create!'

She could feel tears – angry, frustrated tears – threatening to spill over her cheeks. She sniffed hard to stop it happening. God, how *sick* she was of it.

'Hey, them's the breaks, our kid,' Darren said before walking off, whistling, leaving Kathleen open-mouthed in his wake.

An hour later, in the bar, Kathleen kept her 'trap shut', as always. That she must keep her trap shut was one of Irene's most frequent orders, and, having no wish to heap even more attention on her excuse for a family, she was only ever happy to oblige.

Not that she cared that Mary, their regular barmaid, would have already filled all the regulars in on what had gone off. Once perhaps, but she was way past that now. In fact, lately, she realised, she'd even stopped being embarrassed when the locals took the piss over their pints. It was as if they'd even developed a kind of camaraderie with her, complicit in their amusement that Irene could be so thick as to keep falling for all the lines Darren spun her.

'I wish I had a mother like yours, Kathy,' one of the estate lads was saying. 'I'd get fucking robbed every week an' all.'

7

His mate burst out laughing, and handed an empty pint glass across for Kathleen to fill. 'Nah, come on, Gez,' he ribbed his mate. 'Shame on you. You're making out like Darren's lying! Like he's not in the bookies every single bleeding day backing anything that moves. Give the poor lad a chance. He's been robbed blind. *Again*.' He winked at Kathleen. 'Any one of us could be as unlucky as he is.'

Kathleen felt a smile twitch her lips, if only a small one. And for all their ribbing, they were just speaking the truth. She knew it, her dad knew it, Monica probably knew it too – well, if she could find the energy to think about anything other than herself for two minutes at a stretch. No, the fact was that Darren's problems with gambling were common knowledge, and no one could believe that Irene *didn't* know it.

Kathleen pulled a nice top on the beer for him. 'You're right,' she said mildly, glancing from one to the other. 'My brother is the unluckiest lad in the world, he is. Take no notice of all the gossip. He hasn't got the gambling fever at all. He's just got big bloody holes in his pockets.' She allowed her smile to widen. 'That and a face that thieves like to punch ...'

The two lads roared with laughter and Kathleen laughed with them. This shift – the seven-till-nine one – was the one bright time in her day. With her dad and Irene upstairs having their tea (or tonight, perhaps, throwing it at each other) it was a port in the storm before her dad came down and joined her and Irene did likewise – though her version of work was slightly different; more waltzing around the tap room playing the big 'I am'.

But for these two hours, she felt free. She felt able to be herself. And it occurred to her that, actually, it was more than just that. For those two hours every day, people actually wanted to talk to her.

For two hours a day she wasn't invisible.

Chapter 2

Kathleen always tried to wake up before the alarm went off in the mornings, but given how late she'd had to work the previous evening, she was still surprised to find herself staring at the ceiling a full quarter hour before it did.

Not that she couldn't have predicted it. It was always the same when her dad and stepmum had one of their rows: Irene having one of her convenient migraines come on (because of all the shouting, *obviously*) then demanding that her dad stay up in the flat with her for the evening, leaving Kathleen to pick up the resultant slack.

Silly old cow, she thought. *Pathetic*. Though even more pathetic was the way her dad ran around after her all the time. Always had. She lay still a little longer, contemplating the unfairness of it all, then reached across to the brass alarm clock that sat on the chest of drawers that separated her bed from Monica's, and clicked it off before it started ringing.

The air in the bedroom was cold, despite it supposedly being summer, and the lino beneath her bare feet felt icy. This was her dominion, being first up, braving the cold and – for half the year, at least – the dark, but Kathleen had learned to find a grim satisfaction in her Cinderella status. Always the first up. Always the one brewing the tea, opening the curtains and, in the winter, stoking the fire. Only then would she dare to get her stepbrother and stepsister out of bed – then clean the pub. Only *then* would her dad and Irene get out of bed.

As she tiptoed out of the bedroom, Kathleen glanced back at her sleeping stepsister and smiled to herself. It was funny, because today and for the next two whole months, they would be the same age. Both seventeen. Two months during which Monica couldn't drone on about Kathleen being *only* sixteen. Come her own birthday, of course, Kathleen would start being *only* seventeen. But she'd enjoy the hiatus while it lasted.

Not that today would be much different to any other day. Yes, it was Kathleen's birthday, and yes, her dad had promised her he might take her to the pictures to see *The Sound of Music*, but if past birthdays were anything to go by, she wasn't going to hold her breath. Instead, she clung to memories of happier times, when her real mother had still been alive. Before she'd died in the car crash, Kathleen's mum had made every birthday special. Trips out and parties, fancy dresses and visits to family – these were always on the agenda, sometimes all on the same birthday, but that was all a long time ago. Since she was eight – that was the last one, still bright in her memory – a birthday was really no different from any other day. Well, except in so much as they served to remind her of the distance that was growing, and would carry on growing, between her childhood and the place she was now. How much she yearned to grow up, have it gone.

Her arms mottling from the cold, Kathleen pulled a thick cardigan over her nightie and ran downstairs to the bar. It wasn't time to start the cleaning yet, but this was another of her rituals; to make a rough assessment of how bad it was so she could work out how long it was going to take.

She had to factor in extra time today, as well, it being Saturday, because on Saturdays, as well as cleaning the tap room and toilets, the foyer and back of bar, there was also the best room to give a proper clean. That was a particularly long job because in order to vacuum the enormous expanse of carpet, all the chairs had first to be lifted onto the tables.

She completed her inspection. Two hours, she reckoned, heading back into the foyer to go upstairs again, then she'd have some time to herself for a bit. She was just at the foot of the stairs when the letterbox rattled behind her, as Eddie the postie fed a clutch of letters through the slot. 'Morning!' she called out, waving to him through the frosted glass. She liked Eddie. He was a habitually smiling presence in a day often lacking them. He'd also, it seemed, delivered something for her.

Kathleen never got post. After all, who would write to her? Even on this day, her birthday, such cards as she might get would be delivered by hand. She'd had a pen friend once – a wild-looking girl called Ingrid, who lived somewhere in Germany, and would write to Kathleen in halting, sometimes comic English, but once she went to secondary school, it had all fizzled out. Since then, there'd been hardly anything, the only moment of excitement being when she'd written to a nature organisation, as part of a school project about wildlife conservation, and had received several leaflets, a letter and a poster of a tiger, which adorned her part of the bedroom wall for a good two years.

Funny to realise that she actually felt wistful about school now, despite counting the days till she'd left. But perhaps her eagerness to leave was because she saw better things ahead of her, yet, here she was, just over a year later, stuck working in this place, working like a skivvy for a paltry wage.

She scanned the envelope, wondering who on earth it might be from. There was something familiar about the handwriting, though, even if it was all written in capitals, and when she saw the postmark, it dawned on her who the sender might be.

She ripped open the envelope, as she climbed the stairs back up to the flat, smiling as she pulled out what was indeed a birthday card, and from the person she'd thought it might be from – her Auntie Sal. She was thrilled to see a ten-shilling note fluttering out, but then her face fell. This must mean that she wasn't going to visit. And so it seemed, as she read the short message:

Have a lovely day, Kathleen
So sorry I can't be there but our Lisa has the mumps.
Hope to see you soon, though – just as soon as we're
no longer infectious!
Lots of love, Auntie Sal xxx

Sally McArdle wasn't really Kathleen's aunt. She was, in fact, her stepmum's younger sister. Married to a lovely man called Ronnie (who she called uncle, and who was the blueprint for the sort of man she hoped to marry one day) Sally was the complete opposite of Irene. Blonde, slim and pretty, and with the sort of personality that could light up a room as soon as she entered it, she was everything Irene was not, and, as such, that Irene hated in a woman. Which was part of the reason that Kathleen loved her so much.

Auntie Sally lived in Thornton, which was two buses away, so she wasn't able to visit all that often. But when she did, she always spoiled Kathleen rotten. She'd bring her a new jumper or something, and always a bar of Fry's Chocolate Cream. She also shouted at Irene if she was being nasty to Kathleen, which meant she shouted at Irene quite a lot.

Kathleen could never quite fathom how you could have the joy of a proper sister (as opposed to Monica, who she'd never grace with that name, despite her dad, from day one, always suggesting she should) and manage to hate her so much. Kathleen would have loved a sister – or a brother, just a sibling to call her own – but Irene didn't seem to like Sally at all; she called her all sorts of names behind her back, and hated it when she visited. She had even accused Kathleen's dad of fancying her. 'You'd love to get her into the kip wouldn't you, you dirty old get!' she'd yelled once after Sally had left. 'I've seen the way you leer at her.' That had been followed by the usual four-hour argument, with her dad having to crawl round Irene and tell her how beautiful she was and how he didn't ever want anyone else. It made Kathleen want to puke.

The kettle was whistling on the stove so she quickly propped the birthday card up on the breakfast table before filling the teapot. It was a huge blue ceramic thing and weighed half a ton, but a year of working long hours in the pub had built up her muscles. She might be downtrodden, but she was young, fit and strong, and that pleased her, even if it was just another reason for Irene and Monica, both short and podgy, to resent her.

She spotted Irene's cigarettes on the windowsill and pinched one to smoke while the tea brewed. She did this most mornings, and didn't feel a shred of guilt about it. Irene made sure half her wages got taken straight off her for her board and lodgings, so there was never enough left to justify buying her own Woodbines – and certainly not when her stupid stepmother was so careless with her own. It was another ritual she enjoyed before the rest of the family rose. The back door of the flat opened out onto a small section of flat roof with a railing round it, from when the last owners of the Dog and Duck kept their dog there. Now it served as a sort of patio, perfectly placed as a sun trap, and though her table and chair were an upturned beer crate and a wonky stool respectively, it always felt a treat to be out there, out of the way, with just her own thoughts for company.

Despite the nip in the air, the sun was shining and the day looked like being glorious, so Kathleen lingered as long as she could before going back in to start rousing the family. Darren was first; he needed to be off soon for his early start down at the hospital, and as she went into his bedroom her nose was immediately assaulted by the stale, smelly air that filled the room. What was it with lads and their bodily functions? It was the same in the gents downstairs in the pub. The ladies was never half as bad.

'Daz! It's half seven,' she whispered, shaking him awake. 'Time to get up.'

Darren rubbed his eyes and yawned, adding another gust of fetid air into the room. He looked done in and Kathleen wondered what time he'd come in the previous evening. He was a closed one – you never really knew what was going on in his head. Not these days, anyway. Not since he'd left school, really.

He sat up and rubbed the heels of his hands into his eye sockets. 'Ooh, is there some tea on, our kid?' he asked, as if there wasn't tea on *every* morning. Still, at least Darren appreciated how much she did.

'Course there is,' she said. 'But you'd better hurry up. And don't you be falling back to sleep,' she added, fanning her face in the wake of another gale of foul air, 'because I'm not coming back in here again, you smelly get!'

She left Darren and trotted along the corridor back to her and Monica's room. It wasn't much of a room, really – not like the big bedrooms that people always seemed to share on telly – just two beds, a chest between them, a wardrobe and a sink. A tight squeeze for two girls and all their things. Well, all Monica's things, mostly, because she had so many more of them, so she had three drawers to Kathleen's one, and took up most of the space in the wardrobe – in fact, Kathleen had never really considered it to be her room. It felt like Monica's, right down to the horrible brown velvet curtains she'd chosen, which sucked all the life from the room, even when they were open, making everything seem relentlessly dark and dingy.

'Time to get up, Mon,' Kathleen whispered now. Monica wasn't what you'd call a 'good' waker.

'Oh, piss off, Kathleen,' she growled. 'It can't be half past yet.'

'It's twenty to eight,' Kathleen corrected. 'Come on, Mon, get up. And hey, guess what?' she added, unable to resist it. 'Me and you are the same age now. How crazy is that?'

Monica groaned and wriggled herself up into a sitting position. First thing in the morning, before she'd applied all her war paint, Monica looked a lot like Darren. Same eyes, same rounded chin. They weren't that close, though. Darren was too much Irene's golden boy for that to happen. Mostly on account of simply being the boy. Kathleen didn't think Irene liked females in general. 'Oh, yeah, I forgot,' she said groggily. 'It's your birthday today, innit? Well, many happy returns and all that.' She flapped a dismissive hand. 'Now piss off out while I get dressed.'

'Dressed' in Monica's case didn't really cover it. It was a full twenty minutes after Darren had left (and in a right arse because it was the biggest racing day of the week so he hated working every other Saturday) before she appeared in the kitchen, done up to the nines. Monica told everyone she was a hair stylist, but in reality she was no more than a bit of a dogsbody for Carol, who ran the local hairdresser's from her house on the estate. Carol operated from her back room and the majority of her clients were pensioners, and as they mostly wanted curly perms, Monica's job mainly consisted of winding perm curlers around grey hair and sweeping up. Not that she'd ever admit that. Far from it. She liked to give the impression she was working at a fashionable top-end salon, and dolled herself up accordingly. Immaculate hair and make-up, mini skirt and heels – all to go run around after Carol and her pensioners all day.

Still, Kathleen conceded, at least she made an effort. Perhaps it was good that she acted like she did – you never knew. Perhaps one day Monica *would* work in some fancy city-centre salon, whereas Kathleen could see little for herself in the future, other than toiling away in the pub, running around after her horrible step-mother, and for what? Out of some stupid idea that she couldn't leave her dad. That he needed her to stay there. That if she left and found something better, they'd be somehow broken. Like she was abandoning him, leaving him, just like her mum had.

She was busy taking her frustrations out on the beer pumps when her dad wandered down. 'Morning, lass,' he said coming round to join her behind the bar. 'By 'eck, you're doing a grand job of them brasses, girl. I can see my face in them.'

He made a big show of looking, too, turning his chin one way then another. She wondered if he'd remembered that it was her birthday, but decided not to give him an opportunity to prove that he might have forgotten. If he had, then she'd rather not know. So she helped him.

'Morning, Dad,' she said brightly. 'Did you see the card upstairs from Auntie Sal? That was nice of her, wasn't it? Shame she can't come and see us, though.'

'I did, lass,' he said. 'And don't you worry. I haven't forgot. Happy birthday, love,' he added, giving her a cuddle.

She decided she believed him anyway. 'Well, what with yesterday and all that, I thought you might have. I wouldn't blame you if you did,' she added, even though she would – deep down, she would. 'Anyway, we still off to the pictures, then?'

It was only then that she realised her dad had something for her behind his back, but there was something in his expression that signalled not all was well. He handed her an envelope with her name on, and a large paper bag. 'I can't do it, love,' he said, his face a picture of guilt and misery. 'I completely forgot the brewery were due this afternoon. *Completely* forgot. Well, till your mam reminded me. But we'll do it another day,' he promised, gesturing towards the bag now in her hand. 'Go on, take a look, lass. I think you'll like what we've got you, at least.'

Kathleen thanked her dad through gritted teeth. Trust Irene to mess things up on her birthday. Not that she'd expected any less, because Irene was a cow, but couldn't her dad, just for *once*, find the guts to go against her? To tell her that no matter what, he was going to do something with his own daughter, and she could piss off and see the brewery men without him?

But expecting that was like expecting it to snow in July. It wasn't going to happen, and that was that. She opened the bag, already knowing that the present was going to be a record, and it was. And the one she most wanted. She felt a rush of affection for her dad then, for going into Smith's and getting it. For caring enough to know exactly what to choose. It was 'I Got You Babe' by Sonny and Cher, Kathleen's current favourite song – and everyone else's pretty much, because it was currently number one, and might even have been sold out before he got there.

'Oh, thanks so much, Dad,' she said, reaching up to kiss his cheek. 'I'll go give it a play soon as I've finished down here.'

John smiled at her, clearly pleased to have chosen so well. 'Wait till your mam's come downstairs, eh? Only I didn't tell her I'd bought it, and what with Darren losing all his money this week, she'll be in a right mood if she thinks I've been splashing out on you.'

Kathleen's cheerful mood dissolved as quickly as beer foam into a bar towel. 'She's not my mam!' she reminded him. 'And, Dad, it's my frigging birthday! What does she expect?'

'Come on, Kathleen,' he urged. 'You know how things are. Don't make trouble. And don't let her hear you saying she's not your mam, either. She tries her best for us, love, you know that. You might not always realise, but she does.'

Kathleen bit her lip to prevent the words she wanted to say from spilling out, because all she'd get was the usual gentle lecture – which was *still* a lecture – about how she was too young to understand the complexities of life and how, once she was older, she'd understand it better, and so on and so on and bloody so on. But how complicated could it be? Irene wore the trousers. Irene bossed her dad around. Her dad let her. That was all there *was* to know about it.

And, as a consequence, she not only wasn't going to the pictures, she wasn't even going to be allowed to enjoy her birthday present – hell, she didn't even have her own record player to play it on, so had to 'borrow' Monica's, like that was in any way fair! All that, and he still called the cow her 'mam'. That woman who she'd heard so many times point out to people that no, Monica and Darren were hers, but *she* wasn't – she was 'John's girl'.

She opened the envelope. 'Oh, don't worry, Dad, you're safe,' she said, unable to suppress the sarcasm. 'I won't be finished in here till after then anyway, will I?'

In answer, he gently patted her, then headed off to the cellar to sort out the barrels. He was already out of sight when she realised what he'd put in the card. 'Happy birthday', yes, above the usual couple of lines of printed verse, but underneath he'd written 'Lots of love from Dad'.

'What about this?' she called after him, holding the card up. 'Am I allowed to put it up, or is this a secret too?'

He popped his head back round the door. 'What, love?'

'Is this card a secret, too?'

He looked confused, and she immediately regretted what she'd said. However much he infuriated her, he was still her dad and she loved him.

'Doesn't matter,' she said. 'Go on. You're fine. The card's lovely. I'll pop it up with Aunt Sally's once I'm done here.'

But all she could think of was how there was anything else to understand in the fact that her 'mam' hadn't even signed her birthday card. How many brain cells did you need to understand *that*?

She grabbed the duster again and started attacking the final pump. *Happy Birthday to me*, she thought grimly.

Chapter 3

'Haven't you done in that bathroom yet?' Irene was shouting. Kathleen sighed and gave a very satisfying two fingers to the closed door.

'I won't be a minute, Mam,' she called back. The word 'mam', as always, stuck in her throat.

'I don't know why you bother, girl,' Irene shouted back waspishly. 'No amount of bleeding make-up could make that gormless face look any better. Now hurry up, I'm going to pee myself out here.'

Kathleen smiled at her reflection in the mildewing cabinet mirror. The old cow could just bloody well pee herself then. She grabbed an elastic band from the side of the sink and carefully smoothed her shoulder-length hair back into a high ponytail, then eased the hair out at the top so she could make it all bouffant, like all the pop stars like Lulu and Dusty Springfield did. She took her time. She didn't care about her stepmother's bladder, because it wasn't her fault she had to use the bathroom first, was it? It was Mary's.

Well, not so much her *fault*, because she couldn't help being ill, could she? Kathleen understood that. But it was absence of Mary that had put Kathleen behind. She'd sent her husband round with a note for Irene first thing that morning, to let her know that she wouldn't be able to do her shift on the bar. And, of course, Irene couldn't *possibly* be expected to do it – at lunchtime? On a Wednesday? So, of course, it fell to Kathleen, on top of all the skivvying she'd still have to spend the afternoon doing – cleaning the flat, doing the washing, shopping for food and then cooking it, so her poor worn-out step-siblings would have a meal on the table for when they got home from their *much* harder jobs.

The only solace, and one she clung to, was that while she was upstairs and Irene and her dad were busy down-stairs, she could borrow Monica's record player and play her few records, while fantasising about all the pop stars who might whisk her away to a more exciting life than the one she had now.

Her dad was, as usual, down in the pub's cellar at this time, so with Darren and Monica both at work, it just left the two of them in the flat. On a normal day, Kathleen would keep herself out of Irene's way, but, still seething about her stepmother's hand in last weekend's non-birthday, today she felt a powerful urge to dawdle as long as she could, just for the sheer pleasure of wind-ing Irene up.

'Nearly done!' she called, gaily, as she sat on the closed toilet seat and adjusted the straps on her sling-backs. 'I'm just finishing off my hair.'

But she couldn't stay in there for ever. One last check – she liked herself better in a ponytail – and she unlocked the door. The grin soon disappeared.

'Horrible little cow,' Irene spat as she clipped her round the head, before pushing past her awkwardly, having to hobble because of her urgency, and slamming the door behind her as forcefully as she could.

'Now get down them stairs and get some frigging work done!' she yelled from behind the door. 'And I've told you before, madam, you can't make a silk purse out of a sow's ear!'

Or a human being out of a witch, Kathleen muttered to herself as she trotted down the stairs, enjoying the feeling of her ponytail swishing from side to side behind her.

Kathleen was already in place behind the bar before her dad came up to open the front doors, looking out across the sea of neatly arranged chairs and tables, through the sash windows and over the hedges that were threatening to shut the light out, to what little she could see of the bright day beyond. Which was probably all she would see of it, too.

Still, it being a Wednesday, there wouldn't be a queue waiting, and the regulars would stroll in in their own time. You could set the clock by most of them, and each had their own drinking pattern. First would come the drunks, with the day stretching ahead of them, because they were all unemployed, then, from twelve till one, the workers, keen to fit in as many pints as they could before returning to their various jobs, then the pub would close for a bit, and it would be back to washing up and cleaning, while her dad went back to the cellar, getting the barrels ready for the evening – and more than likely filtering a gallon or so of water to the ones that were already on, just to eke the profits out that bit further.

They'd then reopen for the tea-timers. Almost exclusively men, these would be the ones stopping off on their way home, and who'd be rolling home to their wives and kids at about eight, much the worse for wear – or a bit before that, if their wives came looking for them. Then it was the night crowd. The cycle rarely changed. Day in, day out, the same. And Kathleen wondered at the repetitive nature of it all. There should be more to life, shouldn't there? Perhaps they enjoyed it, but sometimes the thought of standing here, pulling pints, for years and years, filled her with a profound sense of gloom. She could almost see herself, hand gripping a pump, a decaying skeleton, rictus smile still held firmly in place.

She was shaken from her reverie by the sound of the front door going, and painted on the smile automatically. Because the smile was important. The most important thing about being a barmaid. Her dad had told her that a while after her mum had died, and she'd

27

asked him how he could joke with the punters when all she wanted to do every day was cry. So he'd told her. He'd explained that once you were a grown-up, no matter how sad you were you had to roll your sleeves up and paint a smile on your face when you were working, and do all your crying on the inside.

It had stayed with her that, and it had been something of a comfort. Where previously she'd thought he hadn't cared as much as she did, it was a comfort to know he was crying just like she was, even if nobody could see. And now she was seventeen, she did it almost automatically. No matter what was going on in your life – whether it was everything or nothing – you forgot about it and smiled inanely at everyone.

Her first customer, for instance, who was a middle-aged regular, who'd been hurt in a demolition accident. It had left him with a limp – he was limping across to her now, very obviously – and though he was only in his forties, a face that seemed much older. Which sort of fitted. He was 'retired', or so his line usually went, though, according to Irene, who never had a good word to say about anyone, he was just a lazy bastard who didn't have a good day's work in him.

'Morning, Jack,' Kathleen trilled, liking Jack because Irene didn't. 'A pint of mild is it?'

'Please, love,' he said, dragging a bar stool to his favourite spot. 'No Mary today?'

'No, she's poorly,' Kathleen told him, expertly pulling him a nice frothy top. 'So you have me to put up with today, I'm afraid.'

Jack grinned. 'Now't wrong with that, kid,' he said, winking at her as he settled on his stool. 'And mebbe Mary'll be off a few days yet, eh? Wouldn't mind that. Have you and that pretty sister of yours serving me any day, I would.'

Kathleen tried not to grimace, because she knew she should be above that. It wasn't like he was telling her she was ugly, after all. And Monica *was* pretty. No doubt about it. Well, when she was tarted up, which she mostly was. Everyone said so. 'Pretty sister' tripped off everybody's tongue. Though not to Monica, she suspected – no, she *knew* – about her. It was her job to be the plain Jane. The dull presence beside which Monica could more easily shine.

She wouldn't normally do it – the smile was all, the smiling attitude very much a part of it – but today she 'accidentally' banged Jack's pint glass into the pump as she passed it across the bar, knocking some of the head off and ensuring it would flatten within minutes. 'Oh sorry, Jack,' she said, smiling sweetly. 'I'm *such* a clumsy mare.'

By mid-afternoon, Kathleen was getting face-ache. It was hard trying to look thrilled to bits all the time about being at the beck and call of the punters, and the minutes seemed to be crawling by today. It didn't help that it was quiet – far too nice a day to be sitting in a smoky bar – but with those that were in were all sitting chatting, full glasses in front of them, at least it meant she could nip out the back for a pee and a quick ciggie, her dad not allowing her to smoke behind the bar – it was either out *in* the bar or in the toilets.

She headed out into the foyer. It was Terry Harris, one of the regulars, who was a long-distance lorry driver – a job that, to Kathleen, always sounded so appealing. He must be here at this time because he'd just finished a local job. He was feeding coins into the one-armed bandit, and he turned when he heard her. 'Alright, lass?' he asked her.

Kathleen felt herself colour. She always did when she saw him because he was so ridiculously handsome. To her, anyway. And tragic. He was only young, but already a widower, his wife having died in a house fire a couple of years ago. Everyone felt sorry for him; some of the older ladies would sigh every time he passed. 'Oh, hello, Terry,' she said, 'I'm just nipping out back.' She gestured. 'But I can get you a pint first, if you like.'

He shook his head, and gripped the machine's arm, curling his long fingers around it. 'No, love, I'm alright for a bit,' he told her. 'You go on.'

She turned to go, happy to hide her blush, but then he called her back. 'I'll wait for you here actually,' he said. 'If that's alright.' He looked suddenly awkward. 'Only, there's summat I wanted to talk to you about.'

Kathleen left him then, feeling the heat in her face as it collided with the cold air coming from the ladies' loo. She stood a moment before lighting her Woodbine, looking at her face in the mirror above the sink, wishing she'd put on a bit of make-up, sorted her ponytail out a bit better and just generally *looked* better. Made that bloody silk purse out of the sow's ear that was stood in front of her, in its dowdy blouse and skirt.

She lit her ciggie. She wished she could stop herself blushing at the sight of him, but she never seemed to manage it. It was something she didn't seem to have any sort of control over. It was a stupid crush – she knew that. He was thirty-three, for God's sake! – and she fervently hoped now she was seventeen she'd grow out of it. But there was just something. Something about his face, the way he smiled, the way he'd let his wavy hair grow. Be longer than hers soon, she reckoned. She liked that. That and the aura of sadness, despite his smiles. And there was a connection, too. Because Terry worked with her Aunt Sally's Ronnie, who was his best mate.

Kathleen took a drag on her cigarette and watched the smoke weave above her. Perhaps that was mostly what she liked about Terry. The tragedy. That he was injured. Mentally scarred. Like a hero out of a book. Because no one else seemed to see in him what she did. Monica certainly didn't. She'd said he wasn't much of a looker. But then neither was Mr Rochester, was he? And there was just something about him that always made her heart flutter. It was fluttering all the harder now. What could he *possibly* want to talk to her about?

She finished her cigarette, had her pee, washed her hands and hurried out again. Terry was where she'd left him, but now he was staring out towards the road, hands in the pockets of his jeans.

'I'm back!' she said brightly, glancing through to the bar to check for customers, but nothing much seemed to have changed.

But Terry's expression when he turned around was serious, and she wondered what on earth he *could* want her for. She hoped he wasn't after a sub because Irene had made it clear that they weren't lending any more money out to the punters. Not until some debts had been repaid, at least. But not from him. And she doubted it would be that, in any case. He might not dress up much but Kathleen had a hunch that was because he didn't want to. Not because he was on his uppers. He had a solid, full-time and doubtless well-paid job. He ran a Cortina, as well as the juggernauts he drove.

Maybe he had a message from her Auntie Sally, then. She'd like that. But then he'd be smiling, wouldn't he? And he wasn't.

At least she was no longer blushing. 'Go on then,' she said. 'What is it you wanted to talk to me about?'

Again, he looked awkward. 'Well, I don't know if I should be telling you this,' he said, 'but it's about your Darren.'

Kathleen felt her heart sink. She should have guessed. Her bloody stepbrother! Did he have any shame at all? Pound to a penny he owed Terry money. She pulled a face, waiting for the inevitable. Darren really needed to sort himself out! 'Go on, then,' she said. 'What's he done now?'

Terry stared at Kathleen for a long moment, as though he wasn't sure how to start. For so long that she had to drag her eyes away. 'Well, I might as well just come out and say it,' he told her finally. 'After all, it's no secret he's got gambling fever, is it? Thing is, Kathy, I think he might be getting in over his head.'

The blush returned with a vengeance. Terry was the only person since her mum had died who had ever called her Kathy. She wondered if he even realised. Probably not. She waited for him to continue.

'Only I've been hearing tales, love,' he said gently. 'Serious shit, actually.' He lowered his voice and glanced behind her. 'I think he must be planning a robbery or something. He's been trying to get hold of a gun.'

'*What?*' Kathleen was confused now. A *gun*? Their Darren? She shook her head. 'You must have that wrong, Terry. Surely. Our Darren is a prat but he's no need to go out robbing. He gets all he wants from bloody Irene! You know that. Everybody knows that. A *gun*?'

Terry shook his head and she could see how troubled he obviously felt. He meant it. He might be wrong, but he meant it. 'I'm not mistaken, Kathy,' he told her, as if reading her mind. 'He's definitely been asking about where he can get hold of one. I've been told by more than one person. So it's either a robbery …' He paused. 'Or he needs it for protection. Either way, he's getting himself involved with some bad people.' He touched her wrist. 'Love, I'm telling you because you need to warn him.'

The rest of the shift passed as quickly as the first half had dragged, Kathleen's mind in a whirl, trying to process what Terry had told her. Trying to fathom what her stepbrother could possibly want a gun for, trying not to think about quite how much money trouble he might be in. It must be bad – Terry was right; he had gambling fever pretty badly. But was it that much worse? How much did he owe that he couldn't get it from his mam? Where Darren was concerned she'd do anything … But then she wasn't made of money, was she? So could it be true? That he was getting a gun so he could go and rob someone at gunpoint? Or getting it for someone else? Who were these bad people Terry was talking about? Did he know them?

She wished she'd asked him. And protection. What was that all about? Did that mean he owed money to the sort of people who might hurt him? Because there was no doubt his addiction had been steadily getting worse, so much so that perhaps he'd been driven to borrowing from people he'd no business going near. And struggling to pay them off? These days he never had a penny to call his own and he was bleeding her dad and Irene of the pub's takings most weeks.

So what should she do? The idea of facing Darren himself seemed impossible. He'd just tell her to bugger off and mind her business. She knew he would. So perhaps she should tell her dad and Irene what Terry had told her, and let them deal with it. Her dad would surely know what to do.

But would he? And what about Irene? She could imagine it all too well. The very idea of her passing on anything negative about her golden boy was unthinkable. She'd probably slap her halfway across the room. And if she just told her dad … well, then he'd have to tell Irene anyway.

No, on balance, she decided, as she hung up the last beer towel, and made her way back upstairs, she'd have to be brave and tackle Darren himself, when he got home from work. But Darren? A *gun*? Even the word felt unreal. Perhaps Terry had got it all wrong. She hoped so.

Chapter 4

It was the following day, Thursday, before Kathleen managed to get Darren by himself, the weight of what she'd learned pressing down on her in the meantime, always inching into her thoughts. And nothing she heard in the interim had put her mind at rest. The night before, he'd been home late from work, and she'd heard him telling Irene that he'd been made to do some overtime – some nonsense about someone having called in sick. And she'd known it was nonsense because she'd already heard from one of the customers that he'd been down the bookies trying to borrow money to put on the horses.

So she'd chosen to stay silent, for that night at least, because his foul mood had made it obvious that whatever he'd borrowed he'd lost, all adding fuel to the fire that didn't even need any stoking – was Terry right? Was he already in dangerously deep? Was he trying to gamble his way into amassing cash to pay back a previous gambling loan?

Mary hadn't turned into work again which meant that Kathleen was back on the bar at lunchtime, and just before closing in he walked, surprising her.

She tried to gauge his mood as he wove his way round the chairs and tables. Was he happy? So-so? He certainly wasn't scowling. Which was what decided her. Perhaps this would be her moment.

'Alright, Kath?' he said, smiling as he walked behind the bar. He picked up a pint glass. 'Am I in time for a quick drink?'

Kathleen returned his smile. 'Course you are,' she said, stepping aside so he could get to the pumps. 'What are you doing back so early anyway?' she asked him. 'I thought you didn't finish till five.'

Darren poured himself a lager and returned to the other side of the bar, where he pulled up a stool and sat on it. 'They owed me a day's holiday,' he said, once he'd taken an inch off his beer. 'And after the shitty day I had on the gee gees yesterday, and the sun being out like it is, I thought why not?' He leaned towards her. 'Good thing I did, too. I just won twenty quid. But don't you dare tell my mam, okay? She'll be in my pockets for it quicker than the frigging artful dodger!'

He laughed, and Kathleen felt the anxiety inside her ease a little as she picked up a cloth to clean the tables in the bar. It was always better when Darren won. It was like a light turned on inside him. He was like a different person when he had a few quid in winnings in his pocket. Generous, too. She knew she'd only have to ask if she needed something and he'd give her it, no question. She went around the bar to start the cleaning.

'Don't worry, Daz,' she told him. 'You know better than that. I won't be telling my wicked stepmother *anything*.'

Darren laughed again, and she wondered if now was her moment. When he was like this he was always happy to take the mickey out of his mam with her, often mimicking her voice to make the punters laugh. There were just two left today, however, over in the far corner, and seeing her come round, they drained the last of their drinks, and headed out into the foyer with a nod.

She followed them out, so she could bolt the front doors behind her. Now was the moment, with them alone, and Darren only halfway through his pint. Now or never. She cleared her throat as she went back in.

'Daz, you know Terry – Terry Harris?' she asked him. 'Uncle Ronnie's friend?' He had his back to her and she waited for him to turn around before continuing. 'Well he was in yesterday,' she went on, grabbing the punters' empty glasses. 'And he said something really strange to me. Something about you.'

Darren grinned at her. 'Well? Spit it out then, kid. Go on …' he seemed relaxed about it. 'What am I supposed to have done now, then?'

'It's probably just gossip,' Kathleen said quickly. 'But, well, he said …'

'Yes, he *said* …'

'Well, he said there'd been some talk about you asking around for a gun. What's he on about?' She put the pint glasses down on the bar.

The change in Darren's expression was instantaneous. His eyes narrowed and – was she imagining it? She didn't think so – all the colour seemed to drain out of his face. He'd drained his pint while she'd been speaking and now he slammed the glass down on the bar. Then he raised a finger and jabbed it towards her, the ready smile long gone.

'You better not repeat that to anyone, Kathleen, do you hear me?'

'I wasn't saying I was –'

'Not a word, you hear? You *hear* me? God, I am that fucking *sick* of all the gobby twats in this pub! Not a word, do you hear?'

'Not a word!' she parroted back at him, his threatening tone – he'd stood up now – making her take a step back. But she couldn't just *leave* it. 'So it's true then?' she carried on, almost in a whisper. 'Darren, *have* you been asking to buy a gun? Why?'

Her stepbrother grabbed her by the shoulders, hard, his fingers digging in. She couldn't remember the last time she'd seen him so angry – so properly angry, not the half-pretend ranting he did whenever Irene really got on his nerves. That was for effect. This wasn't. He meant it.

He looked straight into her eyes, the blue of his own like ice. 'I'm warning you, Kathleen. You need to mind your own business about this and keep your trap shut. You need to *button it*. What I do is nothing to do with

Terry Harris, you hear me? Or you, or any fucker else. Now I mean it, I don't want to hear another word about it, and if anyone else cares to mouth off about me, you just send them my way, alright? Terry fucking Harris! Who the *hell* does he think he is?'

Kathleen nodded vigorously, feeling even more frightened now. She had never seen Darren this angry. He was usually so laid back and unruffled by anything. What on earth had he got himself involved with? Who on earth, more to the point? 'I promise, Daz, I won't say anything,' she tried to reassure him. He let her go. 'I just thought I should tell you, that's all. I didn't mean to make trouble. I was just worried about you. That you're not *in* trouble, that was all.'

He exhaled, tugged his jacket straight. Patted her shoulder, almost warmly. 'Good lass,' he said finally, as if having satisfied himself about her. 'Keep this between you and me, our kid, eh? Okay? And stop taking notice of idle gossip from folk who know nowt about nowt. Now, let's forget about it, eh? How about me and you sneak another quick half before your dad comes down, eh?'

Shaken as much by the turnaround in his mood as his failure to deny it, Kathleen quickly pulled two halves of lager. She'd never normally drink in the daytime – she didn't drink hardly at all, really. Barely even at the weekend, let alone on a weekday. But she knew her stepbrother was hiding something, and that, whatever it was, it was serious. She needed something to settle the butterflies in her stomach.

John came in just as they finished them, having settled into silence, her clearing up and wiping, Darren staring straight ahead. Thinking what? She wondered. Thinking *what*?

'Alright love?' asked her dad. She hoped he couldn't see she wasn't. 'You look nice, Dad,' she said, trying to cover her own anxiety. And he did. He always did at this time in the evening. Tall, slim and handsome, in his nice suit and tie. Making an effort, as he always did, for the customers.

He patted Darren's arm as he passed him. 'Terry Harris?' he said lightly. 'What's he been doing to get you niggled?'

So he'd heard them talking. Must have popped down to the cellar first and heard Darren raising his voice. Kathleen shot a look in Darren's direction, but he wasn't looking at her.

'Oh, it's nothing,' he said breezily. 'Just giving our Kathleen some advice. I was just telling her' – now he glanced at her – 'pick on someone your own age. What is he – thirty-two? Thirty-three? Much too old for her to be sniffing around with that daft look on her face.'

Kathleen felt her cheeks begin to flush. She didn't know where to look, let alone what to say.

Her father looked at her. 'Terry Harris? You sweet on Terry *Harris*?'

The answer came quickly, automatically, out of anger more than anything. It might have been quick thinking but it was too bloody quick! And way too close to the mark for comfort. Darren had actually *noticed that*? When? How?

But perhaps he was just thinking on his feet. That wouldn't be unusual. 'No, I am *not* sweet on Terry Harris,' she snapped, bridling genuinely as she said it. 'We were just chatting about Auntie Sally. Which' – she glared at Darren – 'is allowed. He is *best* friends with Uncle Ronnie, or had you forgotten that?'

Her father's expression told her he didn't believe her. So had he noticed too? He chuckled. 'If you say so, love,' he said. 'But Darren's right. He is a shade old for you. Still –'

'I am *not* sweet on Terry bloody Harris, Dad!' she thundered.

'So nothing to scrap about then,' he said mildly. He almost chuckled. 'Anyway, what you doing home so early, lad?' he asked Darren. He got the same answer. 'Well, there's a nice bit o' stew in the pan up there if you're hungry.'

Darren headed off, giving Kathleen a final warning look as he did so, reminding her – as if he needed to – that that was that as far as she was concerned. Well, so be it. That would teach her not to get involved in his business. He was twenty. A grown man. He could fight his own battles. Even so, a *gun*. And had he got one? She realised she didn't even know.

She finished up with the tables, while her dad got the bar ready, glancing across from time to time, feeling his eyes might be on her. They weren't – he seemed as absorbed in his work as he ever was, but, even so, it rankled that he'd said what he'd said – even with the twinkle in his eye as he'd said it.

And as for bloody Darren – Darren who she often liked, and at worst rubbed along okay with – possibly getting himself in trouble. Yet another thing to worry about. A secret she didn't want to keep for him. Should she tell her dad? Put him straight? But everything in his body language had told her not to. Not now, when, for all his dapper looks and ready smiles, he carried the burden of being married to that harridan upstairs like a physical weight around his neck. And with money always so tight, and her constant selfish nagging ...

'Right, that's me done, I think,' she said, smiling across the pub at him. 'I'm off upstairs. What sort of mood is she in?'

'She's having a nap just now,' her dad said. 'But I'd keep out of her way for a bit. Migraine's still niggling ...' he tailed off. He didn't need to say any more.

And hopefully she'll bloody stay napping, Kathleen thought irritably as she made her way up the stairs. For forty days and forty nights, ideally. But no such luck – she could hear her and Darren talking in the front room.

43

And about her, it seemed. 'You pissing little trollop!' Irene said to her, as she entered the room. 'Terry frigging Harris! He's a *widower*, you little slut. Have you no respect?'

Once again, Kathleen found herself glaring at Darren. He'd obviously come up and given his mam the same ridiculous story. Talk about covering your tracks and creating a diversion. This was ridiculous!

But Darren, presumably seeing her fury, was equally quick to defend her. 'Oh, don't go off on one, Mam,' he said.

'Go off on one?' she rounded. 'We keep a respectable pub here, if you don't mind, and that's the way it's going to stay. Showing us up …'

'Mam, you're being *ridiculous*,' Darren said. 'So what if she is sweet on him? Who's it going to hurt? It's not like he's going to look twice at a girl our Kathleen's age anyway.'

'The way she looks at them? I've seen her. I've seen you, I have, young lady. Making eyes at all the lads –' She made a move as if to slap her but Darren put himself between them.

'I was just talking to him about our Sally and the kids!' Kathleen shouted back at her. 'I was just being *friendly*! There's a law against that now, as well, is there?'

'No there's not,' Darren said before Irene could protest further, placing an arm around her shoulder and leading her to the door. 'Come on, Mam. I was supposed to be making you a cup of tea, wasn't I? Special treat, since I'm home early. Take advantage while you can.'

He manoeuvred her through the doorway and then he turned around.

Then he knitted his brows slightly. Not quite a frown. Just an indication of what had passed between them. Then he smiled and disappeared off to the kitchen with his mother. 'Now, Mam,' Kathleen heard him say, 'how about you tell me *all* about your day?'

Kathleen flopped down onto the sofa and considered her churning feelings. As grateful as she was that Darren had stopped Irene having more of a go at her, she was still angry; angry that she still didn't know what was really going on with him, and angrier still that he'd made such a good job of deflecting things by turning all the attention on *her*. She wished she *did* have a lad – one of *any* sodding age – just so she could, even if only for the tiniest time, get out of this miserable place.

Chapter 5

'Why don't you come down and have a drink, lass?'

Kathleen looked up from the TV as her dad came into the room. It was Saturday night and, as usual, the pub downstairs was buzzing, the raised voices, loud music and gales of drunken laughter all conspiring to drown out the sound of *Z Cars*.

Not that either source of noise seemed to be getting through to Darren. He'd been drinking steadily since he'd returned from work and eaten his tea, and was now fast asleep in one of the two armchairs, a row of empty beer bottles by his feet.

'Is it busy, then?' Kathleen asked her dad, not quite trusting his 'have a drink' line. 'You don't need me to work, do you?' She knew what Irene was like – chances were, she'd get her down there and then trot off to join the punters while *she* worked – specially the male ones, who she always enjoyed flirting with. Her dad didn't seem to mind that, but *she* certainly did – particularly after a full day of bar-tending and cleaning already.

Her dad obviously read her mind. '*No*, silly!' he said, laughing. He was quite merry already, by the look of it.

'It's just daft, that's all – a young lass like you stuck up here on a Saturday night. It's not right.' He jerked his head towards Darren, who was snoring now, his lower lip hanging open and his fringe over his eyes. 'You don't want to be stuck up here. Come downstairs and enjoy yourself. I've just nipped up to change my tie – managed to get bitter splashed all over it – but I told your mam I'd pop my head round and ask you down for a bit. She's in a good mood, I promise,' he added after a pause.

'Okay,' she told him. 'I'll be down in a minute.' Then she uncurled her long legs from under her and went across to turn off the telly. Darren would be out for the count for the rest of the evening now probably, and there was no point in it playing to itself. She stretched, having stiffened up, then went across to the mirror above the fireplace. She looked respectable enough, she decided. Well, almost. She'd definitely have to go and run the brush through her hair. Not that she was actually *that* bothered about spending time in the pub this evening. She'd have far rather gone off to the Bull as she'd planned – there might well have been a few people she knew in there tonight. But with her mate Linda down with a bug, her evening had been effectively over – to walk there and turn up alone required the kind of confidence and courage she didn't possess, even if a girl going to a pub alone wasn't frowned on.

But there was one thing drawing her down, and she wondered if her dad knew it. Terry might be in for a bit.

You never knew, anyway. Worth running the gauntlet of the battle-axe for that.

There was no *law*, that was the thing. That was the thing that really rankled. That was the thing that had *really* stuck in her craw in the week that had passed since Irene had called her a slut, for possibly – just possibly – being attracted to Terry Harris. Who was a widower. No longer married. Whose wife had been dead over two years now. *How* did that make her a slut exactly? By what rule? That was the thing that *really* got to her. The sheer lunacy – even over and above the name-calling aspect – of Irene thinking there was something so fundamentally wrong about a single girl being interested in a similarly single man; it wasn't like Terry's wife had died a month back or anything. It had been two whole years. Why on earth *shouldn't* she like him and him her?

If he even did, which wasn't a given – Kathleen was too aware of her own naivety to kid herself too much – it might well just be a case of wishful thinking anyway. It probably was, much as she always felt his eyes staying on her just that little bit longer than normal. But even so – there was still the principle. That was what mattered.

She glanced back towards Darren. It was a rare Saturday night when her stepbrother wasn't out till the small hours. It was very out of character for him to be slumped where he was on *any* night, in fact. There were few evenings when he didn't go out at some point.

But then Darren had been behaving oddly ever since she'd confronted him. And not just with her – with everyone else in the family too; he'd been grumpy, uncommunicative, unwilling to engage. And had been slumped in that armchair pretty much every night this last week, downing beer, dropping off, and then waking up ratty, before stomping off again, with a grunt, to his bed.

She kept thinking she should ask him again – why a gun? Who was he scared of? Or, if he wasn't, what was he up to? Instinct still told her he'd tried to get one because he was frightened someone was after him, but now the idea of him being involved in some sort of crime had taken root in her mind, she couldn't seem to shake it off. Time and again she had wondered if she should say something to her father. She almost had, too – the previous night, when he'd got home from work late – but she'd got no further than 'Look, Darren ...' before being subjected to such a mouthful that she vowed that she *would* keep her 'fucking nose out' as instructed, as the slap he'd suggested she might get if she didn't – again, completely out of character – didn't appeal.

No, best leave him to it. Whatever 'it' was. That was clearly what he wanted. And she wasn't *that* naïve. If someone was after him, he'd presumably sort it out. He'd have to. And if they weren't – if he was planning to do something criminal ... well, perhaps Terry *would* be in and she could speak to him again. Perhaps, she decided, as she went to get her hairbrush, *he* could even speak to Darren instead. At the very least, he might be able to give her some advice.

She went to get her brush – perhaps she'd add a lick of Vaseline to her lips, too – to find her and Monica's bedroom in its usual Saturday night state of disarray – a wasteland of discarded tops, laddered stockings, open pots and spilled powder, much of which would be swept to the floor when she tottered back home again, significantly worse for wear, gusting alcohol fumes across the space between their beds.

Which was reason enough, Kathleen supposed, to go down. If she had a couple of halves herself she'd probably sleep all the better – the better not to be awake when Monica crashed in.

She ran down the stairs, the swell of noise and cigarette smoke rising to meet her, and the first thing she noticed was that she'd been right on one count – Irene was perched on a chair at a table near the bar, holding court with a gang of her favourite cronies from the estate. She was half-cut, by the looks of it, despite it still being quite early, and laughing just a little too loudly and raucously for it to be natural; she was playing to her audience. She saw Kathleen almost as soon as Kathleen had seen her and it was the expression on her face that would stay with Kathleen later – and expression of such confident, unthinking, everyday contempt, the like of which she wouldn't be seeing again.

'Oh, Jean, that's priceless!' she said, nudging her friend and turning slightly. 'But hey up, better keep it down, girls – big lugs is here. And you know what she's like for spreading the gossip.'

The other women laughed. Why would they not? She was a figure of fun to them. And if she'd learned one thing since becoming part of the fabric of a public house, it was that the insight of drunk people was every bit as lacking as their inability to realise how boring they always sounded was immense.

She glanced around in search of friendlier company. Mary, now recovered, seemed to be coping fine behind the bar, which was presumably why her dad wasn't there.

'If you're looking for *him*,' Irene called across, without any prompting, 'he's in the best room playing dominoes. Meant to be bloody helping, he is. Lazy old git. And her …'

Kathleen let the sentence drift away as she headed to the best room where, up till ten or so minutes ago, a band had been playing, the members of which were still busy getting their leads and amps together, and who nodded a hello to Kathleen as she entered. She knew them well. They played regularly – had done for as long as she could remember. A trio of men, nearer her dad's age, all from the Canterbury Estate, who sang country music, folk songs, some unbearably sad to listen to; one in particular which Mike, who did most of the singing, and had known her dad back in his printing days, had always told her had been a favourite of her mother's.

The jukebox was still blaring in the main bar – to which many had now decamped – but in contrast this room could have been somebody's dining room, so was a choice spot for the older customers to drink and play their dominoes in peace.

Her dad seemed pleased to see her. 'There's half a lager here, love,' he called as she glanced around. 'And we've nearly finished this game if you want to join in the next one.'

Kathleen quite enjoyed the odd game of dominoes – it was one of those childhood things that had always bound her and her father – but it was Saturday evening and she couldn't quite escape the feeling that a seventeen-year-old girl playing dominoes with her dad represented a tragedy just that bit too big to be borne. She pulled up a chair, though, to be friendly, and accepted the drink.

'No ta,' she said, smiling, 'I'll just have this half and watch, then I might go give Mary a hand behind the bar.'

'I told you, love,' her dad chided, 'there's no need for you to do that. Relax, love. Enjoy yourself. Mary'll be fine.'

'But it's getting busy now,' she said, glancing back across through the foyer to the tap room as a couple of new people came in. 'Pictures probably turned out, and in a bit, she'll be swamped with –' She stopped, feeling her face flush. Terry Harris was standing watching her from the foyer. He was with a mate, but he'd stopped, and had obviously been waiting to catch her eye. He grinned and waved, and she immediately lowered her gaze. But at the same time …

'You know what, Dad?' she said. 'Think I'll head back to the bar after all. Can I take this?' She raised the glass.

'Course you can, love. I told you. But –'

'No, it's fine, Dad. I don't mind. You know what Mam's like. I'll go and help Mary, or she'll be hollering for you instead, won't she?'

Kathleen picked up four empties in her free hand, and then pushed through the door, back into the foyer. Terry was still there, now watching the reels of the bandit spinning. He stopped when he saw her and reached to pull the taproom door open for her.

'Here,' he said, taking the empties. 'Let me carry those for you.'

'No, it's fine,' she told him. 'Honest.' But it was to no effect, since he already had them anyway.

'Nice to see you down here on a weekend,' he said, smiling back at her as she followed him to the bar itself. 'You don't normally work on a Saturday night, do you?'

No, but I'm glad I'm down tonight, she thought but didn't tell him. 'I'm not really working as such,' she said. 'It's just that my mate's ill and I'm at a loose end, and –'

His eyes widened. They were dark-lashed but pale. An unusual greeny grey. 'Ah, so that means you could maybe have a drink with me then, doesn't it? If you'd like to,' he added, turning to look at her as he plonked the empty pint glasses down on the bar.

She thought she'd like that a great deal. And not just because she was keen to talk to him about Darren. But Mary *was* getting busy. And there'd be fat chance, if she did go and sit down with Terry, of Irene not ordering her to go and help out anyway – or at least, given it was Kathleen's night off, and she had no business doing so, making an enormous 'thing' out of her sitting down with Terry.

But you never knew. In a bit she might be teetering on her usual brink – either too pissed to care, immersed in stirring the cauldron with her cronies, or too pissed to stand, in which case she'd disappear off to bed.

'That would be nice,' Kathleen said, and hoped he could tell that she meant it. 'But I really should give Mary a hand first. Just for a bit … I'm coming, Mary,' she called across.

But it seemed Mary didn't want or need her help. Or perhaps there was something more. She certainly glanced behind Kathleen, towards Terry, as she approached.

'Thanks, love,' she said, her tea-towel-covered hand moving rhythmically around the inside of a pint glass. 'But I'm fine at the moment, honest. Why don't you pull yourself a drink and then go have a sit down with Terry. I can always shout you if I need you, can't I?'

'Good idea,' Terry said. 'You're hardly ever out from behind that bar, Kathy. Come on. Come sit with me a bit. Rest your feet.'

'You make me sound like a little old lady,' she said indignantly, as she pulled herself a half and topped it up with lime cordial. 'I can rest my feet when I'm dead, thanks.'

'Alright. So we'll stand up, then.'

'Now you're just taking the mick.'

'No, seriously. I spend that much time on my backside ... Still, now we're here.' He gestured to an empty table he'd found, on the far side of the pool table, miles from Irene. 'Unless you want to challenge me ...'

'I could too.'

'I'll bet.'

'Seriously, I'm good.'

'Seriously, I'll bet you are,' he said again, smiling at her over the rim of his glass. 'So we'll have to make that a date, won't we? Anyway, *pour tu, mademoiselle,*' he said, pulling one of the chairs out and gesturing to it theatrically, while she tried her best to relax and to not keep thinking *date, he said date ...*

And she did relax. Almost immediately, too, even though she knew Irene was sneering across at her. Even though she knew they'd be gossiping about her. Let them, she thought. Let them say what they want. She didn't care. *Pour tu*, he'd said. French. The familiar form of it. She remembered that from her French lessons in school. Terry and her Uncle Ronnie went to France quite a lot, she knew, driving all the way down south and taking their enormous lorries onto the ferries. It sounded so glamorous, even though Terry had more than once told her it wasn't. That she'd have to take a look inside one of his lorry cabs some time. That it was probably about as glamorous as keeping pigs.

He was chatting about it now, about a recent trip to Paris – him and Ronnie; some anecdote about a missing wallet, or was it pallet, or *something*, at any rate – and she was perfectly content just to listen. To listen and, in fairness, to drift a little, too. What she wouldn't give, she thought, to wake up every morning and not know where in the country – or even the world – you were going to end up. In a lorry cab. With him.

'It sounds magical,' she told him. 'Paris! How could Paris *not* be magical?'

'As wondered by a girl who has clearly never had the good fortune of spending three hours going the wrong way round the *Périphérique*!'

Périphérique. Even the word sounded magical.

He stopped speaking then, and rolled his empty glass between his palms. 'I'm rabbiting on a bit, aren't I?' he said, looking suddenly sheepish, disarming her. 'Nine to the dozen. Sorry. I've a tendency to do that when I … well.' He coughed. 'How about another half?'

'No, it's fine,' she said. 'It's *fine*. And, no. This'll do me for a bit. But you go and get yourself one. And I'll put some music on, shall I?' she added, the silence between them suddenly so loud. Though hopefully not as obvious as the blush she could feel already inching up her chest to her neck.

'Good idea,' he said, and headed off, then seemed to check himself and turned around again. He was wearing a loose shirt, a checked one, with the sleeves folded back. Terry never looked like he cared much what he wore – Irene had once commented on it, in her usual negative fashion – but far from thinking him a 'scare-crow', which was obviously how she saw him, Kathleen found it attractive. She liked the way he didn't care. That he didn't spend time dandifying himself all the time. She loved how her dad was always so smart, but he was older. Terry dressed young. He *was* young. Perfectly young enough for her. Their eyes met. Had he noticed the way she'd been looking at him? 'Here,' he said, fishing in his jeans pocket for change. 'For the music.'

He placed it in her hand and as he did so, she felt it. Just the touch was enough. Just that almost impercepti-ble tremor that told her he was nervous too. Which told her something even better. That perhaps her thinking hadn't been quite so wishful after all.

It was the thought in her mind as she went to the jukebox. The thought in her mind as she scrolled through the choices. The thought in her mind as she chose 'Anyway, Anyhow, Anywhere' by The Who, which seemed so perfect. The thought still in her mind as she scanned the bar for Terry – and quickly found him – and at the point when the air in the bar seemed to be rent in two. Not by an explosion of laughter from Irene's table. But an explosion of sound that was unlike any other. A sharp crack. A *boom*. Then a thump against the ceiling.

The sound of a gun going off upstairs.

Chapter 6

The silence that followed was like a living, breathing thing. It mushroomed around her like a rising, rushing tide, pushing up – pushing eyes up – pushing everything above it, snatching half-spoken sentences from mouths that hung open, as everyone's heads seem to tip, almost as one; tipping back as they looked to the ceiling above them and then, to a new sound – which again, came from nowhere – a keening sound, a half-scream, from where Irene had been sitting. But now wasn't. She was rising to her feet, trying to push through the crush, scrabbling at backs, shouting 'Please! Let me through! Let me through!' Then the sound of the glass Kathleen had picked up hitting the table, then falling, with a thunk, onto the carpet.

She moved forward, stepping on the glass, feeling the dull crack of it breaking, seeing her dad – a suited blur – and all the shocked, confused faces, moving forwards, and then, suddenly, a hand on her arm.

'Stay here.' It was Terry. 'Stay here, Kathy. Let them go …'

But she couldn't. It was a gun. It had been a gun going off. She shook her arm free. 'I've got to …' she began. 'Darren – Darren's up there!' Still he stopped her. 'I *must*!' she said again, shaking him off. Stepping forward. Barging through now, aware, as she did so, of a way being made for her. Opening up, like a flower. Through the bar. Round the back – Mary, cloth in hand, white-faced – to the stairs, thundering up them, two at once, to the landing, to the doorway to the living room – the room she'd just come down from – to see Irene, almost as if her entire body had become liquid, fold up into a writhing, screaming heap on the carpet, and her dad, trying to stop her, almost folding up with her, but just checking himself enough, with a lurch to the side, to allow her to see what her stepmother had just seen, which was Darren, on the floor, by the armchair he'd been asleep in, asleep now – curled up, curiously foetally, like a baby – his boyish features blank in repose, one of the beer bottles on its side, by his face.

'Jesus Christ.' Her dad's voice. 'Jesus *Christ*!' His voice rising. And a smell. A powerful smell of burning. And then seeing it, a mere half a dozen inches from him. The gun.

The beer, the beer, the *beer*, leaving the bottle, foaming, soaking into the carpet. It held her gaze. Had to. *It must*. Almost in fascination. It must have been an almost full bottle he'd knocked over, she decided, because it wasn't flowing so much as spewing, coming in malty-smelling gouts. Slow, rhythmic hiccups of foam.

60

She tried to focus, while her stepmother screamed and writhed and screamed. Not on the hole in Darren's temple, which was so small – so incredibly, stupidly, *impossibly* small – and ringed with a perfect starburst of tiny brown flecks. Concentrate. Concentrate. On *anything* but that. *Entry wound*, her brain told her, even though she tried so hard to stop it. *Entry wound*. She remembered it from something she'd seen on TV. And where there was an entry, there must be an exit … and little by little, that too revealed herself to her. Not so obviously, not at first, just in the strangeness of his position. In the fact that it seemed that he'd fallen so precisely – just so, face towards her – but strangely, oddly canted. As if the back of his head – all that hair, all those ropes of curly hair – nestling in what must be a hole in the floor. But there *was* no hole. No dip. No gap in the floorboards, under the paisley patterned carpet. There was no dip. Darren's head wasn't nestled in anything. It looked strange because half of it was no longer there.

The beer, she thought. *The beer. Look away. Look at the beer. Look at the beer bottle*. But her eyes wouldn't listen. Now her brain had worked it out, all she could see, bar the bloom of blood darkening the carpet, was the half-missing head and the gore. The unspeakable gore.

She felt an arm on her. Terry's? No, a different arm. Mary's. She felt sick rising in her throat. Realised she could smell it as well. Irene, on the floor in front of her, now was arch-backed and heaving, the hot liquid spurting, rat-a-tat, on the carpet, flecks of it hitting Darren's dead, outstretched hand.

'Jesus Christ!' her father shouted. 'Someone call the police!'

'My boy!' Irene screamed now. 'My *boy*! Help him, John!' She was clutching handfuls of her hair now, as if to drag them from their roots. 'My boy, my boy, my boy!' she screamed. 'Oh help him, oh help him!' She was pawing at his legs now, and Kathleen's father rushed to stop her. Pulled her back. Pinned her arms. Wrapped his own tightly around her.

'Don't touch anything,' he said softly. 'Mary, ring the police, please.' He glanced back at Kathleen. Mary had already gone. 'And an ambulance, love. Okay? Tell her an ambulance. Tell her to fetch an *ambulance*.'

Though the look in his eyes confirmed he knew what she knew. That the time for an ambulance was long gone.

Chapter 7

It was 1 September. Just a few days before the kids went back to school, and the long summer holidays were over. It was also the day that Darren Dooley, aged just twenty, was laid to rest.

Like all unnatural deaths, his had been the talk of the whole estate, and like all unnatural deaths, it had had to be investigated. So passed a week – maybe ten days – in a fog of comings and goings. An ambulance coming for the body, everyone interviewed, separately. The endless questions, both spoken and unspoken, the chores undone, the room abandoned. All to a backing track of awful, animal crying.

But somehow, unimaginably, they had pulled it all together. Kathleen wasn't sure how it had happened, but somehow they'd done it. Given her stepbrother, to use the parlance, the funeral he deserved.

Like all funerals around Canterbury Estate, that meant a big, showy affair. With Darren being the son of the landlady of the local pub, it was always going to be, but it was also because he'd been a porter at St Luke's Hospital; despite his gambling, his resultant debts and his constant scrounging, Darren's sense of humour and devil-may-care nature had won him a large number of friends.

The main reason, however, was that Darren had been so young. It was that, more than anything, that pressed on Kathleen's mind. That twenty – an age full of energy and potential – was an unspeakably young age to die.

She fixed a black ribbon round her ponytail, not bothering to primp and preen, her only concern being quite how she'd find the strength to get through the day. She just didn't feel strong enough, either physically or mentally. Since that horrible, heart-stopping, never-to-be-forgotten night, she had barely stopped crying herself – it was as if she *couldn't* stop crying, no matter how hard she tried.

In the days following Darren's death, it had seemed that life had lost all its forward momentum. She'd wake up, and it would be there, this huge, looming reality. Like a boulder in her path that could not be moved. He was dead. It was final. He was never coming back again. Everything else seemed to be happening just out of reach, beyond that, the only thing able to pass it being the sound of Irene's screaming, then wailing, then sobbing, then gulping as if choking, then, as if struck by it anew, screaming again.

In the midst of this, her dad – face set in place, as if made of plaster – quietly set about doing everything that needed doing. He'd cleared the living room of furniture the very next day; it had sat in teetering piles on the landing, half-pushed into his and Irene's bedroom, a jumble of armchairs and ornaments, settee cushions and pot plants, while he set about the business, Stanley knife in hand, of ripping up and cutting up the heavy, ancient carpet, so that, piece by piece, it could be transported down the stairs and out the back, ready for the bin men, where no one would have to look at it ever again.

He'd scrubbed the floor – the smell of disinfectant seemed to permeate everywhere – and, in what seemed like no time at all – Monday or Tuesday? – some men he knew with a truck had arrived with a new carpet and had laid it. The new-carpet smell – one she'd once loved – was now lingering, and, though the furniture was back, the ornaments all positioned, it was impossible for Kathleen to even think about going in there, unable to stop pictures forming in her eyes, of Darren's body, and his hair – of the way it had glistened with blood and bits of brain. The way his head seemed to be sunk into the floor.

There was a tap on the bathroom door and she started, newly fearful of the animal Irene had now become. Glazed and crazed. Barely functioning. Unpredictable and frightening. While understanding – the unthinkable had happened, she understood that – she was more terrified of her stepmother than ever now. Only yesterday, while seeming outwardly quite calm, she had taken a saucepan full of potatoes and almost boiling water and hurled it at the kitchen wall with such force that it had left a dent. Her dad had come running, and had quietly shepherded Irene out, but the look in her eyes when they chanced upon Kathleen's had chilled her to the core.

It was her dad now. 'Are you nearly ready, love?' he said. 'Only the car's outside in the car park.'

Kathleen coughed and straightened up. 'Coming, Dad,' she said, opening the door. 'I won't be a sec.'

'I'll wait outside for you then, love,' he said. 'Your mam and Monica are already in the car, so don't be long, will you? And make sure you lock the door,' he added, as he headed back down the stairs. 'We don't want a burglary to add to our bloody misery, do we?'

She watched him go, then ran back into the bedroom for her bag. Trust her dad to be so practical, but then he'd done all this before, hadn't he? When she was eight.

It was an odd thing, Kathleen decided, as she took her place opposite her stepmother in the funeral car, to feel sorry for someone you've so hated. Well, not so much hated, she supposed, as been so fearful of. She liked to think – she *hoped* – hate wasn't something she'd ever harboured. But this new thing – this sympathy, this pity she felt for Irene – was so alien that she didn't quite know what to do with it.

What she did know was that Irene seemed to have aged ten years. She couldn't imagine what it must be like to bring up a child and then lose it, but she had enough intelligence to realise that it was probably a different business to that of a child losing their mother. It was the wrong way round. It was a loss above all others. The stuff of nightmares.

It certainly seemed so from the way Irene had been. She looked haggard now, desperate, unhinged, without hope; as if she meant what she'd said over and over and over this last week – that she could *not* bear the pain. That she just wanted to die and be with him.

Her eyes were red and swollen, her face doughy and grey, and her hair – that thing she most hated, and on which she lavished daily attention – was a cloud of faded amber frizz around her face. It was difficult to even look at her.

The car took them through streets lined intermittently with people, some there to pay respects, some just to watch the procession – with the schools not gone back yet, there seemed to be children everywhere, too, and Kathleen wondered what thoughts might be going through Irene's mind, of the little boy she'd raised and had now come to this – moving slowly, in his coffin, just ahead of them.

It took only ten minutes to get to St Joseph's Church, but it seemed a great deal longer. Where did you look? How did you act? What did you say? Kathleen had been to her mam's funeral, and though she could remember few of the details, bar the posy of anemones she'd been given to throw onto the coffin, the sense of horror – of impending chaos, even – had never left her. That fear that, with all the adults behaving so oddly and looking so distressed, anything could, and might, happen.

Monica, strangely, seemed completely composed. She'd cried little, said little – almost nothing to Kathleen personally. Like Kathleen's dad, she had rolled her sleeves up and got on with it. It had been Monica who'd rearranged the photos on the mantelpiece, Monica who'd prepared meals, who'd insisted her mother eat a little – on Monday and Tuesday she'd even gone to work, saying that Carol's pensioners needed doing and couldn't wait.

Kathleen wasn't convinced by her outward composure. She and Darren might not have been that close, but they were still siblings. She'd lost her only brother. Again, Kathleen found herself confused by her own feelings in this; by the genuine respect she currently felt for her stepsister; for the care she was taking of her mother.

'We're here, Mam,' Monica said to Irene as the car pulled up outside the church. 'And I'm right here beside you. Try to stay strong, okay?'

Irene's only answer was a blink and a deep shuddering moan; a sound from deep inside her and unlike any

Kathleen had ever heard. 'Come on, lass,' said her dad, gesturing that she should get out first.

It was only now, in the light of a glorious late summer morning, that she could see just how tired her dad looked. He'd lost weight from his face, and his body too, she reckoned, though it was difficult to tell under the heavy black suit.

He'd barely got a breather. They'd closed the pub for two days, out of respect, but after that, on the Tuesday, they'd re-opened. Which meant that as well as sorting out the funeral, the priest, the order of service and everything, he had the usual round of chores still to deal with too.

Perhaps that was key – to keep busy. They always said that. Keep busy. As with when her mum died, he kept going, kept the smile plastered on his face. Well, not so much the smile, but the control, at least – more often than not, there were few people smiling. It was too much of a tragedy, too much of a waste. That was what everyone said, all the time. 'What a waste.' And he'd nod and he'd sigh and he'd keep changing barrels, while Irene stayed curled up on Darren's bed, howling like a baby – you could sometimes hear it, even with the juke-box on loud. Kathleen could certainly hear it reverberating in her head.

Her guilt was a tight knot that moved in her stomach. If only she'd said something. If only. If *only*. Why hadn't she? Why else had Terry warned her? He had purposely sought her out and told her what he'd heard about the gun, and instead of doing the right thing and telling her dad or Irene, she had spoken to *Darren*. And now he was dead.

It all seemed so obvious now. She should never have said anything to him. She should have told her dad and let *him* decide what was best to do. If she'd only done that, then might he still be alive? But what could she do now? Tell her dad after all and get it off her chest? But what was the point? What would *he* be able to do? No, she'd done the wrong thing and there was nothing she could do to change it. She desperately wished she could talk to Terry.

Irene began wailing as she made the unsteady walk from car to church, the same animal sound she'd been making since the night Darren had died, as if she'd discovered a language that no one else could share. Kathleen walked behind her, Monica and her dad holding Irene between them, having to physically support her. Had they let her go, it was clear that she'd simply collapse, and lay keening on the gravel between their feet.

As they walked slowly up the aisle, the church more packed than she'd ever seen it, she could see that the length of one of the front pews was clear, ready to receive them. The organist was already playing – 'The Old Rugged Cross' – and it was that, together with seeing the photograph of Darren sitting on a low table, next to where the coffin would be placed, that caused Kathleen to shed her first tears of another day. She was suddenly overcome with grief, in fact – not just for the loss of Darren, which still overwhelmed her, but also for the loss of her own mother. It might have been almost a decade since her mam died, but it suddenly felt as if she was right there, again – the terrible loss of her all rushing back.

She opened her bag to find her handkerchief as quietly as she could. The hymn had ended, and everyone was suddenly still.

'Stop snivelling!' Monica hissed in her ear, making her jump. 'He wasn't even your family, for God's sake! You're just looking for attention.'

The reply came out of her mouth the moment she'd thought it. 'Piss off!' she hissed back, through a mist of still-to-be-shed tears, her previous respect for her stepsister dissolving away like the tears into the fabric of her hankie. Attention? Was Monica mad? That was the *last* thing she wanted.

The service, once it started, was mercifully quick – either that, or Kathleen lost herself in the middle of it. Because after a couple of hymns which she couldn't sing for the lump in her throat, and a eulogy to Darren by the vicar (which she could hardly hear for Irene's sobbing – something she was glad of) they reached the point where the next stage of the funeral was to begin – transferring Darren's body to Bowling Cemetery.

This would be the worst part, particularly for Irene, and again Kathleen found herself quaking at the prospect of the next hour that still lay ahead of them. But there was comfort of a sort in that, as they were walking back down the aisle, she caught the eye of her Aunt Sally, a couple of rows behind them, here with her husband Ronnie and their little ones, Stuart and Lisa. It hit her that Stuart was the same age as she'd been when her mam had died and, once again, seeing the way Sally gathered the children close to her to reassure them, felt a pang of yearning for the mothering she had missed.

She nodded in acknowledgement and Sally smiled at her reassuringly. Kathleen wondered how hard Darren's death might have hit her. She and Irene might not get on, but she'd been a good aunt to her niece and nephew, never forgetting a birthday, being generous with them at Christmas. Today was a tragedy for her as well.

In the event, Irene managed to hold herself together for the burial, not least, Kathleen thought, because her dad had been supporting her – at one point giving her a couple of tots of something he had brought with him in his hip flask. Kathleen had hung back, not wanting to see the coffin being lowered, and was first back in the car for the journey home.

Once again there was no conversation; Irene couldn't speak, and her dad was too busy trying to soothe her to talk of anything but that, and Monica, with the same unnerving composure she'd shown all day, held her mother's hand and stared steadfastly out of the window. So Kathleen did as well, musing that they were in the 'family' car, yet no four people could feel less like a family – not now that Darren was no longer there to glue them together. And as they turned the last corner, she almost felt closer to the group of relative strangers who'd gathered outside the pub to greet them.

As was expected of them, Irene and John had put on a big spread for after the burial. Mary had got her niece in to help and as the funeral car pulled up to drop the family off, Kathleen could see the pub car park was full.

She got out and joined the small crowd who were milling out front, keen to get inside out of the fierce noontime sun, but not wanting to go in before Irene, as a show of respect. The Jaggers were there, the Hudsons, the McNallys and Delaneys, the McNultys, Burnetts and Hostys … in fact, it seemed like almost everybody from the estate. No doubt a lot of them had come for the free grub and the free first pint, but most of them, she thought, because they had known and liked Darren. She pushed away a stray thought that one or two might have known him in ways that contributed to his death. That would be unfair. As of now they knew nothing. Darren had *left* nothing. No explanation. No note. Just debt.

'There you are. How are you holding up, sweet-heart?'

Kathleen turned to see her Aunt Sally walking across to her just as her father reached her, Monica having left him to greet everyone while she took her mam inside; it would probably be a while before she could compose herself sufficiently to speak to anyone. She patted her dad's arm. 'I'll be in in a minute, Dad,' she told him. 'I'll just go say hello to the kids.'

'Alright, lass,' he said, then, half a second later, 'You okay? You coping? Not a nice business, all this.'

She was touched. She reassured him that she was.

Although Sally was as perfectly made up as she ever was, beneath the baby-blue eye shadow, her eyes were red. She'd been dabbing at them with a handkerchief, which now fluttered in her hand. 'What a *terrible* time for you all, love,' she said, throwing her arms around Kathleen. 'I just can't *believe* it, even now. Our bloody Darren – so young and so full of life …'

Sally's voice faltered, which, strangely, made Kathleen feel stronger. 'I know, Auntie Sal, I know,' she said, 'it's just awful, isn't it?' Then she squatted down on her haunches to speak to her step-cousins, for whom this must all be so strange. 'Now then, you two,' she said, kissing them on the cheeks in turn, 'have you been good for your mammy? I bet you have,' she finished. 'Because you're good kiddies, aren't you? Shall we go inside and get you some pop and crisps?'

Sally smiled gratefully and they headed into the pub, Ronnie following, and as they did so, Kathleen noticed

Terry coming to join them, peeling off from a group he'd been talking to. He expressed his condolences to Ronnie, while Sally and the kids went ahead, but just as she was about to do likewise, as Ronnie was doing, Kathleen felt his hand brush her arm.

'How are you doing?' he said. 'Tough day, eh? Tough *week*.'

He took her hand and squeezed it, and the sensation surprised her. Even in the midst of all this, all this *misery*, it felt good and right. Like a port in a storm.

She felt a sudden need to unburden herself to him. To say all the things she'd not had a chance to that night. That night ten days and what felt like a lifetime ago. She'd not seen him since – he'd been on a foreign job. One of the regulars had told her. 'Oh, Terry,' she said, 'I've been feeling so terrible. About what you told me. I didn't know what to do about it. I should have told my dad, but I didn't – I had it out with Darren. And he denied everything. Gave me hell. Told me to keep my nose out of it. And so I did, and now he's dead and I feel so bloody awful, and I can't say anything – what's the point? It's not going to bring him back, is it? I just wish I'd told my dad. I feel so bloody *awful*.'

Terry placed a hand on each of her arms. More and more people were drifting past them into the bar now, but he stood like a rock in the midst of them, causing them to part ways. His green-grey eyes were on hers, sure and steady. 'The *hell* it was your fault,' he said quietly. 'Kathy, that's just daft. If he told you to button it, then you did right to heed him.' Then he sighed. 'I shouldn't have told you. Shouldn't have put that on your shoulders. But you know what? If your Darren was determined to do something like that – which it looks like he was, doesn't it? – then he would have done it anyway. At some point. *No one* could have stopped the silly lad. Not you, not your dad and not his mother, neither. Love, trust me. There's no need for you to feel guilty about this.'

'I wish I could tell myself that,' she said.

'Then *do*.' He moved his hands to her shoulders. Then he kissed her on the forehead. 'Come on,' he said, taking her hand and leading her to the door to the bar. 'We both need a drink. Let's go toast your brother, eh? Enough tears. For today, at least. And we'll worry about tomorrow tomorrow, eh?'

'Live in the moment, then?' Kathleen said, remembering something she'd read somewhere.

'That's about the size of it,' he agreed. He still held her hand. 'Because you never know what's around the corner. How can you?' There was a half-smile on his lips, as if he was remembering something that mattered. 'Because that's in the *nature* of corners,' he finished.

It was only then that it struck her. That he'd been here as well. His wife had been – what? – twenty-seven or twenty-eight when she'd died?

She looked sadly at Terry, seeing more of him suddenly. Feeling a connection she'd not realised was there before. 'We're too young to have so many ghosts in our life, Terry, aren't we?'

He nodded and opened the door. They walked in together.

Chapter 8

Although it was still only mid-September, there was a definite autumnal nip in the early morning air. Kathleen put out the stub of her cigarette against the brick wall, and hurled it across the back yard and into the bushes. Then she glanced at her watch. It was only twenty to seven, and the sky was a stunning orangey-pink. The sort of sky that promised a beautiful day. Well, outside. Inside, it would be anything but.

Kathleen had been getting up earlier and earlier since Darren's death. With Irene having lost all normal patterns of sleep and waking, time to herself had become a precious commodity. Even more precious than it ever had been, too, because, as far as Irene was concerned, Kathleen's main crime – far more heinous than having been born to her husband – was that she hadn't been the one to die.

'There's no logic to it, love,' her father had explained, when Irene had railed against her the previous evening. She was half-mad with grief and she railed all the time. Always at her stepdaughter, for having the temerity to still exist. 'No logic and no reason – it's just pain, terrible pain. Don't rise to it. She doesn't mean it. I mean, I know she can be short with you at the best of times, I *know* that. But this is different – she's just lashing out. I'm getting it too. And she's got it in for Monica as well, love. Why d'you think she's been making herself so scarce, eh?'

Kathleen had tried to accept this. To be reasonable – not least because she so worried about her father. He was taking everything on his shoulders, and Irene could barely function, and to throw her own toys out of the pram wouldn't help him one bit. And he was right about Monica absenting herself currently – for all that she looked after her mam in those first few nightmare days, now she was hardly ever home, working ridiculously long hours, then coming home only to check on her mother, before buggering off round her mate's house, as quick as she could.

But her dad wasn't right in saying Irene had it in for everyone. She didn't. Oh, she'd rant and wail and cry and give nobody any quarter. But when they were alone, which was often now, Kathleen understood perfectly. Irene could hardly look at her, such was the depth of her loathing – and when she did, it was with a new level of fury in her eyes. The term 'if looks could kill' could not have been more apt. And it wasn't just because Kathleen was still alive, though that was much of it. It was because she'd also been the last person to see Darren alive, and Irene had convinced herself she must have played a part.

'You were up there *with* him!' she'd yelled at her the previous afternoon, while her dad had been out buying spirits and crisps. This was her thing now; when awake she would follow Kathleen around, drifting from bar to bar, from room to room, behind her, drawing on cigarette after cigarette, aimless, unseeing, unkempt. 'What did you say to him? What were you talking about? You must know something! Must have *said* something! Something must have triggered it! There must have been a reason! What did you *say to him*, you little bitch? What are you *covering up*?!'

'I have told you ten *times*!' she'd shouted back at her. 'The story's never going to change! He was asleep! We didn't exchange a single bloody word! Not one! He was asleep when I went in there and he was still asleep when I went down!'

But this wasn't the answer Irene wanted, and she wouldn't let it go.

'I'm his frigging mother!' she'd screamed. 'His *mother*! He wouldn't have killed himself without leaving me a note. He just wouldn't. He just *wouldn't*! You have got to know something –' She jabbed Kathleen painfully in the ribcage. 'You were the last person to see my boy alive, so you'd better give me something! You'd better tell me what you said to him, or I'll …'

'What?' Kathleen had retorted. 'What? Or you'll *what*? Well just do it! Do your worst! It's not going to change anything, is it? It's not going to bring him *back*!'

Which, of course, was the point at which her father had come upon them, and Irene, as was her way now, because she was all over the place, obviously, collapsed against a bar stool, sobbing like a baby, her fists beating out a tattoo on the bar.

Kathleen slipped back inside to start cleaning the main bar and tried to think how things might be made better. Time. That was her father's line, and she supposed he knew what he was talking about. There was only one 'cure' for bereavement, and that was time. It was the only thing that could effectively blunt the pain. But this was Irene's *child* – her favourite child, and that made such a difference. She had already figured that perhaps her dad was partly right – perhaps Monica's frequent absences derived from always having known that; perhaps knowing her mother (had she ever been made to choose) might wish it had been her instead of Darren meant her sympathy now only stretched so far.

But there was also the nagging guilt that, in fact, Irene was right. She *did* know something Irene didn't about what Darren had been up to and though her instinct was that his decision had been an act of sudden impulse, if he'd not had the gun, he wouldn't have been able to do it. And no matter how much Terry had tried to convince her otherwise, she knew that even if he would have done it anyway, he wouldn't have done it *then*, and not in that way.

The picture appeared before her eyes, just as it kept doing, all the time. She seemed powerless to stop it happening, and it seemed to have no pattern. Her thoughts would drift and then – bam – it was there right in front of her, the colours and textures, the whole revolting, unspeakable horror of it, all heightened to a grim glorious technicolour.

She shook her head to clear it and tried to think less dangerous thoughts. Thoughts of Terry. All those trips to the phone box she'd been making. He'd given her his work number (though not he hers yet; she couldn't having him calling the pub and risking getting Irene) and she'd slipped away several times to the sanctuary of the red box on the corner of Park Avenue, and they'd talked and they'd talked and they'd talked. And twice more they'd met – she hugged herself mentally – the first time to his little two-up two-down on Louis Avenue. All this time, she'd thought, and he'd been living just a couple of streets away.

It was a neat house. A man's house. It had little in the way of feminine touches, apart from a photograph of his dead wife, hung in a frame next to the fireplace; a pretty, dark-haired girl, with huge, expressive eyes. It had been professionally coloured. Done by a proper photographer. She wondered if he could really bear to look at it.

There was little furniture in the house, not that she could see. Not downstairs, anyway. Just a cellar-head kitchen – a tiny space at the foot of the stairs – and in the front room an oval coffee table, a TV stand and a small beige settee, with cushions that had hunting scenes on them, on which they'd sat to drink a brew and where he'd told her about how grim it had been having to move there after his house fire, and how it still didn't feel quite like home since he was away so much of the time. Which he'd been happy with, he pointed out; always happy to take the really long jobs, rather than go home to a place that didn't feel like a home. She didn't say so, but she knew how he felt.

'Might just opt for a few shorter ones now, though,' he'd told her, and the shyness in his tone had made her heart swell.

Then she'd seen him again, albeit only briefly. He was leaving shortly to go to Europe, and after her lunchtime shift there was little time left, so they'd agreed to meet up at the café in John Street Market. They'd talked and talked – the time had just vanished – and when they left he took her hand, and continued to hold it all the way back to where he'd parked his car. He'd then dropped her outside St Luke's – heaven forbid anyone saw them together and it got back to Irene – and before she got out of the car he'd leaned across and kissed her.

It had just been one kiss, that was all. Not even meant. He'd just pecked her cheek and then, somehow, they'd looked at one another, then rearranged their faces, and kissed each other properly.

It had stunned her and made her stomach churn and been everything she'd imagined it might be, but Kathleen wasn't fanciful enough to start weaving romantic stories around it. Yes she was, she supposed, 'seeing' him, and he obviously liked her. But she wasn't stupid, or soppy, or anything like that. She certainly wasn't childish enough to do as Monica had a couple of years back, practising her married name – the name of a boy she'd hardly been out with half a dozen times, and who finished with her a couple of weeks later.

But she knew that what she felt for Terry had nothing of the breathless quality of the crushes and infatuations she'd had before this. There was nothing of the knight on white charger about him, or the jack-the-lad, either; he couldn't be *less* like that – but perhaps because of that, she was drawn to him even more. That and the fact that they'd both lost someone dear to them? Perhaps. It didn't matter anyway.

Lost in her thoughts, it was only the sound of a chair being stacked that made her realise her father was in the bar with her. She'd been emptying the ashtrays – one of those horrible jobs that always seemed to be *her* job – and she realised she'd no idea how long he'd been there. It made her start. What was he doing, creeping up on her like that?

'Bloody hell, Dad,' she ticked him off. 'I nearly jumped out of my skin! What are you doing up at this time anyway? It's not even quarter past seven!'

He was still in his pyjamas and dressing gown and, like Irene, looked like he'd aged a decade in a week. 'Your mam's just gone off, love,' he said, nodding towards the ceiling. 'Bloody wretched night, we've had.'

'Then go to sleep as well,' Kathleen told him. 'God knows, you look like you need it!'

But her father shook his head. 'I've got to go and have a bit of a sort-out in our Darren's room ...'

Kathleen raised her eyebrows. '*Really?*' Darren's room had already become something of a shrine. No one was allowed across the threshold, let alone in to touch any of his possessions; well, bar the police, who she'd no choice but to let look around. Which they duly had, even after the funeral, because they needed to establish if there were any factors that might have had a bearing on things, but once it became clear that it was a straightforward suicide (which the extent of Darren's debts clearly hinted at, on top of the forensics) they'd not been back, and probably wouldn't. Since then, only Irene had ventured past the doorway, something she did at least three or four times a day, often sleeping there as well.

'I just feel I need to see if I can get to the bottom of it, love. I know it won't bring him back' – Kathleen flinched slightly at the way he said that – 'but if there's any little thing. Anything that might give her a crumb of comfort ...'

'I can't see how anything could do that,' Kathleen said. 'When people kill themselves, well … there's not much that can be said, is there?' She wanted to go on – to point out that there probably wouldn't be. That, to her mind, it had been a completely spur of the moment thing. No, more to the point, would be to find out what was happening on the outside. Had someone been threatening to hurt him? To kill him, even? There were plenty bad enough and mad enough on Canterbury Estate. She wished she had more of an idea of what he'd wanted the gun for. To commit crime or in fear that it was about to be committed against him? But she decided to say nothing. Not to her dad. Not right now.

A thought occurred to her, out of the blue. 'What will you do with his things, Dad?' She asked him. 'You know, when eventually, they have to be – well, you know, sorted out?'

'What, his clothes and that? Go to charity most likely, I suppose,' he said. 'I doubt your mam would be happy to pass them on to anyone local – don't think she'd cope well with seeing anyone prancing around in one of his fancy suits, do you?'

'Your mam.' It never rankled any less. Kathleen shook her head. Was that what had happened to her real mother's things? That her dad couldn't bear the thought of seeing anyone in them? She thought of the welfare shop down on Great Horton Road, and all the fuddy-duddy stuff they had hanging in the window. Dead people's clothes? It wasn't a nice thought. She thought about Terry then. Had he kept stuff? Was there anything left for him to hang on to, or had everything been burned in the fire? Or was he like her, cast adrift with only memories to hang on to?

She wished her father had kept something of her mum's for her. Anything. Just a blouse, or a favourite cardigan or something that she could have sniffed.

'D'you want me to help you?' she asked him.

'Would you?' He seemed pleased that she'd offered. 'Once our Monica's up and gone. I gave your mam a couple of those pills the doctor prescribed for her. She'll be out for a good while.'

'I hope so,' Kathleen said ruefully, managing the first smile to him in days. 'There'll be hell to pay if she finds us in there. She'd bloody murder us!'

Which wasn't the most diplomatic thing to have said, but it at least raised a smile from him too.

They finished off the early morning chores together, John dealing with the back of the bar, while Kathleen, having taken Monica her tea and checked she was up for work, finished off the big room and went and dealt with the toilets.

Monica was back down in what seemed like no time, hair and make-up immaculate and only the grim set of her mouth giving any indication of how she was feeling. It was still very early, and Kathleen had the impression that getting out of the pub was her first priority every morning – only once she set off up the road could she breathe out and start her day. Oh, how she wished she could do just the same.

'Mum's spark out,' she told her stepfather, not even glancing in Kathleen's direction.

Kathleen's dad nodded. 'And will be for a good while, I'll bet,' he said, their nods of acknowledgement confirming that was much the best thing for everyone.

'Anyway, I'm off,' she said and now she did seem to acknowledge Kathleen's presence. 'Some of us have proper jobs to get to.'

It was her way, Kathleen decided, of excusing her disappearance. Point-making, to deflect any negative comments about how little she was currently around. *So let her*, she thought. *I really don't care.*

Not so her dad. 'Enough of that,' he said. 'Kathleen works every bit as hard as you do. Just get gone,' he added mildly, 'and less of the gob.'

It was the first cheering thing Kathleen had heard from him in days.

Less cheering was the business of entering Darren's bedroom, which was dark – Irene had obviously decided to keep the curtains closed now – and smelt musty and stale.

The bed was all awry from where Irene had been climbing in and out of it, but apart from that, it looked as bare and neat and characterless as it always did. Darren had been as tidy in his personal habits as he'd been with his clothing. It was just such a tragedy that his personality had led him so inexorably to the chaotic world of the out-of-control gambler.

Now she was in here she really didn't know what she could help with. Riffling through Darren's personal papers was the last thing she felt like doing.

Her father, however, seemed to have no such concerns. Perhaps conscious of the clock ticking, he immediately went to the wonky old wardrobe, getting down on his knees to see what he could find in the bottom – the place where Darren apparently shoved his paperwork. Out of sight, out of mind? She studied her father's back. He'd said little of his personal feelings, but he must have them. Darren had been his stepson for a long time, after all. And he'd liked him. They'd rubbed along fine.

She went to join him, aghast at just how much stuff was jumbled together at the bottom of the wardrobe – who knew so much was hidden behind the thin wooden doors? There were piles of boxes and files and she accepted a shoebox he'd handed her, and was soon lost in a thick sheaf of sundry documents. Many payslips, a bunch of bank statements, a bundle of handwritten letters that she recognised as being from a girl he'd been going with for a while a couple of years back, and betting slips – all of them old ones, for small, seemingly insignificant amounts, but which had still amounted to the seeds of his destruction.

It was difficult to know what to look for, she realised, and, again, her thoughts strayed back to the business of having to be here – like a pair of snoops, in a room they had no business being in, with the weight of its absent owner pressing down.

She could have sat there on the edge of Darren's bed for hours, no doubt, she realised, but for a sound, through the wall. Was Irene stirring?

Her dad obviously heard it too, because his head jerked up, listening. She wasn't sure what he'd been going through – he now seemed like an island in a sea of bits of paper – but he quickly closed the lid on the box he had in front of him, and gestured to her that she should do the same, and hand it back to him.

She did so, glad to leave, unsure what purpose could be served here, and was just heading out again, her dad close behind her, when she heard a rustle.

She turned. He seemed to be stuffing something into his dressing-gown pocket. 'What've you found?' she whispered.

'What?' he said, before putting a finger to his lips. Then he shook his head. 'Nothing.'

She continued out of the room, her dad following, switching off the light with careful fingers. It was only when they were back on the landing that she saw his face was white.

'What have you found, Dad?' she said again.

He shook his head. 'I told you,' he mouthed. '*Nothing*.'

And she knew he wasn't telling her the truth.

Chapter 9

Kathleen stood back against the wall behind the bar and tried to listen. It was late afternoon, just a few days before Bonfire Night, and whoever was at the other end of her dad's whispered telephone conversation must have things to say that he didn't want anyone else getting wind of – presumably Irene – because he'd stretched the phone cord all the way out from the end of the bar and taken the receiver out to the bottom of the stairs.

But he wasn't doing much of a job of keeping the conversation private. He was obviously getting angry. He was certainly raising his voice.

'Well you can't get blood out of a bleeding stone, can you?' he snapped, his voice close to a shout now. 'So there's no point coming here, pal. No point whatsoever! I owe you nothing,' he hissed, obviously checking the volume of his voice. 'And there's more than me here if you're thinking of coming mob-handed.'

There was a long pause then, whoever he was speaking to obviously giving as good as he'd got. Then, 'Step one foot in my boozer and see what happens *then*, eh? I'm about sick of this – folk chasing us for money we don't owe! It's the police next if it doesn't stop. I mean it!'

Kathleen jumped away just as her dad burst back through the door into the bar. He looked angry and stressed and she wished she could help him. This wasn't the first of that sort of call he'd had to deal with – far from it. And it was almost as if Darren's creditors were working together. Nothing for ages – not a peep out of anyone – and they were suddenly all coming out of the woodwork. As if they'd waited for what they thought was a respectable amount of time before calling up en masse to try to get what they were owed out of her dad. Was one of *them* the reason Darren had got himself that gun?

'Creditors again, Dad?' she asked after he'd slammed the phone back on the bar, and tried to impose some order on the now-twizzled cord. She hadn't forgotten that he'd hidden something from her in Darren's bedroom. Perhaps his debts were a lot more than they'd thought. 'Dad, I told you, *I'll* deal with them for you. I'd be more than happy to. You know that. No point in you getting it in the neck all the time, is there?'

She would too, she thought – which had been something of a surprise to her, as much as it evidently was to her father, who'd looked at her when she first suggested it as if she'd gone batty.

'*You?*' he'd said then, glancing nervously upstairs. He'd seemed obsessed with keeping all of it from Irene, and she sort of understood that. But it was surely only a matter of time before she found out for herself.

'Yes, *me*,' she'd countered, looking at him defiantly. 'I'm not a child, Dad. And I'm not as wet as you obviously think I am, either. I'll tell them straight. No nonsense.' She knew she would, too. And it wasn't just because she saw it as a way to help with the guilt, either. It was as much because she had that much pent-up anger and frustration and hurt inside her that it would be good to have a way to let some of it out.

John shook his head now, just as he'd done the last time. 'No,' he said, and in a tone that made it clear there was to be no more discussion. 'Some of these people … They're … *No*, lass,' he said firmly. 'Okay? *Forget* about it. I can sort it out. I just wish they'd have a chat among themselves and get the blinking message. That they'd bugger off and let that be an end to it.'

'They will,' she reassured him. 'Sooner or later they will, Dad. They have to. It's not fair that they're chasing you for money our Darren owed. It's just not *fair*.'

But fair or not, the creditors had kept on coming. Friends Darren had borrowed from, apologetic but still insistent. Loan sharks who'd loaned him silly amounts of money at ridiculous interest rates. Bookies who had happily let her stepbrother rack up credit on the horses. Heated phone calls. Letters and threats in person.

She watched her dad as he served the last customers of the day shift, and she worried about him. Worried about the painted-on smile that was now conspicuous by its absence, by the fact that he wasn't chatting to the punters like he normally did, but sitting up on the high stool at the far end of the bar, staring into space, as if in a world of his own – a world full of threats from nasty people? She supposed it must be.

Not that the real world they were inhabiting was any better. Irene had started coming down and working again a bit, here and there, but she was so volatile and unpredictable it was as if she'd been possessed by some demon, and everyone – including Monica, who usually gave as good as she got – tiptoed around her as if she was an unexploded bomb. Which, in some ways she was, because the slightest and most unlikely thing could set her off. And in one of two different directions as well – either to breaking down, sobbing hysterically and rushing off upstairs again or, worse, flying into a rage that could turn violent in an instant, particularly if she'd been drinking, which she was now doing a lot.

Kathleen continued to observe her father, and felt a welling of frustration. Always so quiet and even-tempered, he'd been a different man these past couple of weeks. He'd found a temper; a tone that meant Darren's creditors knew they shouldn't mess with him, yet that was the rub of it. He still seemed unable to use it where it was most needed – on his wife.

But now as then, it seemed, he couldn't. Or wouldn't. 'Cut her a bit of slack, love,' he'd say. 'She's in a terrible way, you know that. Be patient. We've all got to make allowances at the moment.' And as a consequence, it was as if they were living with a sleeping dragon, who could wake at any time, breathing fire, and destroy anything in its path. Or perhaps more accurately, as if she was the mad woman in Mr Rochester's attic, every so often screaming and rattling her chains.

So Kathleen made allowances, for her dad's sake, because he had more than enough on his plate. She did as Monica did – well, as far as she was able, given that, unlike Monica, she couldn't go off to work – in that she tried to keep out of Irene's way as best she could, and counted out the days till she'd next be seeing Terry.

And now the day had come. It was Firework Night and, just returned from his latest job abroad, he'd be round pretty soon to pick her up. He was taking her to the huge Firework Night celebrations that were being held around the enormous bonfire that now sat in pride of place in the middle of Ringwood Road and which, among other things, included a pie and peas supper.

November 5th had fallen on a Friday this year, which made it even more special – for lots of people it would mark the start of the weekend. And while Terry had been driving to somewhere in Holland and back, everyone on the estate had been preparing for it. It wasn't strictly legal – they held it on the corner field by the youth club, which was land owned by the council – but

Canterbury Estate being what it was, i.e. a law unto itself, there was about as much chance of it not happening as Guy Fawkes himself rising from the grave.

Best of all was that she didn't need to work tonight, not at all. Her dad had promised her the night off because the pub wouldn't be busy anyway; a lot of the regulars would be at the party with their wives and kids, enjoying the fireworks; it would be just the hardcore and the moaners; the ones who disapproved of anything that involved lots of people having fun.

But they were in a minority. Almost everyone on the estate looked forward to it, so the group that organised it – the Jaggers and the Hanleys – had been collecting bits of money from everyone who could afford it for weeks. Enough to buy plenty of fireworks, and, of course, hundreds of sparklers for the little ones. After all that effort, having fun was non-negotiable.

And fun she knew she would have; excitement was already bubbling up inside her. That and the butterflies that took flight in her stomach every time she thought of seeing Terry again. Despite her generally level head, and her sensible pragmatism when it came to romance, Kathleen knew she was falling, headlong – had already fallen, in fact, and too far to be able to haul herself up again. It would have happened anyway, because Terry's looks and his kindness had always drawn her to him, but it was also because he seemed to feel the same way as she did, which could only fan the already blazing flames.

She tried her hardest not to but she couldn't help the frisson she felt whenever she thought of him kissing her, or her pulse from racing whenever a shadow walked past the pub window that might be his. In that sense it had been something of a respite, him being in Holland. Out of sight, he was very much *in* rather than out of mind, but at least it gave her a chance to come up for air.

She'd taken great pains, however, not to let the depth of her feelings show – not to Monica (who'd taunt her mercilessly), and especially not to Irene, who'd already made it more than clear what *her* feelings were about them; that there shouldn't be a 'them' in the first place.

And, on that score, things were even more complicated than she'd thought. There had seemed to be a bit of a sea-change in that regard since Darren had died – a very unexpected one, as well. Had she not known it to be ridiculous, and even making allowances for Irene's drinking, Kathleen wouldn't have considered it outside the bounds of possibility that Irene was even making a play for Terry herself.

At first, she'd dismissed that; even been cautiously optimistic. Irene being *nice* to them? Coming over to chat to them? Had her dad said something? Had he pointed out to Irene that they were doing nothing wrong? And had Irene, understandably preoccupied with losing Darren, finally decided that her perspective needed changing? That life was short, and there was nothing wrong with her going out with Terry after all?

But she was soon disabused of her now naïve-seeming optimism. Terry had been in the pub just the night before he'd gone away, having a drink with a couple of his mates. And Kathleen, who'd been working, had stood and watched, open-mouthed, from behind the bar, as Irene had gone over to collect some empties from their table, and, while leaning across Terry to pick up some glasses, had actually pressed her satin-clad bosom hard against his shoulder.

It had been an action so obvious that it left no room for doubt, and as Irene had returned with the glasses, to the far end of the bar, Terry's bemused glance at Kathleen had said it all.

But tonight they'd be free of her – free of the pub, free of the gloom there – and as she wriggled into her slip she felt a thrill of excitement that it would be *her* body pressed against his later on, huddling close, as they'd need to, to keep the bitter cold out, as the fire-works leapt and danced in the sky.

'Jesus Christ, girl – what the *hell* do you think you look like?'

Since Irene and her dad had been busy eating their dinner – which *she* had cooked for them, as per usual – Kathleen had hoped she'd be able to finish getting ready for her date unmolested. No such luck, clearly, as she emerged from the bathroom to find Irene, fist aloft, ready to rat-a-tat-tat it against the door.

Kathleen had changed her outfit several times. Which was quite a feat, given her meagre wardrobe, and the need to wrap up to keep warm. But her eventual choice – a roll-neck sweater and her navy knee-length kilt – seemed about as unlikely to incur her stepmother's wrath as would a head-to-toe boiler suit.

But it wasn't the fact that her knees were on show that seemed to attract Irene's ire. 'What *do* you think you look like?' she sneered. 'You're actually going out like *that*? You look like a twelve-year-old, off to see the bleeding vicar!'

Darren's dead, Kathleen intoned to herself. *She's deranged. Make allowances. You'll be gone in half an hour. It doesn't matter what she says. Don't rise to it. Just DO NOT rise to it!*

And you look like a whore, she answered, even if only in her head. *An old one, as well. With your old-lady bosoms bursting out of your nasty satin blouse, and that ridiculous short skirt, and that horrible red lipstick ...*

'It's cold out,' she said, sidestepping Irene. 'I'm dressing *sensibly*.' Then she half ran, half skipped down the stairs.

Unusually, given how eagle eyed she was these days, she heard Terry's voice before she saw him. 'Now there's a sight for sore eyes!' he said, picking up his pint and slipping off the stool he'd been sitting on at the far end of the bar.

Her father, who'd been chatting to him, smiled his agreement.

She slipped through the hatch, wishing blushes could be turned on and off like radios, to stop the static crackling between them as their eyes met. 'You look nice too,' she told Terry brightly. 'I like your jumper.'

'This old thing?' he said, pulling at the front of it and frowning. It was a big chunky jumper, like a fisherman might wear. Sort of stone-coloured, flecked, with a big floppy roll-neck. It suited him. It also looked home-knitted. She wondered by who. His mam and dad lived hundreds of miles away. He'd come to Bradford with Iris. Had his mam sent it up for him? She hoped so. 'About a million years old, this is,' he told her. 'I'm lucky the moths haven't had it. Like a drink before we go, love? While I finish this up?'

'Half of lager, please,' she said, but her dad had beaten her to it. One had appeared by her arm even before she answered. Terry handed it to her, grinning. 'How's that for service, eh?'

She sipped the head off it. 'How was Holland, then?'

'Flat and full of cheese.'

'When did you get back?'

'Three quarters of an hour ago. Traffic's been murder.'

'Only three quarters of an hour back?' Kathleen said, shocked. She remembered him saying he'd be driving overnight to catch a dawn ferry, too. 'God, Terry,' she said, 'have you slept at *all*? You must be shattered!'

He raised his glass to her. 'Got an hour's kip on the boat, but you know what I always say? Plenty of chance to sleep when I'm dead.' Then his expression became thoughtful. He glanced at John, who'd moved off down the bar, and he grimaced. The weight of it was everywhere. The sense of life being so fragile was always in everyone's minds. 'Anyway,' he said, dipping his head closer to her, 'more to the point, Kathy. How are *you*?'

Kathy. She loved how he always called her Kathy. 'Oh, okay,' she said. 'So-so. Ups and downs. You know how it goes. But all the better for …'

'Seeing me?' he said, his eyes meeting her gaze and making her blush again. 'If so, I have to say the feeling's mutual.'

She batted him lightly on the arm. 'I was *going* to say all the better for having a Friday night off, for a change. But, since you mention it …' She buried her face back in her glass, all too aware that the colour in her cheeks had probably already finished the sentence for her.

'Ooh, look at *you*!'

They both looked up. Irene had evidently come down, then. She was now standing, hands on hips, behind the bar. She was also smiling idiotically at Terry.

'Alright, Irene?' he said, before finishing the last inch in his own glass.

'Look at *you*,' she said again, extending an arm and then a finger, which almost reached but didn't quite connect with Terry's chest. 'Hmm,' she said, her eyes running past Kathleen in a point-making fashion. 'Who's dressed *you* tonight, eh?'

Now it was Terry's turn to blush. He seemed lost for words. Then eventually found some. 'My fairy godmother, evidently,' he said, glancing at Kathleen and smiling.

But Kathleen was still standing there, agape. 'Mam!' she hissed. 'What *are* you on about? You're embarrassing him.'

Irene didn't bother to answer. Instead she winked at Terry. 'Oh, I think *he* knows.'

To which there seemed no kind of answer. At least, Terry didn't make one. Instead he turned to Kathleen. 'Done with that?' he said, gesturing towards her two-thirds empty glass.

She put it down on the bar, unfinished. 'Definitely,' she said. 'Don't want to miss the fireworks, do we?'

And even then – even *then* – Irene wouldn't let them alone. 'Plenty of fireworks to be had here,' she simpered, again looking suggestively at Terry. Had she already started on the gin tonight, or what? 'So make sure you hurry back here, eh?' she finished, her painted lips puckering then parting, in a come-hither smile.

Kathleen looked over at her dad, who was serving a customer at the far end of the bar. What on *earth* would he make of all this ridiculous carrying on? So she felt rather than saw Terry's hand wrap around her own. 'Oh, I doubt we'll be back,' he told Irene. 'Not before closing time, anyway. I told this young lady here –' he squeezed Kathleen's hand as he said this – 'that I was taking her out for the night, and the night is still young, so …'

'Young *lady*?' Irene scoffed. '*This* one?' She nodded in Kathleen's direction.

Kathleen sensed Terry stiffen. He nodded and cleared his throat. 'That was the word I used, Irene, yes.'

Irene made a sound that was halfway between a huff and a puff; the sort of sound she was apt to make when passing judgement on female customers who dressed not to her liking, or on punters who refused to succumb to her charms. A sort of dismissive 'pah!' She began to turn away, muttering, grabbing a tea towel and flicking it. Terry watched her, but made no move to lead Kathleen away.

Then he spoke. 'Young *lady*,' he said. 'Yes. Do you have an issue with that, Irene?'

He was talking to her back, but now she slowly turned around. Kathleen glanced towards her dad again, who was still chatting to the same customer, arm resting on pump, still oblivious to what was going on.

'I *beg* your pardon?' Irene snapped at Terry, her face pinched and pallid.

'I said, do you have an issue with that, Irene?' he repeated.

'An issue?' Irene blinked at him. 'What's an "issue", when it's at home?'

Once again, Kathleen felt Terry's hand tighten around her own. His was hot. So was hers. It was difficult to work out where one began and the other ended.

Irene flapped the tea towel again, glaring hard now at Kathleen. She looked expanded now somehow, as if being pumped up, like an airbed. She fixed on Kathleen. 'And you can wipe that smug look off your chops, while you're at it, you little madam!'

Kathleen said nothing. Just looked despairingly towards her dad. But far from noticing what was happening, he'd now got embroiled in another conversation – discussing something in the paper with one of his other regulars. But it seemed Terry was happy enough to finish this on his own. 'You know what?' he told Irene mildly. 'You're a nasty piece of work, you. I'm sorry for your loss – *truly* sorry too, because I liked Darren. He was a nice lad, a good lad, and he'll be very much missed. But, you know what? *All this*' – he raised the hand that still had Kathleen's curled within it – 'is just *nasty*. Uncalled for. Offensive. What's Kathleen *ever* done to you, eh?'

'Terry, don't …' Kathleen entreated. She couldn't help herself.

He squeezed her hand. Nodded. 'No, you're right, love,' he said. 'Let's blame it on the lack of sleep, eh? Mine and hers,' he said, nodding dismissively towards a now open-mouthed Irene. 'Let's get off to the bonfire, shall we? Got your coat? Let me help you. Let's get going,' he finished, his eyes glittering as they met hers. 'Get outside, where the air's a bit less poisonous.'

'You cheeky bloody *bastard*!' Irene began, as Terry helped Kathleen into her coat. 'How dare you! How *dare* you come in here and start mouthing off at me! How *dare* you –'

But neither of them heard any more. Just the sound of the foyer door sighing closed behind them.

Chapter 10

As it turned out, Irene had been right. There were plenty more fireworks to be let off that evening – a whole box, a *big* box, full of rockets.

They'd skipped out onto the empty street, arms as well as hands now entwined, and for a few lingering moments, Terry had said nothing to her at all. Just pulled her towards him and smiled, and kissed her hungrily on the mouth, under the benign gaze of the street lamp outside. His skin was cold – the air was bitter – but his lips and arms were warm, and as he snaked the latter round her, she buried her own up inside his jumper. 'Blimey, Terry,' she admonished him, once they finally separated. 'Haven't you got a coat with you? You'll catch your death out here!'

He tipped his head back to look at her. His hair was haloed gold by the street light. Then he grimaced. 'Guess what? It's on the coat hook, back in there.'

It was too cold to even think about going to the bonfire without it, so, after some whispered deliberation, it was Kathleen who fetched it, sneaking into the foyer, keeping low, avoiding the glass-panelled inner doors, and emerging with it moments later, almost doubled up with stifled giggles.

Terry kissed her again then, reeling her in as she tried to help him fasten it – it was a donkey jacket, which fastened with big, troublesome buttons, and with the temperature so low now they were out in the night air, he was having some difficulty doing them up.

'I can't believe you did that,' she said finally. 'I can't believe it.'

'What, *that*? I've been waiting to do that for days now, I can tell you.'

'No, not *that*! I meant taking on my stepmam like that.'

'Earned the kiss, then?'

'Earned several,' she said, threading her arm through the crook of his.

They set off up the road, walking fast, to keep the cold from creeping up on them, heading towards the snicket, where they could cut through to the rest of the estate.

'I'm not sure I can quite believe it myself,' he admitted, after a moment. Then he sighed. 'It was just on the spur of the moment. I couldn't help myself. I hope I've not caused you a lorry load of trouble now.'

Kathleen shook her head. 'No. Well, no more than I'm usually in just for generally existing anyway.' She hugged his arm, still feeling stunned by him. By the bulk of him. The maleness. The heroic way he'd fought her corner. 'And it was so kind …'

'It wasn't that,' he said immediately, surprising her. 'I bloody meant it!'

'I didn't mean *that*,' she said, touched. 'Not that you didn't *mean* what you said. I meant, you know, as in standing up for me with my stepmum like that. No one's ever done that. Ever. Not like that. *Never*. I'm surprised she didn't fall down in a dead faint behind the bar.'

He stopped on the pavement. The sky ahead of them glowed now behind the houses – a low arc of orange, fading into charcoal, then navy, then black – and every so often a spray of sparks would spatter up above the rooftops, and leap into the darkness. It must be a very big bonfire, Kathleen decided.

'That wasn't kind either,' Terry corrected her. 'I was just doing what I needed to. What's *wrong* with the woman?' He seemed genuinely stumped. 'I mean, I know what she's like; she'd always had a sour tongue on her, but that *really* takes the biscuit. That she thinks she can just calmly treat my girlfriend like that, and expect me to stand there and do *nothing*?'

He exhaled, and his breath formed a white cloud in front of them. Kathleen didn't think she could possibly feel any happier. At that moment anyway, despite everything. Despite *anything*. It just wasn't possible that she could feel more full up with joy. If she did, she decided, she might burst. She glanced up at him. 'And who said I was your girlfriend?' she teased him.

'Your boyfriend did,' Terry told her firmly.

The bonfire party made it obvious why her father hadn't needed her behind the bar. It seemed like everyone from the entire estate was there. She saw the Williamses and the Hostys, a gaggle of old girlfriends from school and the usual gangs of lads, who now, compared with Terry, seemed so immature and silly and gauche. And all about there were the Hudsons, the biggest family on the estate, who'd now swallowed up the equally notorious Jaggers, and who, together, seemed to be at the centre of everything, while their half-feral children – or so Irene always described them – roamed like good-natured packs of animals round the periphery.

The feeling persisted. She really couldn't have been happier, and as they oohed and aahed at the fireworks and sang along with all the singing, she didn't even need to make an effort to forget about the row waiting for her at home; she was living in the moment, just as Terry had said they ought to, because you never knew what was just around the corner.

And in this case, it had come from *right* around the corner – the only difference being that they *had* seen it coming. Which was why Terry had insisted on seeing

Kathleen right inside, when he walked her home again, despite her entreaties that they say goodbye just up the road.

'I *know* her,' she'd told him. 'She'll have been getting crosser all evening. Sitting stewing. She'll be waiting and if you're with me, it'll only make her worse.' But Terry had refused to budge. What sort of boyfriend would he be, he'd pointed out, if he'd left her to her fate when it was him who'd lit the spark under the old witch?

So that was that, and though Kathleen had managed to extract a promise from him that he'd do absolutely nothing (well, except if he had to) he was allowed to escort her all the way back to the pub.

And here they were and, unusually, her dad was out front.

It was just past closing time – only a scant minute after her 11 p.m. curfew – and for a moment she didn't quite believe what she was seeing. Standing outside the front, looking at his watch, simply wasn't her father's style. But then, Kathleen mused, as they walked down the street towards him, being late home – going out, even – wasn't really *her* style.

He was smoking, and as they approached he dropped the cigarette on the ground in front of him and, just as Kathleen knew he would, ground it out and picked it up. He then popped it in his jacket pocket, ready to throw away – not in the kerb, never that, but in *the correct place, the bin.* She could almost hear him saying the words in his head.

'You okay?' Terry whispered, when they were twenty yards away from him.

She nodded. 'Bit strange, my dad being out, though.'

'Not really. I imagine he wants to talk to me, don't you?'

'Oh, I wish … I wish …'

'What?'

'I wish … I wish *everything*,' she finished lamely. 'Wished everything was different … Wish I could just climb into that lorry of yours and disappear …'

'I know.' He gave her hand a reassuring squeeze. 'So do *I*, believe me. Because it doesn't look like we're going to get that goodnight smooch you promised me otherwise, does it? And me off to Andorra tomorrow …'

'Don't remind me,' she whispered, feeling all at once as if home was the hand she was holding, and the place she was headed was no sort of home at all. Like enemy territory, almost. But for her dad.

'Hello lass,' he said, as they neared him. 'Hello, Terry.'

'John, look,' Terry began, letting go of Kathleen's hand and plunging both of his into his jacket pockets. 'What I said …'

John nodded lightly. Then turned to Kathleen. 'Get inside, love. Go on. You'll catch your death.'

'But –'

'No buts, lass.' His voice sounded tired rather than angry. 'I'll be in …' He made a flapping motion with his hand.

'Till you're back, then,' she said to Terry, who was nodding at her too, urging her, she knew, to do as her father asked her. She turned to him, albeit reluctantly. 'Is Mam up still?' she asked him.

'What do you think?' her father told her. So she reached up and kissed Terry's cheek, which felt a small act of defiance in itself, then turned on her heel and went inside to face the music.

Irene was still behind the bar, stacking glasses on the draining board, ready to be washed by Kathleen in the morning, and for a moment, when she looked up, having heard the interior door bang, Kathleen almost felt sorry for her. It was almost a knee-jerk reaction – *Irene's bereaved, and she's broken, so be kind to her* – but at the same time the feeling was genuine. And Kathleen clung to that, not just because it made her hold her tongue more than she might have, but because it re-affirmed that she must be a good, decent person – that she had the ability to care about how others might be feeling, which meant that, despite the sadnesses and losses she'd suffered, her spirit and her heart were still in place.

The feeling of pity, edged with guilt, was only fleeting, though. 'You little bitch,' Irene said to her, from behind the sea of dirty glasses, and Kathleen knew straight away that she'd had too much to drink. Her eyes flicked down to the pint pot she had in her hand. Kathleen wondered if she might be about to throw it at her.

Marooned in the middle of the carpet, waiting for her dad to come and rescue her, she couldn't think what might be the best thing to do or say. So she said nothing. Did nothing. Just stood and waited for the explosion. Pondered the idea of heading behind the bar and up the stairs, but only briefly as that would mean getting past Irene in any case. Should she bother? She felt sure Irene would simply follow her up there, screaming non-stop abuse, as was her way.

'Mam,' she began, almost reflexively.

'Don't you "mam" me!' Irene screamed at her. 'You're no daughter of mine, you little bitch! How *dare* you!'

'Dare me *what?*' The words tumbled out by themselves, surprising her. 'Dare me what, Mam?' she said again. 'What exactly have I *done?*'

'The way he spoke to me! Humiliated me! Spoke to me as if I was no better than a dog turd on his shoe! Spoke to *me*. Had the nerve to *speak to me like that*! The little shit! Who the *hell* does he think he is? And don't bother looking for your father, because he's not going to help you. Or for that fancy-pants boyfriend of yours neither, for that matter, because he's barred from here – you hear me? *Barred.*'

She pulled herself up – the same gesture with her arms that Kathleen had seen so many times before. As if gathering up her breasts, like a shield placed in front of her. As if waging war on the world. Were her face not so full of hate, it would be almost comical, like that female character Dick Emery played on his show. 'Speaking to me like that!' Irene shrieked, oblivious to the thoughts running through her stepdaughter's brain. 'In front of you! In front of your father! In front of everyone!' She swept an arm around. It held the glass and, as if the idea had only just occurred to her, she launched it, not at Kathleen but at the door into the foyer, as if aiming it at Terry's ghost.

Kathleen was just about to point out that no one had listened, no one had heard, no one *cared*, for God's sake. And that, actually, all Terry had done was point out just how ridiculous and cruel *she* was being. But a door banged out back, causing both of them to turn.

'Jesus Christ, woman!' said Kathleen's dad, who'd returned via the back way. And probably with good intent, Kathleen thought distractedly, so he could put his fag end in the bin on the way.

He ran across to Irene, who was looking down at her hand now as if it wasn't actually a part of her. She'd been lucid enough, but her eyes seemed unfocussed now, and she swayed.

John put an arm around her, and, as if on some sort of automatic programme, Irene crumpled into his embrace, sobbing noisily. 'Off you go, love,' John whispered, and Kathleen crossed the room gratefully. There was nothing she could do to make the situation any better, much as she hated leaving her dad to deal with it.

'Leave the broken glass,' she mouthed. '*I'll* do it. First thing in the morning, promise.' Then she crept up to bed – no sign of Monica yet, which was a blessing – and wondered wretchedly what her dad had said to Terry.

Kathleen had no idea how long she'd slept, only that sleep had been a long time coming. She lay in the darkness for a while, trying to guess what the time was, the heavy brown curtains giving nothing away. She turned her head. Still no Monica. So she'd not come home *again*.

With the room to herself, and no worries about noise, Kathleen reached for, and put her hand on, the clock that sat between them, then leaned the other way, far enough to grab a corner of the nearest curtain, her effort rewarded by a shaft of greyish light. She squinted at the alarm clock. It was already just past eight. She groaned. And the glass … the broken glass. She'd said she'd clear that up, hadn't she?

She pushed the blankets back and climbed reluctantly out of the warmth of her bed, pulling her old cardigan over her nightdress and, because Monica wasn't around, her feet into her step-sister's princessy pink slippers. The warmth enveloped her, reminding her just how thin and battered her own were, and also of Terry, who'd be asleep, she hoped, before leaving for Andorra. *Was* it Andorra? Was that right? She would need to go to the library and look it up – the place that was not quite in France, and not quite in Spain, but, either way, a horribly long way away.

As she suspected might happen, the lounge bar was clear. Knowing her dad, you'd need a microscope – and a very high-powered one, at that – just to have a hope of finding so much as a single speck of broken glass, and she cursed herself for not having set the alarm clock.

'Alright, Dad?' she said, finding him on his knees behind the bar, lining up bottles of mixers on the shelves.

She got down to help him, pulling a crate towards her. 'I'm sorry,' she said.

'Sorry? What've you got to be sorry for, lass?'

'For not getting up in time to clear all that glass up. For everything. I don't know … Mam asleep still?'

'She's had a pill,' her dad said. That was the way of things these days. Gin for the night times and pills for the day.

'Dad, about Terry. What he said … I don't know what she's told you …'

'Who's she? The cat's mother?' he corrected gently.

'What Mam's told you. I don't know what she's said, Dad, but all he did was point out that she was being nasty.'

117

'To you, lass?'

'Yes, of course to *me*. She said some wicked things, Dad. That's why he said what he said.' She doubted her father would have heard a word of what his wife had said. So she told him, more or less. As accurately as she could. It wasn't hard. There wasn't much, was there? It might have sounded rude in the utmost to Terry, but it was something and nothing here. But it was also the truth, and it *was* cruel, and it addled her that the truth was such poor currency. 'He was just trying to stick up for me, Dad,' she finished, adding, 'which, not unsurprisingly, didn't go down too well,' and then, almost immediately regretting it.

Because her father wasn't stupid. He knew how Irene spoke to her. It was normal in their family. That was the trouble. It was normal. And in a flash of understanding, she realised it was *not*. And not just because she was sick of trying to ride it. Because it *was* cruel and nasty. And that's what Terry saw. Why could her dad not see that too?

'I know, love,' he said. 'And I *do* understand. Sometimes, I know … well, I *know* she can be unkind to you.' He turned and smiled ruefully, and she felt a rush of pity for him. For the lines on his face. For the aches in his back. For the blindness that she was coming to understand no prescription was *ever* going to help. 'You and me both, love,' he said, and in such a forlorn way that she immediately put her arm around his shoulder.

'Times are tough right now, aren't they?' she said. 'Bloody awful.'

'Yes, bloody awful,' he agreed.

'And Terry *knows* that. He understands … It's –'

'It won't make any difference, love. You know what Mam's like. He's –'

'What d'you mean? About barring him? But that's ridiculous, Dad! *She* started it!'

Her dad's eyes flashed towards her.

Kathleen sighed in frustration. 'Dad, it's not *fair*. He was trying to defend me!'

'He was very *rude*, love … and in her own bar. He humiliated her in front of folk. That's not on, love. That's not respectful. Specially not from a young 'un to an old 'un.'

Kathleen fumed. So he was an old 'un when it came to seeing her, but in this, he was a young 'un – as if respect was just assumed. Didn't need to be deserved. And it was not *her* bar, she thought, it was *their* bar. Or, more correctly, *his* bar, till she came along. 'Dad, did you actually hear any of it?' she said. 'No, you didn't! I was there.'

They both stood up, the mixers shelved now, and faced one another. 'Love, don't start. Please. *Leave* it. Let it lie for a bit, eh? For me.'

'Of course,' Kathleen said evenly, feeling the anger rise within her. 'Let it lie. Let it stew. Let it come out in the wash. Is that the plan? Bar him from the pub for hurting her – *Mam's* – feelings, but what about me? What about *my* feelings? Don't they count for anything?'

There was a silence, which stretched, as her father considered. It was always the same, this quiet thinking things through. 'Of course they do, love,' he said. 'You *know* that, and I know your mam's not herself, but right now, for *everyone's* sakes, let this lie a bit, can't you? If I go against her now, it'll only cause more trouble. I know you think it's straightforward but when you're older and wiser … give it a week or two … that's all …'

'But it *is* straightforward, Dad! It's the *principle*!' She felt her throat cracking and it made her even angrier. *Go against her* – as if he was being a defiant child, rather than a husband.

'And, well, love, the thing is …'

'The thing is *what*?' she snapped at him.

'Don't you think, well, given *your* age, and given *his*, and …'

'And *what*?'

'Love, you're only seventeen,' her dad finished.

He let it hang there, looking at her sternly, if not unkindly, over his glasses. 'Still a bit young to be so serious?' he suggested. 'Still a bit young to be off –'

'What d'you mean off?'

'Off getting ideas in your head. He's almost twice your age, lass.'

And a bad influence. She could almost hear him thinking it. A bad influence on his silly, naïve, impressionable child. It was the worst thing he could have said to her, and also the best. Because it made it so abundantly clear how things were, how things stood. How her father really didn't know her at all.

'Love, wait,' he called after her as she stalked up the stairs. But only quietly, so the dragon wouldn't stir.

Chapter II

Kathleen's first thought was to go round to Terry's. But as the idea took shape, so the doubts began gathering. He'd be asleep. He was off to Andorra that evening. To turn up at his house would be to make his day hard, if not impossible, and her mind was soon visited by frightening scenes of carnage, as he fell asleep at the wheel, on some distant Spanish highway, and plunged to his death over a cliff.

And if she could accept that she was being melodramatic, which she knew she was, she was still plagued by the very words her father had proffered – that she was only seventeen, and it would be a very seventeen-year-old thing to do, to pack a bag, turn up on his doorstep, tearful and pathetic, and let him sort things out on her behalf. No, running to Terry at this juncture would never do. It was the very last thing she should be doing.

But what to do instead? How to *deal* with it all? Her anger boiled in her, like a hot ball of lava, spitting and spurting – rolling around in her stomach, making forays to her temples, bunching her fists and making tears spring in her eyes.

But what to do with it? Where to go? Could she conceivably go anywhere? All she knew was that the last place she wanted to be was home, because home, in as much as it had ever really felt it since Irene joined it, didn't feel at all like home any more.

She sat for a while on her bed, trying to calm herself down. To think of her dad and what a difficult life he'd had. To lose his wife. To be left with an eight-year-old daughter. To leave their home and go for the pub job, trying to make a new home for them, free of painful memories. And then Irene, who he'd not so much found as been invaded by (she'd long since understood that, how her stepmother had reeled him in), who he'd taken in, with her children, who he treated as his own children, working so hard to provide – to provide for all three of them. And now this – the crushing tragedy of Darren's death and her stepmother's unravelling ... And now her – his own daughter – taking him on as well. Should she *not* wait? Should she not do as he asked and be patient? *Did* he have a point? Did he have a right to expect that she do as he say?

But it was no use. She couldn't talk herself out of her anger – an unusual anger, in that try as she might to be mature about it, she couldn't find it in herself to put her dad's needs before hers. Much as she loved him, she also had a right to her own life. And if it turned out that her choices were the wrong ones and she'd regret them, then so be it. That would be her choice as well.

She felt claustrophobic in the airless room she so longed to escape from, reminded now, more than ever, how that had been invaded, too. When they'd moved here – her bewildered, her father gaunt and exhausted – this room had been a safe haven, full of her things and toys. But for so short a time – six months? Maybe seven? Before into it came Monica, just that few months older than she was, and who'd asserted her right, as the *eldest*, to take charge of everything, to put her own stamp on the room with all her rows of golliwogs, gonks and dollies, just as the drawers and wardrobe were stuffed with piles and rails of her many clothes.

Kathleen stood up. Half-packed a bag and then furiously unpacked it. There was nowhere for her *to* go, not for more than a walk. So her act of rebellion, her act of principle, was reduced, in the end, to taking to her bed (still no Monica, which was still such a blessing) and not doing her Saturday lunchtime shift. She then composed herself, and though a part of her still ached to run to Terry's (how she wished she had a key; he'd even offered to give her one) she instead had a bath, tied up her hair, dressed 'appropriately', then came down to the bar and worked her usual Saturday night shift, the smile never leaving her face.

What Irene thought of all this, Kathleen truly had no idea, as she'd clearly decided her best course of action was to keep out of her stepdaughter's way. At least it seemed that way; Kathleen didn't know if it was by accident or design, but when she emerged at about four, Irene was nowhere to be seen upstairs, and when she went down, she was nowhere to be seen there either. She'd finally turned up – having apparently been out shopping, yet so skilfully did she manage to skirt around Kathleen that she wondered if her dad had finally given Irene a warning.

He'd certainly been solicitous and kind to Kathleen; not exactly apologetic, but with something in his manner that made her think he *had* done – had told Irene she was treading on a very sticky wicket. Had stood up for his daughter, after all.

Which should, she knew, make her feel less angry towards him, but somehow, though she wanted to, she couldn't seem to feel it; what Terry had done, almost unthinkingly, had created a new standard – and being stood up for wasn't all it was cracked up to be when the action had to be wrung as if blood from a stone.

She went to bed as soon as she finished work on Saturday night and wrote to Terry. He couldn't call her – from Spain (or France, or wherever Andorra turned out to be) it would cost him a small fortune, even assuming he could find a phone box that worked, which, from what he'd told her about where he was going, might be difficult. So she wrote, reassuring him that everything was okay, and spinning him the same yarn her dad had spun her – that in a couple of weeks it would all have blown over and that – *seriously, Terry, I'm not just saying this, honest* – she didn't care if they never went in the Dog and Duck again, because she'd seen enough of the blinking place to last a lifetime.

It was soothing to write to him, to feel connected to him somehow, even though all she could do was post it, or perhaps deliver it, for when he was home.

Then, on the Monday, just because it would connect her to him more, she phoned her Aunt Sally, while her mam and dad were up at the cemetery, seeing to Darren's grave, to ask if she'd heard anything from Uncle Ronnie since they'd gone, and, in doing so, to double check when Terry might be home.

And somehow, though she hadn't planned it, it had all come tumbling out.

'Oh, my giddy aunt, love!' Sally had declared, once the last drop of emotion had been wrung from Kathleen and the telephone cord was wound, noose-like, around her wrist. 'That *cow*. 'Scuse my French and respect to the recently bereaved and so on, but, oh, I could swing for that sister of mine, I really could. You must come to me,' she added.

'Come to you?' Thoughts of moving out – moving in with Sally and the children – swirled invitingly. But what about Terry? Two whole buses. The beguiling images disappeared.

'Yes, come and stay, for a visit. Come and stay a few days while my Ronnie's away. The kids will be ecstatic.

Beyond ecstatic, in fact. As will I. Oh, my poor love. We need to get you out of there. No disrespect to your dad, and I'm sorry if it puts him in a bind and that, but he's not doing right by allowing Rene to bully you. Which I've no doubt he knows, but …' She tutted down the line. 'Well, anyway. You're coming. That's if you want to, of course,' she added, as if the thought had just occurred to her. 'You do want to?'

'I want to,' Kathleen said.

Kathleen didn't own a suitcase of her own – mostly because she'd never had need of one, but she remembered that Monica had a small purple vanity case under her bed that would be enough for her needs.

Monica was at work, and wouldn't be back till after Kathleen had left, and it seemed a strange irony that, at this point, when so much depressing stuff was happening, she and Monica had found a connection; a thin strand of kinship.

She had come home from her friend's eventually, early on the Sunday evening, but had said she was going out again soon after, and after the ensuing row with her mam, which had gone on for the best part of an hour, had stormed into the bedroom and thrown her bag on the bed with such force that the little alarm clock had bounced off the chest of drawers and onto the carpet, where it pinged once, pathetically, before suddenly bursting to life, and ringing as if its very life depended on it.

Upon which Monica, with an impressive roar, had stamped on it. 'And you can bleeding shut up as well!' she'd yelled at it. Then she looked at Kathleen, who'd been reading over the letter she'd written Terry, who first stared, and then found herself grinning.

Which made Monica smile too, and then giggle, and then laugh, and before they knew it, they were both laughing uncontrollably, almost hysterically, stifling the noise with hands clamped over their mouths, for fear of Irene hearing them. It was the best and longest laugh they'd had in years.

Monica wouldn't mind, Kathleen decided now, drawing back the candlewick bedspread and reaching into the dusty gloom to lay her hands on the case. It was home to a couple of pairs of old stilettoes and a plastic bag of hair rollers, and these she put back neatly, where the case had sat before.

She didn't have to think for long, as she had very little to choose from, and with space tight – the case was no bigger than a couple of shoe boxes – had thrown in clean underwear, two pairs of slacks, a couple of blouses and her good sweater – along with her nightie and her wash bag, it should be enough to last her for the two or three days – four at most – that her dad had allowed her to be away.

'I wish you'd let me drive you,' her dad said, as she appeared downstairs, ready. 'If you can just hang on a bit, Mary'll be here and I can leave her and your mam in charge.'

Kathleen shook her head. 'Dad, it's fine. I'd prefer to get the bus anyway. Get to know my way around a bit better, independently, on my *own*.'

If he'd noticed her pointed tone, he gave no indication of it. 'If you're sure, love,' he said instead. 'Just don't you be talking to any strangers bearing sweeties.'

He smiled – it was a shared joke, another memory of after her mam died and he'd get off to work at the printers, leaving her to make her own way to school. Which he'd hated – though she hadn't; it had given her her first taste of independence – and, fearing for her welfare between home and the playground, those were the last words he'd say to her every morning, before he left.

But Irene had come up behind him, and hadn't seen the smile that had passed between them.

'For God's sake, John,' she snapped, 'I should think she's old enough and ugly enough to look after herself, don't you?'

Kathleen saw her father's jaw clench, but was happy enough to let it pass – *it's just an expression. Which says more about her than about me. Don't rise to it. Ignore it.* Instead she picked up her case and smiled at her stepmother, who had just had her hair done down at Carol's. It put Kathleen in mind of a Brillo pad, gone rusty. 'Oh, *more* than enough,' she agreed.

Her dad opened the door. It was dull out and drizzling. They kept saying on TV that there was heavy snow coming, and once again she worried about Terry getting home. She patted the letter in her pocket – she would deliver it on her way to the bus stop – and stepped out into the morning, flipping her hood up.

'Ring and let us know you got there safe,' her dad said as he kissed her. 'And give your aunt our love,' he added, 'and those two little nippers.'

Kathleen heard Irene's 'pah!' just as the door closed. 'Same to you!' she trilled, heading briskly up the road.

Thornton, where Sally and Ronnie had moved to the previous spring, was two longish bus rides away.

It felt a world away, in fact, and as Kathleen got off the second bus, it felt more like a universe away. It felt like she was stepping straight into the pages of one of the Enid Blyton books of her childhood. *Mr Pink-Whistle*, that was it, where the streets were tree-lined and clean, and the houses were uniform and neat. She half expected to smell the scent of freshly washed laundry filling the air. Sally had always had a lovely house – not council, either, but bought and paid for. Kathleen knew this new one would be just as bright and neat and lovely.

She kept repeating Sally's instructions, which she'd memorised before she'd left, just in case she mislaid the scribbled notes on her piece of paper.

'Walk straight down the road, take the first right then the second left.' Which assumed, she thought anxiously, that you got off at the right bus stop. But no, she told herself sternly, it had been the right bus stop. She'd checked with the conductor – she was definitely in the right place.

But which way to walk along the street she'd been deposited on? Sally had said 'down' but which way was down, given that for the most part it was flat as a pancake?

But with only two choices she reasoned she might as well set off – if she was wrong she could simply retrace her steps and set off again in the opposite direction. And after walking for ten minutes it seemed she'd done exactly that – she'd taken a right but it was a right that seemed entirely without lefts, and by the time she'd returned to the place where she'd started, a second bus had pulled up at the stop. Happily, this disgorged an elderly lady carrying two heavy-looking shopping bags, who had the look of a person who knew where she was going, so Kathleen ran across the road to catch her up.

'Can you tell me where Sandal's Green is?' she asked the woman breathlessly.

She smiled from under a transparent rain-hood that had slipped down at the front and, with her hands occupied, clearly couldn't pull up. 'This way,' she said. 'I'm headed there myself. Follow me.'

Kathleen resisted the urge to push it back into position. 'Can I help you with your bags then?' she suggested instead.

'Would you, love? That'd be grand,' the old lady told her, allowing Kathleen to take the two bags into one hand while the other hung on to the case.

'You on a visit?' the lady said as they took the right right this time.

'Yes, I'm off to see my aunt.'

'In Sandal's Green? What's her name?'

'Sally McArdle?'

The woman stopped. 'Young Sal? You're her *niece*?'

'Well, sort of. Her step-niece,' Kathleen explained. 'She's my stepmum's sister.'

'Well, she's a grand lass is Sal. She's a real gem, she is. Truly. Anyway, there you are – third door down. This is me.'

Kathleen took the bags to the doorstep of a neat little semi, with white net curtains and a garden full of neatly trimmed shrubs. And, in the summer, no doubt serried rows of flowers. The air was colder here but there was a warmth seeping out of the place even so. And Sally – 'young Sal' – was a grand lass. A gem. How nice it would be to be able to pass that news on. It would tickle Sally greatly, and, of course, it was true. How nice to be known in that way by your neighbours.

How nice to be known in that way by anyone, anywhere, she thought, her spirits lifting as she lifted her aunt's knocker.

Chapter 12

Kathleen wrapped her hands gratefully around the teacup Sally had given to her. It was small and dainty – almost translucent, because it was made of bone china, and decorated with sprigs of forget-me-nots. A memory surfaced, of having cups a bit like this when she was a little girl; a tea set that had originally belonged to her nan and had been passed down. The same nan who'd died only weeks after her mam had. From a broken heart, or so everyone had said. What had happened to those cups and saucers? It bothered her that she didn't know. She'd have liked them. Something solid from her past.

'I just don't understand,' she said, sensing the feeling returning to her fingers, after having carried the two shopping bags in one straining hand.

'Understand what?' Sally asked.

'How you and mam can be so different. There's you a gem, and a grand lass, whereas Mam …' She grinned but didn't elaborate. 'How *can* you be so different and still be sisters?'

Sally popped the cosy on her cheerful blue-and-white spotted teapot, then pulled up a chair and sat down on it, on the other side of the little kitchen table. The children were still in school so they had a good hour for a natter before she'd walk up with Sally and fetch them. And surprise them, Sally having decided not to tell them in advance. She'd been tickled pink to hear the reports of her sparkling reputation, laughing loudly and commenting that Mrs Hughes obviously hadn't seen her and Ronnie rolling home of a Saturday night.

But she now considered the question as seriously as it was asked. 'Oh, it can happen,' Sally said. 'Believe me, it can. It's not just the genes you're born with that matters, is it?' She shook her head. 'Look at you,' she said. 'You're frozen. I wish you'd let me come and meet you at the bus stop, like I said. Shall I get the blow heater out for you?'

Kathleen shook her head. 'It's not that cold, honest. And I'll be fine once I get this tea down me. I'm warming up already.' She took a sip of the tea, which was hot and strong and perfect, as was the pretty kitchen, as was all of it, in fact. 'Oh, and thank you *so* much for having me,' she said, feeling emotional all of a sudden. Perhaps her heart was beginning to warm up as well.

'Anytime, love. I mean it. *Anytime*,' Sally said. 'Anyway, tell me all again. Slowly. Every last bit of it. What's that *cow* of a sister of mine been up to this time?'

Despite how she felt herself, Kathleen still found herself shocked at the vehemence of her aunt's tone. Since Darren had gone, it felt strange hearing anyone speak like that about her stepmother, whether within her hearing or out of it. Well, till Firework Night anyway. And, angry as she was, and despite feeling so thrilled Terry had stood up for her, she even felt bad about *that*.

She supposed it was all down to being brought up a Christian, about God. However much she still hated Irene, for what she'd done over the years, Darren's death had changed everything in that respect somehow. It was a kind of guilt, because Irene had lost the thing that was most precious to her. Had the worst thing imaginable happen to her as a mother – had been made to pay the ultimate price for her sins. So it seemed almost as if you were no longer allowed to even harbour bad feelings about her, because God had already punished her so much.

But did that mean she could do what she liked now? Treat Kathleen so badly and just be allowed to? What did God say about that? Was that right? The questions bubbled away inside her, confusing and strange. Should Irene be let off being brought to account for *anything*, ever again? Sally obviously had no such confusion in *her* mind. And Kathleen wished she had her aunt's confidence in how things should be.

She sighed. 'She's got it in for us. She has since the start. And now he's given her a reason to make it impossible for us ... She's determined to split us up. I know she is. Me and Terry,' she added shyly, still a little self-conscious about the business of them being a proper couple.

'No surprises *there*, then,' Sally said. 'I'll *bet* she is. She's jealous! And what'll she do for a slave if you go waltzing off into the sunset with him, eh? Fat chance of that niece of mine helping her, is there?' Kathleen shook her head, and explained about how Monica was more and more avoiding being at home now. 'Can't say I blame her,' Sally said. 'Anyway, go on,' she urged. 'I need to know the facts. Tell me all. Get the lot of it off your chest.'

So Kathleen did. About Terry and how they felt about each other. About Irene being unkind to her in front of Terry and how he'd leapt to her defence. How he wouldn't stand for her being so nasty and how it had all gone on from there. How she'd barred Terry from the pub and how her dad had just let her. How he'd even suggested that she shouldn't be with him anyway. And how Irene was making her life a complete misery …

'And here we are,' she finished, sighing. 'For two pins I'd run away, I really would.' She drained her cup and smiled ruefully. 'Except for one problem. I have no money and nowhere to run away *to*.'

Sally said nothing for a moment, then pushed back her chair, went and got the teapot and topped up Kathleen's cup.

'I've changed my mind,' she said, as she took her seat again. 'You know, you're right. I don't understand how we can be related to each other either. Well, maybe not so much that. But I'm ashamed to call her my sister, I really am.'

Kathy sipped at the fresh tea, which was by now dark and tangy. Just the way Darren used to like it, she remembered. No more. 'I always wished I had a sister,' she said. 'You know, particularly after Mam died. Just someone to share everything with. 'Specially when Dad took up with Irene. Just a friend, really. Someone who knew how I felt.'

Sally nodded sympathetically. Perhaps she was musing on that too.

'Did you ... you and Irene ...' she went on, '... were you *ever* friends? Ever close? You know, when you were younger?'

Sally shook her head. 'I'd like to say we were, but, no. We never were. I was the evil little cuckoo in her nest ...'

'Cuckoo?' Kathleen asked, not understanding. They were full sisters, weren't they? Not like her and Monica and Darren.

'Oh, not in *that* way,' Sally said. 'We had the same parents, so it was nothing like that. But she was the eldest – and by quite a long stretch, as you know. She was twelve by the time I came along, and she wasn't happy about it at *all*.' She grinned. 'I'm not sure Mam was that happy about it when she found out, either, truth be told! But Dad ... well, that's a man for you, isn't it? Well, some men anyway. None of the grisly bits to deal with, so what's it to them? No galumphing around like Ten Ton Tessie – and remember, our mam was by now pushing forty – and no giving birth. Men don't *know* they're born, do they? So, yes, it was a shock, but they took it in their stride – what else was there to do, really? And then I came along, and – well, you know how it goes – I was a bonny baby, by all accounts. A happy one. No bother much to anyone. So I suppose I just became the apple of his eye.'

Kathleen smiled back at her aunt, seeing exactly how that could happen. 'I'll bet.'

'And the agent of destruction in my older sister's previously charmed life ...'

'But you were only a baby! God, if Mam was still alive and she'd had another baby, I'd have loved it.'

Sally drew her brows together, looking amused. 'Really?'

'I would. I'm not just saying that. I'd have *loved* a baby sister.'

'You're too broody for your own good, Kathleen Adamson,' Sally chided her. 'And beware wanting a baby for all the wrong reasons, too,' she added. 'You think you can create your own little family, but, let me tell you, they are not a solution. They are hard work. And they have a habit of compounding problems rather than solving them, too.'

'Oh, I *know*,' Kathleen said, even though lying in bed on Firework Night she had harboured those very thoughts. 'But you and Irene. How could she *hate* you?'

Sally studied her. 'Truthfully? Because my father doted on me shamelessly, that's why. And Mam – well, she was back dealing with nappies and everything, wasn't she? Rene had had them to herself all those years – the cherished only child – and now I'd come along and spoiled things, hadn't I? And it must have been hard. Don't forget, she was a teenager when I was a toddler – and an unhappy teenager at the best of times, too.'

'Do you remember all that?'

She shook her head. 'No, not much of it, not while I was little. But, yes, by the time I was five or six, it was all *too* obvious. Don't forget, our dad had been away a lot when she was growing up, and by the time I came along, he was home that much more. And there were the obvious things …' She paused. 'Well, you can see for yourself, can't you? I'm no Marilyn Monroe, but I was lucky. Got my looks from my nan, who was a bit of a beauty in her day. And then I grew, and I grew. And I was blonde, as well – God, how Rene hated that. I tell you, love, she *raged*. I was the thorn in her side, I was. The irritating little sister. The reason she was miserable. The reason she could never get a boyfriend … or keep one.'

Kathleen thought back to Irene's constant preening and flirting with the customers. Even with *Terry*. 'But that's ridiculous! Even by the time she got married, you must have only been twelve!'

'Oh, I know, and it wasn't till I was in my teens myself that it really properly hit me quite how much she'd always resented me. I'd stolen her dad's heart – or so she had decided, anyway – and I was a *femme fatale*, wasn't I? 'Specially once I'd starting seeing boys myself, and that. Didn't matter what I did, how hard I tried, she never had any time for me. Jealousy's a very powerful emotion.'

'D'you think it's true, then?' Kathleen ventured. 'About her first husband, and Darren? D'you think she *did* get pregnant on purpose, just to trap him into marrying her?'

Sally sat back and sighed. Was she thinking about Darren again too, and what a tragedy it all was? 'I don't know, love,' she said finally. 'That's the truth of it. I don't know. I mean, it's possible. Maybe even probable. But I can't say it's what happened. And, you know, when he upped and buggered off back to America, I was proud of her for being so strong about it. Couldn't have been easy, could it? Left with a toddler and another one on the way, doing it all on her own.

'And I tried to help her, too. And for a while there, I *did* help. I used to babysit while she was at work –' She grinned again. 'You're not the only one who's young and broody, love! But … well, we never could get past it. *She* could never get past it. I was young, free and single, wasn't I? So I could still do no right. And you reach a point – well, I did, anyway. Some more saintly types might not have – when I realised I was never going to make it go away. All the barbs, all the resentments. All the jealousy she had against me. Just for existing, pretty much. She needed me yet she hated me. That's about the size of it really ...'

'So did you have a big falling out?'

'Not exactly.' Sally stopped. Seemed to consider. 'Let's just say she crossed a line. With a boy. Who I was very sweet on ...' She paused again. 'But let's not drag all that up. That water's long since flowed under the bridge. I suppose the main thing is that, really, it's down to Mam and Dad – 'specially Dad, God rest his soul. Like I say, it's not just genes, is it? Not like it is with being blonde or ginger. There's sowing seeds ...'

'So you forgive her, sort of?' Kathleen asked, trying to make sense of what sounded like Sally's understanding. That she didn't necessarily *blame* her for being the way she was. 'You realise she couldn't help it? Is that it?'

'Occasionally, when I'm feeling particularly thoughtful. But, no. Not now. Not so much. Yes, I think I *understand* now. But we're all adults. We're none of us slaves to our backgrounds, are we? She could have the same thoughts herself, couldn't she? That I didn't *ask* to be born then. That I'm not responsible for what our dad did or didn't do, any more than she is. She could try to do that, couldn't she? But, as far as I can tell, she never has.'

She was silent for a moment, then she tipped her head back and laughed. 'Hark at me! That's far too much philosophising for one day, I think. Drink up.

And wrap up. Now you're all thawed out. Typical! But we need to toddle down and pick up the little ones from school soon. Aww, it's *so* good to see you, Kathleen,' she said, as they both got up from the table. 'And you know what?'

'What?'

'Everything is going to be just fine, you'll see.'

'I wish I had your confidence. Terry must think I come from a family of maniacs. He must be having second thoughts …'

'Nonsense. Trust me, he's *very* sweet on you.'

The knowledge thrilled her. Just hearing it, knowing that Sally already knew that. 'But Dad's right about the age thing,' Kathleen said. 'That's what I keep on coming back to. I don't care a *fig* how old or young Terry is. But *he* might. Once he thinks about it. People talking and that … worrying that he's cradle-snatching. Judging him. *He* might.'

'Love, I *know* him,' Sally said, putting an arm around Kathleen and squeezing her. 'He's not the sort of man who cares one bit about idle gossip. And if he was – if he was that weak; didn't know his own mind? Well, you wouldn't want to be with someone like that *anyway*, would you? But he's *not*. And another thing, to keep in mind at *all* times, you hear? It's *your* life, okay – yours to do whatever you like with. So, don't let that old witch tell you any differently.'

Chapter 13

Kathleen had been back from Sally's not twenty-four hours when she got Terry's letter. Which was a bitter irony, because it was only the thought of seeing him that had convinced her she shouldn't stay longer than she'd planned.

This was despite Sally entreating her to stay at least over the weekend, when Ronnie would be home and they'd been invited to a party at one of their neighbours'. 'And you never know,' Sally had pointed out, 'we might even be able to persuade your Terry to come, too.'

No, she'd said. She was needed, she had to think of her dad. And besides, she'd not wanted to wait till the Saturday to see Terry. Couldn't bear to. Ronnie wasn't coming home till the Friday, because he'd had another job to go straight on to, but Terry had come back to England on the Wednesday – Sally had confirmed it – and it was impossible to think of him, back in Bradford, so close, and *not* want to see him, alone. To curl up with him on his beige settee, nestled among the hunting-scene cushions his dead wife's mam had made for him

– *them*. And which she'd not quite finished making before their old house was burned down. There was a rightness in him keeping them, she'd decided.

So, no, she couldn't stay. This despite her dad being only too happy to let her. 'Grab the break while you can,' he'd said, when she'd spoken to him on the phone. She should take a proper break before the final weeks running up to Christmas, when, with all the parties and knees-ups and general festive mood, none of them would have a minute to draw breath. 'Stay a while, love,' he'd told her. 'We're managing just fine without you,' and he'd been so insistent that Kathleen had already made an early New Year's resolution – that she'd be eighteen the following August and soon after that she'd be twenty-one, so she must stop thinking she had to be the pub skivvy pub for ever; that if she didn't things would all go downhill.

So, on the Thursday, she'd left as planned, with Sally walking her back to the bus stop, and despite knowing she was going back to the misery at home, the butterflies in her stomach travelled the whole journey with her, bringing warmth to her mood, even if not to the weather, which had suddenly turned bitterly cold. Perhaps they were right. Perhaps the snow was on its way now.

She didn't care what her dad said – that had been her other resolution. If Terry remained barred from the pub then so be it. She would simply meet up with him else-where – in the Red Lion, or the Bull, or over at his. Because whatever dad had said, she didn't believe for a moment that he would actually forbid them from going out with each other. Even if it did go against her mam's wishes, she refused to believe he would go as far as stop her, not if he knew that it was what she wanted.

And it was what she wanted. There was no doubt in her mind. She'd thought long and hard at Sally's, lying in bed, in their pretty spare room, and now they'd talked and they'd talked – and they'd talked fit to bursting – it all seemed so obvious that they'd never get any of it sorted out.

She felt she understood now – could make sense of why Irene so disliked her. It was the same thing as Sally had described about their childhood. She was jealous, that was all. A furious, consuming jealousy – of the close bond Kathleen had always had with her father and, by extension, with her mam, the wife he'd laid to rest.

'Think about it, love,' Sally had explained, very gently. 'Think about *why* your dad married Rene – what might have been going through his mind. I hesitate to suggest it, but do you think they were ever like you and Terry? Like me and Ronnie? I don't think they ever were. I think your dad, if I'm being honest with you, never felt quite like that about her, do you?'

Kathleen knew the truth of it immediately. Her dad and Irene were *never* like that together. She'd thought, as she'd got older, that that was just the way things were. That once people had been married a bit, things changed in that regard. That all the kissing and the butterflies and holding hands and so on just, well, became less important. But then she thought about Sally and Ronnie, always larking about and giggling, often looking at each other in a way that made it clear that that side of things hadn't disappeared at all.

'Perhaps he saw a family,' Sally had suggested. 'A mum for you. A sister and a brother ...' She'd let it hang, and Kathleen suddenly knew the truth of it so clearly. And as for Irene – well, of course she felt jealous. What had *she* hoped for in marrying John? Security for her and her two fatherless children, certainly. Love? Perhaps that, too. And perhaps she'd never got it. Not in the way she wanted it, for her husband's love was still burning so bright – for the daughter, yes, but also for the mother who'd given birth to her. So there'd be no softening of her feelings towards Kathleen, not ever. Because she had what Irene wanted, her father's unconditional love. And it had soured her, just the same way it had soured things with Sally. And knowing that brought a new sense of determination to Kathleen. That her own life was ahead of her and she had the right to be happy – so it was also her right to choose how to live it.

* * *

But on Friday morning – very early, if not yet remotely bright – Eddie the postie had trotted up and, since Kathleen had the front door open to shake out the big coir mat, placed the letter – the letter to *her* – right in her hand, along with another one, which looked like a bill.

'Another birthday, then?' he'd quipped before turning on his heel, and heading off with his sack of post, whistling.

Kathleen took it into the kitchen, in order to savour it before Monica came down, placing it on the worktop, separate from the other letter, while she poured herself a second cup of tea. She'd not seen Terry yet, but then she hadn't expected to. If he'd been home the previous day he would have had to catch up on lots of sleep, and with him not coming in the pub – which she'd told him in her own letter would likely just inflame things further – she was content to wait to hear from him, which she assumed would be today, either via one of his mates, or perhaps, since there was no other way of contacting her, risking telephoning the pub, and the wrong person picking up the phone.

It was with a rush of excitement that she slipped her thumb under the flap of the envelope. Then she turned it over, wondering for a moment if he'd sent it from Andorra, and thinking how romantic that would be.

But no, it was postmarked Bradford, and the date on the stamp was yesterday, confirming he was home, yes, but then a new, less welcome thought occurred to her – perhaps he was already off on another job and she might not see him now for several days.

It was a single sheet of paper – cheap exercise-book paper – covered in his small slanted writing, and folded in two. She'd never seen his handwriting in this way before. Only here and there; a short list on the back of a fag packet, a scribbled-down phone message on a napkin. Seeing it like this, written *for* her, caused another thrill to suffuse her. Seeing someone's writing was such an insight into what they were like – from the whorls and curls formed by her wild pen pal in Germany, to the neat rows of letters and numbers that her father always formed, as if straying too far from the line was a dangerous business, and that scrawled numerals might spell disaster.

She unfolded the letter slowly, still savouring the look of it. From the way he'd written the pub address so precisely in the left-hand corner, to the date, which he'd separated by long, decisive lines, to the way he'd written 'Kathy' – not dear Kathleen – just 'Kathy', which made it seem so much more romantic.

And then she read:

Kathy
I really don't know how best to say this, and I can't tell you how sorry I am not to be saying it to you in person, as I wanted, but I'm going to be away for

another week now, and I didn't want to leave without
writing to you. I've thought long and hard and I'm afraid
I think it's best if we don't see each other anymore,
because I'm not sure it's going to work out. It's very
complicated, as you know, but I now realise that I have
to do the right thing. Perhaps I should never have
started seeing you in the first place, given everything.
I'm so sorry if I've hurt you. It's the last thing I want.
Yours, always affectionately
Terry

The room seemed to spin, and then settle, and then, as
she turned, spin again. She placed a hand on the worktop to try to steady herself a little, and even as she did
so she berated herself. What was she? A heroine in a
blinking Jane Austen novel? Swooning so pathetically
over being dumped by a bloke she'd barely been seeing
three months?

Not even quite three months, she reminded herself
furiously. This was ridiculous behaviour – no, it was
more than ridiculous. She had half seen this coming,
hadn't she? She'd said as much to Sally. So why was she
so shocked? Why so dumbfounded and distressed?

She could hear movement from the bar. Her dad, no
doubt, coming down to take a delivery. She snatched up
the letter, slid it into the envelope, and hurriedly stuffed
it into her pocket. Then reached across and switched
on the radio, to drown out the clamouring in her head.

'Hello, love,' her dad said, shuffling into the kitchen, in vest and trousers, pushing his glasses up his nose. 'Gawd, that's a bloody racket that is,' he added, as he made for the empty kettle. 'Who is it, the screaming ab dabs?' This was another joke between them. The screaming ab dabs, the dippy doodahs, the fancy nancys – there was always a new one. And for a moment she stepped outside herself and cherished his cheery grin.

But not for long. The radio was blaring with something altogether too jolly. Her eyes swimming with tears, she fled the room.

As she'd known he would, because it was impossible to hide her feelings from her father, he left her for long enough that she'd be able to compose herself before coming to find her out the back, in the yard. This was the long-standing, but unspoken thing they had between them – no scenes of hysteria, no histrionics, no weeping and wailing; it had been that way since not long after Kathleen's mam had died. She would sob and sob, until she realised it was actually *worse* if she did that, because when she cried it made her dad cry and she couldn't bear to see him crying – his strength was the rock that she clung to, for dear life, and if he crumbled it was as if she was falling off a cliff, and would never be able to clamber back up.

It was snowing, adding a fresh layer of swirling, spinning flakes to the crusted heaps that already lay around her. She didn't care – in fact, she welcomed the sting on her cheeks and up her nostrils, but as she battled with a screwed-up bit of old tissue that she'd plucked from her other pocket, her dad said 'for heaven's sake, lass, if you think I'm coming out there, you've another think coming. Get back inside. Let's go back upstairs. I've brewed us a nice pot of tea.'

So she went back into the kitchen and she took the proffered cup and, since there seemed no point in doing otherwise, she told him about the letter and, stiffly, how everything could get back to normal because she and Terry had broken up.

'I'm not pleased, love,' he said in answer to her unspoken question, correctly interpreting the ferocity of the challenge in her eyes. 'I'm sorry. Love, the *last* thing I want is for you to be so upset, 'specially now, but –'

She sighed. Softened a little. There was no point in fighting him. 'There *isn't* a but, Dad,' she said quietly. 'Please don't offer me any buts. And if you say anything about fish in the sea or pebbles on the beach, I will tip this cup of tea over your head.'

'I reckon you would, too,' he said. 'You're like your mam, you. Full of spirit. I had to keep my head down with her a good bit, too.'

Had. It took all of half a second for Kathleen to register that he was talking not about Irene, but about *her* mother. Touched, she laid a hand on his arm. Despite

151

his attempt at lightness, which she could see through, and if it were even humanly possible, he seemed almost more upset about Terry than she did.

'I'll be okay, Dad,' she told him, even though she knew she wouldn't. 'Give it time. Isn't that the thing? You know, keep myself busy ...'

'I wish I could tell you,' he said, pushing a hand through his wisps of greying hair. 'I've not much experience of broken-hearted teenage daughters ...'

And I've no experience of *being* one, she thought wretchedly, feeling the tears spring at the thought of the note stuffed inside her pocket. More tears. And more tears. The very thought of it all was wearying. Unfixable, except by waiting. By time. She sniffed them back. Finished her tea, all the while looking across the top of the cup at her dad's thoroughly miserable face. She missed her mam *so* much. Always had. And so did he.

She arranged a smile on her face. It was the best thing. The only thing, really. She'd never been much of a one for histrionics anyway. Being the centre of attention. Being gawped at. Being pitied. 'Dad, it's *fine*,' she said. 'Come on. Let's get that till and bag of change sorted.'

'I'm so sorry, lass. I *really* am,' he said again.

Chapter 14

Kathleen knelt on the carpet in the taproom and tried not to cry. No one was around so it wasn't as if anyone would see her, but she was sick of it, sick of being on the edge of it constantly, and, most of all, sick of being so bloody *pathetic*; so much the *drip* she didn't want herself to be.

She had counted the days. Hadn't wanted to but couldn't stop herself. All fifteen of them now – it was finally December. Around six of them, she'd worked out, when he was away on one of his trips, then another nine where he could be anywhere – abroad again, possibly, or on a job somewhere in England, or perhaps – since he was no longer a regular in *their* pub, in the Red Lion, or at home, or in town, perhaps – anywhere. She wished she could stop herself wondering. Wished it a *lot*.

Irene had responded entirely as Kathleen had expected her to. With 'good riddance to bad rubbish', with 'you needed your head testing anyway', with 'he'll be out seeing a lass more his *own* age before you know it – some say he already is', with 'will you stop that bloody snivelling and grow up!' more than once, often followed by 'some of us have been through a sight worse than you have, my girl!'

Most of all, though, it was as if Terry had simply been erased, as if by one of those thick blue school rubbers, and bar her dad continually patting her, proffering tea, whispering 'that's the way, lass', life carried on in the same mostly miserable way – Monica short with her mother, always out, often staying out, the same round of chores and bar shifts, the same scowl on Irene's face, and all of it building and brewing and looming larger and larger, the business of Christmas coming and Darren dead.

Was it better or was it worse that she was heartbroken at Christmas? On the one hand she had a great deal to distract her now they were so busy, and that constant reminder, in the shape of losing her stepbrother, helped her to remember (as if she needed help, given how often Irene told her) that all heartbreaks must be kept in perspective.

But on the other hand, the spectres still chased and tormented her; of all the things she might do with Terry, the Christmas card she would write for him, the fun they might have if they were treated to the much-heralded snow – she'd thought exactly that on the bus home from Sally's.

And it had certainly snowed. It had snowed almost solidly for over a fortnight, transforming the grey streets of the estate into Christmas-card prettiness and, for a brief while, causing an almost welcome chaos on the roads; punters coming in at unexpected times, moaning and grumbling, and then, philosophical that their days were already hijacked, starting to see the benefits of being in a warm pub with a glass in their hand. 'That's wartime camaraderie, that is,' her dad told her. 'A bigger enemy to fight. Always does the trick, that.'

But here she was crying. *Again*. Well, almost. She looked down at the string of fairy lights that had brought her so close to tears. It didn't matter if a miracle had them light up suddenly between her fingers. It just didn't feel Christmassy at all.

But how *could* it feel Christmassy? Her own woes aside, how could anyone seriously think about celebrating Christmas this year? With Darren dead. With Darren gone. With Darren's absence everywhere you looked – in the shrieking, yelling silence of the words no one could speak, but they were there, perched like vultures set to swoop down and run off with any single Christmassy thing anyone did.

So perhaps the lights – lights that had once been held in her dear dead mother's fingers – were making a protest of their own. Oh, the pub might now be graced with its big artificial tree, the bars festooned with their garlands and paper chains and tinsel, but without the lights – lights that had come out every single year since she'd been little – it had none of that special magic that

155

might have helped to lift her spirits a little, helped her at least *pretend* there was anything to smile about.

The weather wasn't helping much either. The seasonal snow, which had caused everyone so much inconvenience and such fun, had come too soon, and a sharp rise in temperature a couple of days back had melted almost all of it away. And, almost as if brought in especially to match her grey mood, it was currently hammering down with rain.

There were floods, even. Bad ones. 'Biblical' they kept saying. As if sent to make everything that bit gloomier. But, despite that, perhaps the broken fairy lights could help her. The pub tree needed lights, even if the flat was officially a decoration-free zone, so if she asked him she was sure her dad would give a her few bob to nip to Woolies and get a new set, so she could finish the job before the pub opened again tonight.

It would do her good to get out, too – blow the cobwebs away. Finish the job of having the scales fall from her eyes, as well. It would also be good to escape for an hour or so, if only to be released from the torture Monica was currently inflicting on her. She'd bought a copy of the latest Beatles song as soon as she'd got her wages and had obviously decided to spend a portion of her day off playing it. And playing *only* it. Over and over again.

It wasn't that Kathleen didn't like The Beatles – far from it. She thought she could probably listen to John

Lennon's voice for ever. But right now, apart from the endless repetition, the lyrics seemed set to upset her; almost seemed to be invading her very soul, even when drowned out by Monica's off-key wailing.

She was wailing now – in a vague approximation of the lyrics – about seeing things her way and how she was fed up with talking.

Chance would be a fine thing, Kathleen thought. She'd not even been given the chance, because she'd been summarily finished with. She'd been dumped. Perhaps she'd been stupid to imagine they had a future in the first place. After all, as he'd made clear in his letter, by virtue of *not* daring to mention it, he was right – she *was* only seventeen. Silly teenager.

Her dad and Irene were up in the flat, poring over the account books. She hating talking to them then, being reminded how tight money was. Being reminded by Irene how lucky she was to have a job, when so many others had nowt.

But her dad looked up and smiled and said, yes, of course, love. Go and fetch some. And Irene, who'd obviously downed a gin or two at lunchtime, didn't even raise her head to comment. There was a difference in her now – a kind of distracted, glassy-eyed way about her – and Kathleen wondered if, now she'd had the satisfaction of seeing Terry off, she'd nothing between her and her grief.

She pocketed the money and ran back downstairs, the music from the bedroom blaring as she went.

Monica was still caterwauling as Kathleen reached for her raincoat, now about how short life was.

And, Kathleen thought, short and extremely uncertain. The Beatles were right; fussing and fighting were a waste of what little time you *did* have. She thought of her dad, and of Irene, and how they'd set up 'home' together, and how much fussing and fighting had gone on as a consequence.

She wanted better. She understood, and the knowledge was helpful – it made her realise that life could throw all sorts of stuff at you, and that you couldn't know how you'd deal with it till you were actually in the midst of it – but at the same time, she knew she wanted better.

She also wished she didn't feel so lonely. She missed out all the time, working nights most of the week – missed out on parties and pub nights and just being with her friends – but mostly she missed what she'd only just found, the business of being with a lad – well, a man – and having a special someone to talk to.

She opened the door a little and the wind blew it the rest of the way, bouncing it back again, against its hinges. It was probably the worst time to walk all the way to Woolworths, but in her perverse frame of mind, it was also the best. Like Jane Eyre crossing the moor after leaving Mr Rochester, there felt something very appropriate in stomping out into the teeth of a gale.

It was a good twenty-minute walk to the Woolies in town, but once she hit her stride, Kathleen found herself feeling better already, the foul weather so accurately matching her mood that there was a perverse kind of pleasure in letting it soak her. She might be miserable but at least she felt alive.

The drains were overflowing, so she kept close to the garden walls, as car after car sped past, kicking up sprays of dirty water, no one seeming to care that every puddle they drove over sent another shower over anyone walking by. She'd certainly dodged a fair few as she drew level with St Luke's Hospital, which she couldn't pass without thinking about who might have got Darren's job, and a part of her still not quite fully accepting that she'd not see him striding out of the place, hands in pockets, the *Sporting Life* under one arm, more often than not popping into the Red Lion for a quick one.

And perhaps to touch someone for a loan, she thought sadly, remembering the paper her dad had mysteriously stuffed in his dressing-gown pocket. He'd refused to say more when she'd pressed him, dismissing it as unimportant, but she could tell he was lying, and still wondered what it was about. Another debt, no doubt. Which her dad had presumably decided to deal with. She hoped he'd not ended up in trouble himself.

She heard the lorry pulling up before she saw it. Heard the hiss of the air brakes as it pulled to a stop, a little way down the road just ahead of her. At that point, when it pulled into the spot just outside the pub, she didn't even really register its existence. It was just another vehicle that might have splashed her.

That it had stopped here, however – outside the Red Lion – was strange. It wasn't a brewery truck. It was an articulated lorry – a big one, as well – the indicator lights winking steadily as she drew level with it. She kept her head down as she passed it, briefly protected from the swish of traffic, conscious of the giant wheels almost coming up to her waist.

She would have walked on past, too, had she not heard a shout then.

'Kathy! Kathy, wait!'

She stopped. Turned around, and was momentarily blinded. It couldn't have been much after three now, but it was already getting dark, and the headlights, now behind her, blazed white through the rain. She blinked water from her eyes. 'Kathy, hold up!' came the shout again. 'Let me give you a lift!'

She blinked again. Heard a door slam. The cab door of the lorry. And then suddenly, in the road in front of her was Terry.

'Jesus, you're soaked!' he said, striding towards her, off the road and onto the pavement. 'Where you off to? Let me take you.' He gestured back towards the cab.

'Let me take you wherever you're going. I'm on my way back to the depot anyway … Come on. You're bloody drenched!'

She felt the blood thump in her temples and cursed her luck in him having seen her. He was wet too – wherever he'd been he'd been out in the rain as well. His hair hung in thick curling ropes around his face.

'Come on, love,' he said again. 'Come and get in the dry for a bit, at least.'

'Don't you "love" me,' she snapped back at him, the words appearing as if from nowhere. Then she turned on her heel and set off along the pavement once again.

His hand was on her arm within moments. Clasped around her wet sleeve. She whirled around to face him. 'Just bugger off!' she told him, trying to shake her arm free.

But he wouldn't let go of it. 'Kathy, look. Kathy, *please*. Just come up. Just for a bit, eh? I want to talk to you.'

'Yeah, but I don't want to talk to *you*, Terry Harris. Just leave me alone, okay? I want to *walk*.'

'Walk where?'

'None of your business.'

His hand was still clasping her forearm. '*Please*,' he said again. He shifted his weight to his other foot. He was wearing overalls which couldn't be his, they were that much too big for him. They hung off his frame and made him look like he was a boy dressing up in his dad's

161

clothes. He looked tired, too, and she wished she didn't love him quite so much.

But she steeled herself, despite the clamouring of her emotions on seeing him. She felt tears prick in her eyes. Oh, why here? Why now?

'I don't want to talk to you,' she said again, limply.

'You don't mean that.'

'Terry, I *do* mean it!' Anger welled up in her and she was glad of it. 'And what can you possibly want to talk to *me* about? You dumped me, remember?'

He blinked water from his own eyes. 'Kathy, you *know* why I … Look. *Please*. Just come and sit in the cab with me a bit, will you? You're wet through.' He smiled lopsidedly. 'And so am I now. Come on, *please*?'

He let go of her arm, as if challenging her to stomp off up the road again, and she almost did. But something stopped her. Not his face. Not that. It wasn't seeing him again, she now decided. Not really. That had been exactly as she had expected it probably would be, every shift she'd worked since she'd got that wretched letter. The cause of that sick feeling she'd get every time the post came or the phone rang. That feeling of hopelessness mingled with a dollop of self-loathing. He was *not* going to phone her. He was *not* going to write. But still it made her pulse thump. Made her angry. Made her sad.

No, it wasn't exactly seeing his face – was it that she should do what John Lennon had kept banging on about, and try to see his point of view? That she let him off the hook for bloody leading her on?

No, it wasn't what *she* needed. But perhaps, after all, she should let him explain. Decided, she stomped off, not up the road, but back to the lorry, stretching up to reach the door handle and climbing awkwardly up into the cab, where she sat sullenly, soaked through, waiting for him to join her.

He soon did, the heavy driver's door clunking hard behind him, making the air inside the cab shudder. The engine was still running and the vibration of it was coming up through the seat. He flicked off the indicator switch. Turned the key. The cab became still.

She felt, rather than saw him turn around on the bench seat, where between them lay a mess of rubbish and papers. Old delivery chits, an empty fag packet. A crumpled bag from a local bakery. There was a smell of damp and sweat and engine oil. The rain carried on lashing down, almost pouring down the windscreen in an unbroken stream now, making it seem as if she was sitting behind a waterfall.

Now she was up here she couldn't seem to find anything to say to him – apart from a powerful urge to tell him to start the lorry up again. To drive and keep on driving. To take her away.

'I was just trying to do the right thing,' he said eventually. 'You must know that.'

She couldn't meet his gaze. She wanted to – wanted

so much not to seem the sullen teenager she felt she must look like. She had her hands clasped in her lap, and it was only now she could see just how mottled and waterlogged they were.

'That was how it was, Kathy,' he said. 'I was just trying to do the right thing. Except, ever since …'

He stopped speaking and now she lifted her head to look at him. He was sideways on the seat, one arm cradling the enormous steering wheel. And he was looking straight at her. Now she did hold his gaze.

'The right thing? The right thing for *who*?' she demanded. Again, the words seemed to come from nowhere. What she'd wanted to say – what she had *so* wanted to say to him ever since she'd read and re-read that bloody letter – was that she didn't *care* anymore. That he meant nothing to her. That he could bugger off and go out with anyone else he liked. That he was right. She *was* too young for him. That she didn't care about him *anyway*. That was what she'd meant to say, because she couldn't *bear* to be so humiliated. But none of it had come out. Because none of it was true.

'The right thing by *you*,' he said, sweeping the mess of papers into the passenger footwell. 'You know how your dad feels …'

'What's my dad got to do with it?'

'*Everything*,' Terry responded, an edge to his voice now. 'Kathy, you *know* that. 'You're only *seventeen*. Which means –'

'What? That I'm too young to know my own mind? Is that it? That my feelings don't matter because I'm still just a *baby*?'

'No, of course not. Christ, *no*! But it's difficult … you have to see that. I have to think of what your dad's said, and that he's *responsible* for you, and that he …'

'Will you stop telling me what my dad says! I know what my dad says! And it's nothing to do with him anyway! It's nothing to do with either of them – that witch in particular!' She felt exasperated. Furious at the ridiculousness of it all. 'Christ, age is just a number,' she finished angrily. Then a thought came to her. A bad thought. She well knew what her dad thought because he'd told her more than once. But told Terry?

She shifted on the seat, which was sticking unpleasantly to the back of her thighs. Condensation had finished the job the torrential rain had started. All the windows were clouded now, cocooning them in the cramped space, hidden from the hissing traffic, hidden from the world.

'What *has* my dad said anyway? Come on. What's he said to you? He's spoken to you, hasn't he? Was this what it was all about on Firework Night?'

Terry didn't need to reply. She could see the answer in his eyes.

He sighed. 'Not then,' he said. 'No, it wasn't then. It was after. After I'd been away … But it was only what I already knew, Kathy, that's all. Only what I should have

165

thought about before I even asked you out in the first place. I'm *sixteen years* older than you. Almost twice your age …'

'So *what*? Why does that matter? Terry, what exactly did he *say* to you? When? Did he *tell* you to finish with me? Tell you to write that bloody letter?' She felt gripped by a sudden fury. Irene. It'd have been Irene. She'd have put him up to it, for sure.

'Not in so many words … but …'

'But *what*? Did he threaten you?'

'*God*, no! Your dad? He'd never do that!'

'Then *what*? Did *she* threaten you? And when – and *how*? When did all this happen, then? When I was at Sally's?'

Terry nodded, even though, once again, he hadn't needed to. She realised that in the scant time she'd known him, she'd come to know him so intimately, so well. The realisation settled on her weightily, almost like a kind of armour. They had conspired to warn him off her. They had bloody conspired!

Terry shuffled a little closer. He was looking at her earnestly now, putting her in mind of a teacher she'd once had. One who'd been trying to put her straight on a matter about which he knew a great deal more than she did. She couldn't remember what or why. Only the feeling he had invoked. Making her feel her age again.

'Look, please don't blame your dad, Kathy,' Terry said gently. 'He only ever had your best interests at heart.

There was no threatening – I'd just come round – I came straight after Andorra. And Irene was up in bed having a sleep, and he explained that you'd gone to stay with Sally, and that he was concerned, with you being so young still … no, wait. Hear me out. He just thought it for the best, Kathy, that we didn't get serious. That you needed to spend time with lads more your own age … that you couldn't know your mind yet and that it wasn't fair of me to expect that … Far better to wait. You know … leave you be. At least for now. At least till you're a bit older …'

Kathleen could hardly contain herself. She glared at him. 'And you *agree* with him?!'

'No, but –'

'NO! There are no "buts" in this, Terry! It's *her*, can't you *see* that? She's behind all of this! Don't you get it? She just can't bear to see me happy!'

She had a sudden need to get out of the cab. To get away from him and his 'grown-up' explanations. She reached blindly for the door handle. He reached for her arm.

'No! That's what I'm trying to *say*, Kathy … No. I *don't* agree with him! God …' He drew his other hand through his sodden hair and sighed heavily. 'God, what am I supposed to *do*?' He looked up towards the roof of the cab, then back at her, and then down at her hand, his brows knitting, hinting at some sort of emotional struggle within. Then he squeezed it, almost roughly.

Certainly decisively. She looked down at it. And then at him. And she felt her age no more. 'No, Kathy,' he said again. 'I *don't* agree with him. *No*.'

She didn't think she'd have been able to free her hand, even had she wanted to. She didn't want to. His other hand joined the first, which he then slipped from under it, snaking the arm around her shoulder and pulling her towards him. '*No*,' he said again. 'Oh, Kathy … I can't begin to tell you how much I've missed you. How much I –'

'Then don't,' she said, kissing him.

Chapter 15

The rain continued to hammer down on them – or, more accurately, *at* them. The squally wind was still strong, and every so often the rain hit the windscreen with such force that it almost felt as if it was being thrown at them.

Kathleen didn't care. Pulling back, finally, she was breathless and almost swooning. Such a silly word, she'd always felt – for such a silly Victorian notion. Yet here she was, in Terry's arms, the outside world a blur behind the fogged-up cab windows, and that was exactly how she felt.

They didn't speak for several seconds, each alone with their feelings. Kathleen couldn't guess at Terry's but she certainly knew what hers were; that she was still gripped by an emotion that had overtaken her the minute she'd seen him. Almost like a physical hunger, it was. For *him*. She blushed at the thought of it. Or rather, would have, had she not already been so flushed.

Terry leaned forwards and flicked the giant wind-screen wipers into action. 'Hot, eh?' he remarked, as they made their journey over the huge screen and back again. Then he grinned at her.

She returned the grin, coyly now, almost shy of him. 'Me as well.'

He laced his fingers through hers. 'May as be hung for a sheep as a lamb, though, I reckon.' Then he leaned forward to kiss her again.

'So,' he said, at length, while her heart thumped in her ribcage. 'Where *was* it you were off to? You never told me, did you?'

It was properly dark outside now; the street lights had all come on. There would be hell to play at home with her being gone this long. 'To Woolies,' she said. 'To get a new set of fairy lights. Which I'd better do, sharpish, before they send out a search party.' She checked her watch. As she'd thought, it was already nearing five.

'So I can't whisk you off on my white charger, then?' he asked her, smiling. She could see from his expression that he had the same thing on his mind as she did, and, realising, now she *did* blush, at the *enormity* of it all.

'It's not a white charger, it's a not-very-white lorry, Terry Harris. And no, you can't. Not today, when there's lights to be bought. Onwards to Woolworths, please, driver,' she commanded, keen to rein herself in a little and bury the emotional under the practical. Yet still he didn't turn the key in the ignition.

'So what's to do?' he asked her seriously now. 'Since I can't keep my hands off you –'

'Terry!'

'Or my eyes, or my mind …'

'*Stop* it! You're making me embarrassed now.'

'Because I'm telling you the truth about how gorgeous you are?'

She poked him on the arm. 'I mean it. Terry. *Stop* it. You're making me squirm now!'

He tipped his head to one side and considered her. 'You really don't like being complimented, do you? Makes you uncomfortable, doesn't it?'

'It's not that. Don't be daft, it's just that …'

'That you don't quite believe it?'

'No, *seriously*. It's just …' She spread her palms. He might just be right, she realised. 'I don't *know* …'

'I do. It's exactly what I said,' he finished, peering out through the already re-fogging windscreen. He flicked the wipers on again, this time letting them run while he turned over the engine. 'I love you, Kathy,' he said quietly. 'Is it okay for me to say that to you? Is *that* allowed?'

She felt a fresh bout of tears well, and she was happy for them to fall now. She reached for her hanky. 'Hmm. I'll think on it,' she said.

* * *

The Woolies in town was heaving, just as Kathleen had thought it would be. No matter how hard up everyone on the estate always professed themselves to be, it seemed everyone managed to find a bit of extra cash when it came to buying Christmas decorations – blowing hard-earned money on all the non-essentials of life, just to spread that little bit more Christmas cheer.

The decorations aisle, as a result, was choked with people, and Kathleen realised that up till an hour ago she would have hated threading her way through the late-afternoon crush, bent on a mission that was necessary but at the same time felt so wrong. And, in some ways, it *was* wrong. Had they any business celebrating Christmas, a time that for their family (such as it had ever been that) would, without Darren – and, for her, without Terry – feel so dark.

She would have hated it, she knew that, even knowing it was only for the pub. She'd gone out in the blackest of moods, and would have resented the cheery chit-chat, the good-natured squabbling over tinsel and baubles, the scent of damp and sweat in the too-fuggy air.

What a difference an hour could make. As it was, she felt giddy; lightheaded – almost as if she was floating. As if she was being wafted along on a cloud, or more like the inside of a bubble. A bubble of happiness, a cocoon made of Terry's love.

But she had to hurry. He'd never have been able to park up anywhere close by – his lorry was a big one; he was carrying white goods all over the North tomorrow, he'd explained to her, so he'd dropped her off close as he could, so she could run in and buy the fairy lights, and would drive round the block a couple of times before picking her up again and delivering her back home.

'But I'll be fine!' she'd insisted, aware of what an inconvenience it would be for him – not to mention fearing for the repercussions if Irene saw his lorry pull up. But he'd been insistent, and she'd liked that.

'I'm taking you back,' he'd said sternly, 'and that's an end to it, so stop your mithering. I'll drop you at St Luke's, so you don't get it in the neck off Irene. But you are *not* walking. *Or* standing in the rain for the bus, for that matter. Not while I'm here to drive you. We are going to start,' he'd added, his expression set, 'as we mean to go on.'

And he'd be back before she knew it, so she didn't waste time dithering over the different boxes. Just grabbed a set that looked much like the ones that had broken – with the little plastic flowers around the bulbs – and joined the growing queue of Christmas shoppers at the tills. And, as she queued, Kathleen daydreamed about the day when she'd have her *own* Christmas tree. Have her own family. Her own *life*. With Terry? The thought made her colour again – almost as red, she thought wryly, as the cheeks on the Santa on the fairy-light box.

*   *   *

173

Terry's timing was perfect, and, as it happened, there *was* a huge queue at the bus stop, so Kathleen decided she would simply blame the buses for her late return, and if Irene gave her hell for not walking, so be it.

'I should take you all the way,' Terry said, perhaps reading her mind.

'No, honest, I'd rather you didn't,' she said. 'No sense making things any more stressful than they need to be. What's the worst she can do to me, anyway?'

'I dread to think, love,' he said. 'Seriously, I really should take you all the way. I'm not sure I'm happy with the idea of the pair of us sneaking around. In fact, the more I think about it, the more I think I need to speak to your father. Tell him the truth. Tell him –'

'Terry, *please*, no. Not just now. I need time to think how to tell him. I'm still angry about him speaking to you at *all* and I need to think … He had no *right* …'

He glanced across at her, nodded slightly, his dark brows knitting together. Then looked back at the road again, and Kathleen realised he had a perfectly straight nose. She couldn't quite come to terms with the sensations that flooded through her just from looking at him. So this was love. This was how it felt. Had her mam once felt that way about her dad? She remembered what Sally had said to her about her dad and Irene getting together. She couldn't imagine Irene ever having such feelings. But her dad? It seemed so obvious now. For *her* mam, yes, but not for Irene.

'Well, if not just now, then soon, okay? It won't help us any if I run around behind your father's back, will it? I don't care about *her*, but I respect your dad and I must do right by him.' He glanced at her again. 'You'd think less of me if I didn't, wouldn't you?'

Kathleen nodded, knowing he was right. He was a decent man, which was why he needed to do the right thing. And she hated the thought of lying to her father, however much he'd lied to her in not telling her that it had been him who'd warned Terry off. But what if he forbade it? Or the old witch did? Which she could see as being so likely. 'I know,' she said. 'But let me speak to him first, Terry. Let me make it clear to him how much I … how much I …'

'How much you what?' he prompted.

'How much I love you.' There. She'd said it too. 'I'll catch him in a bit, when Mam's getting herself tarted up, and I'll explain to him. I'll tell him how I feel, and how much …'

'… how much you love me.' Terry was grinning now.

She batted his arm. '*And* that. And how I'm seeing you, *whatever* she says. Or *he* says. They can't stop me –'

'Well, technically they *can*,' he said, flicking the indicator switch to pull in by the hospital. 'Till you're twenty-one, they can, anyway.'

'Not physically. Not unless they lock me up, and even *she* wouldn't go that far. No, once Dad realises I'm serious …'

The air brakes whooshed, startling her. 'Seriously, Kathy,' he said, as the lorry juddered to a stop again. 'Just something for you to think about – and don't go taking this the wrong way or anything, but I've been thinking. You know, over this past couple of weeks, and now we've … well, just then, when I was driving around …'

Kathleen had already opened the cab door and the wind was trying to snatch at it. 'What?'

'That, well, you know, if it all gets too difficult at home for you …' He paused and looked at her, his expression now uncertain, his eyes questioning. 'Well, if you wanted to, you could always come and move in with me. If you wanted to,' he said again, quietly.

She gaped at him. 'What, you mean like *live* together?'

'That's exactly what I mean, my love,' he said.

Was it written on her face? Was there some magical power Irene possessed? Was she really that bad at hiding what was going on inside her? Because Kathleen had barely stepped inside the back door before it hit her that Irene seemed to be able to see into her very soul – at the very least to the place in it where the name Terry sat, illuminated as if by its own fairy lights.

'Where the bleeding hell have you been?' she thundered. 'Sneaking out to see him, is it? *Is* it? Off shopping for lights, indeed. *Pah*. You lying little hussy!'

Kathleen had left the cab in a different kind of bubble five minutes earlier. And as she'd hurried along, keeping to the walls and hedges once again, while the rush-hour traffic thundered past her, throwing ribbons of light onto the wet road, she had had to pinch herself mentally to accept she hadn't dreamt it – that Terry had actually suggested she move in with him.

It had thrown her into an entirely new kind of dilemma. Should she do such a thing? It seemed to go against everything. Seemed to fly in the face of all the codes she'd ever had drummed into her. Even the less rigorous, unwritten rules among her peer group. Never let a boy touch you on a first date or a second. Never let them go all the way till … till when, exactly? On that point there always seemed to be an element of approximation; it often seemed a rule till a girl decided to break it. And then the goalposts seemed to shift a bit, to be just that bit more permissive. To fit the permissive society in which they now apparently lived. Kathleen wished now, more than anything, for her mother. For guidance.

Because there was no doubt here. To go and stay with him – to go and live with him – would mean one thing, for certain. That she'd be sleeping with him – going to *bed* with him. Finally crossing that long-anticipated line. The thought was as frightening as it was exciting. And she was seventeen – hardly young; several of her friends had lost their virginity long since. But *should* she? Shouldn't she wait till she was married? Would everyone think she was loose? That she was easy? But, on the other hand, should she even care what anyone else thought?

Terry had been at pains to point out that he wasn't trying to take advantage of her. And she believed him. She didn't doubt that he knew she was his now for the taking. What she'd not said in so many words today, she had readily implied. She would give herself to him willingly when the time came, she knew that. But to move *in* with him. That was so much more than just being a girlfriend. It was such a lot to think about.

Was it that, then? That huge internal discussion she was having with herself? Was that what Irene could so plainly see on her face?

She decided she wouldn't bother denying it either. She slung the box of lights down on the bottom step of the stairs. 'One box of fairy lights, bought as planned. And what if I had anyway?' she added, remembering Terry's words earlier. May as well be hung for a sheep as a lamb in this, too. 'It's none of your business!' she fired back.

It was like the proverbial red rag to a bull. And, from her newly altered perspective, Kathleen found herself not caring any more. Instead she simply wondered how a woman could hold so much hate in her heart and not pop. 'Don't you dare cheek me, my girl!' Irene fumed, her vermillion lips a violent slash in her powdered, too-pale face. 'Or you'll be seeing the back of my hand! You're an hour late, for starters, and there's still the toilets needing cleaning. And you've the front to come in here telling me what is or isn't my business?! I'll tell you *your* business, madam – it's to do as you're told! Not to come and go as you please as if this was a bloody hotel! And you can wipe that superior look off your ugly mug too while you're at it!'

She raised an arm as if to strike Kathleen, and she didn't doubt she would have, had her father not come into the hallway at that moment, presumably alerted by the raised voices he could hear from the bar.

His expression was enough to stay Irene's hand. However much she screamed at her stepdaughter – and didn't care who heard it – she was thankfully more reticent about slapping her when John was about.

'Ah, you're back, love,' he said, and in that instant Kathleen knew how she was going to answer Terry's question. 'Ah, you're back, love', in that low conciliatory way he always adopted when he was fearful of Irene's rants escalating into a full-on row. No 'Don't you raise a hand to my girl!', no 'What's all this shouting about, Irene?' Just the usual damage limitation – as if he was trying to turn down a gas ring or a thermostat. Just cooling the temperature and keeping the peace, which she knew probably enraged Irene as much as it did her.

And which kept no peace. Just left the bile on a low simmer. Kathleen yanked off her sodden raincoat and wished she'd agreed then and there to what Terry had suggested. That he drop her off at the pub. That he come into the pub *with* her. That he tell her dad *with* her – *and* her *cow* of a stepmother – that she was moving in with him. As it was she could only seethe.

'Got the lights okay, then?' her dad said, nodding towards the box on the bottom step. 'Good.' He picked it up and started shaking off the lid. 'Best get these out and strung then. Cheer the place up, eh?'

Kathleen felt a pang of conscience, imagining the 'place' without her in it. How sad her dad would be. How much it would upset him to see her leave. And something else occurred to her. Did Irene even know about her dad warning Terry off her? Did he speak to him on the quiet? Had that been damage limitation too?

Not that it mattered. 'I'll give you a hand, Dad,' she told him.

'Oh, no you won't, girl,' Irene snapped. 'You'll clean the toilets, like I told you. And be quick about it, too. We're due to open in ten minutes.'

There was half a second when Kathleen thought her dad might overrule her stepmother. Tell her that, first, Kathleen would help him string the lights *she'd* been out and bought. But he said nothing.

The pang of conscience withered and disappeared.

Chapter 16

Kathleen hoisted the last of her things over the pub wall into Terry's waiting hands. She was feeling warm from the effort, despite the bitter cold. Warm and energised. She didn't think she'd ever felt so powerful, so strong. So in charge of her own life. So in *control*. In mere minutes from now she'd have officially left home – the home that had for so long not really felt like a home – and there was nothing her vindictive stepmother could do about it.

Terry's two-up two-down on Louis Avenue was only around the back of the pub, so as his car was off the road with a flat tyre – and, thanks to the earlier snow and him being away, a flat battery, too – it made more sense to move her stuff this way than walk the long way round via the road. She had so little, after all – far from owning a record player, she didn't even possess a transistor radio – just her small collection of clothes and toiletries, and her few precious books. Gathered together, they amounted to very little to show for a life, she thought, but, in some ways, that only strengthened her sense that leaving was the right thing to do.

And climbing over the wall like this made her feel giggly. As if they were eloping, almost – even if only to a terraced house round the corner – and Terry's answering smile as he helped her over, so she didn't slip on the icy concrete, only added to her rebellious mood.

Irene was looking down on them, sour-faced as she smoked a cigarette up on the balcony, and as Kathleen looked up and met her eye, before taking a last look back at the pub, a surge of courage inspired her to stick two fingers up at her. 'Good riddance to the silly old mare,' she said, slipping an arm around Terry's waist as he caught her. 'Thank God that's over with. Good bloody riddance!'

Terry pulled her close. 'I wouldn't get too cocky with her, love. You've still got to clean there, remember.'

'Yes, but I won't have to *see* her. She's still in the land of nod long after I've finished cleaning. And what can she do to me now anyway? Sweet Fanny Adams, that's what.'

Privately, Kathleen knew that wasn't strictly true. Irene would find ways to make life difficult for her; she had no illusions on that score. But the knowledge that she had escaped filled her with too much happiness for that to bother her. Not now she had Terry by her side, sticking up for her.

* * *

And in the end, it had been ridiculously straightforward. With Terry out of reach, delivering his last-minute fridges and spin-dryers the following day, Kathleen had thought she'd take her time, rehearse what she'd say to her father, pick her moment, but it was Irene, in the end, who'd set things in motion.

She'd been up in the living room, on her own, doing some paperwork the following lunchtime, and when Kathleen had passed by on her way back up for her break, she had called her in and told her to go down and get her a packet of fags. This Kathleen had done, and duly returned with them, plonking the packet down on the table and then, since it was her break time and her bedroom was like a bombsite after one of Monica's intermittent clothing crises, had gone and got her book, returned with it and sat down on the settee.

Irene had looked up. 'What d'you think you're doing?' she'd said.

'Reading a book,' Kathleen had answered.

'Well, go and read it somewhere else,' Irene had responded. 'I'm in here.'

She'd had a drink at her elbow, a glass of something clear. Kathleen remembered that very well. Could have been water, could have been gin. Perhaps it didn't even matter.

'So what?' she'd replied. 'I'm not exactly bothering you.'

'Yes you are,' Irene said. 'How am I supposed to concentrate with you over there? Go on, piss off somewhere else to read your bleeding book. I have work to do.'

'Piss off somewhere else.' Kathleen had repeated, standing up.

'You heard,' Irene muttered, back looking at her work again.

'Okay,' Kathleen had said brightly. 'You know what? I will.'

Terry had found her on his doorstep when he came home from work. Not distressed, not disturbed, not in any way anxious. 'Hello,' she told him. 'I came to give you my answer, which is yes.'

Since then it had been an interesting couple of days, to say the least. She'd had to tell her dad, of course, and fully expected him to forbid it (and if he had she'd already decided she'd go anyway). But for once, Irene's hate for her worked in her favour. 'Let her go,' she'd told her husband, with no small amount of feeling. 'Let the silly little bitch go and good riddance!' she'd railed. 'Let her find out what *real* life is like for a change! She'll soon come crawling back with her tail between her legs, just you wait and see. Go on,' she said again, 'just piss off out of my sight! Ungrateful hussy. Go and play at being a grown-up.'

And now she was. She was off to play at 'being a grown-up' and her principal feeling – other than the joy of it all – was that if Irene and her dad were anything to go by, 'being a grown-up' was the last thing she intended to be playing at.

She couldn't hold Terry's hand as both of his were occupied carrying her bags full of belongings, but she could link her free one through his arm, so she did. 'Feels all Christmassy with this frost, doesn't it?' she said, looking down at the sparkling pavement.

He squeezed her arm and grinned. 'It'll feel even more Christmassy in a minute. I've got us a tree. Off a guy who came selling them at the depot yesterday. Not one of your fancy aluminium ones, or anything. Just a real one.'

'*Just* a real one?' Kathleen could hardly contain her excitement. How could he understand quite how much the idea of that thrilled her? They'd not had a real tree in so long – not since her mam had died. She couldn't pass one without the smell of pine conjuring such bitter-sweet memories. Blurry fragments of the time before Irene and the pub. 'Oh, a real one will be perfect,' she said.

'And I picked up some trimmings and that, too,' he added. 'Thought I'd leave all the artistic stuff to you.' He smiled at her as he opened the front gate to his house. 'Thought it would make you feel at home and that.'

Kathleen could hardly find words to express the depth of her feelings. The expected ones, of love and excitement and anticipation – all of those. But in this – having a home, decorating her *own* tree – there was something more. A feeling of an important step having been taken. She suddenly felt very worldly, very adult and very, very excited about this new chapter in her life. She felt like a *woman*; imagined going to bed and waking up with her lover every morning, washing his clothes and cooking all his favourite meals. She felt so happy she could burst.

Terry popped the bags down on the step and fished in his pocket for his door keys. 'Come on then, girl,' he said as he put the key in the door. 'Might as well do it right.' Then, to Kathleen's surprise, he scooped her up in his arms and carried her over the threshold.

'Terry!' she shrieked. 'You bloody nutter! You're only supposed to do that after you've been married!'

He winked at her. 'Well, think of it as a practice run then.'

He took her through into the little living room, and set her down on the beige settee, among the cushions. Then he rubbed his palms together and went to turn the fire up. 'I left it on low,' he said, 'so's you'd be nice and warm when we got back.'

The tree was already in a bucket, stationed in front of the window and, drinking in the scent, and watching Terry fussing around her, Kathleen felt no compulsion to move. It was all just so novel to have someone running around after her – to have someone who seemed interested in attending to her needs. 'Cup of tea?' he said, heading off to the little cellar-head kitchen to put the kettle on. 'The Christmas stuff's in that Woolies bag behind the door if you want to make a start.'

But Kathleen was scanning the wall above the fireplace, where beside the gilt mirror a belt of horse brasses now hung. Where was the photograph of Iris? She felt another rush of love and tenderness overwhelm her. He'd taken it down.

She stood up then and went to fetch the bag of decorations. He'd bought so much it stunned her. It must have cost a fortune. She took the bag back to the sofa and began to sort through it. There was a light set, lametta, two boxes of baubles – one box of the kind she remembered from her childhood, with the dimple in one side in which nestled a little snow scene. There was also tinsel, and little bags of chocolates to hang up – some little squares wrapped in foil, others miniature umbrellas – in recognition perhaps of that day that changed everything – less than a week, but now what felt like a lifetime ago.

Terry returned, bearing two mugs of tea, which he set down on the little dark-wood coffee table. Kathleen wondered what it must have been like to lose almost everything, as he had in the fire in which his wife had died.

She set down the little bag of shiny umbrellas. 'Oh, Terry,' she said. 'You've taken down Iris's photo.'

He sat down beside her and put an arm around her shoulder. 'You're observant,' he said. 'And you're right, yes, I did. I didn't want to upset you so I took it down.'

Kathleen twisted to face him. 'Oh, Terry, bless you. But put it back. *Please*. I don't like it not being there. I mean, I know what you must have been thinking, but there's no need to have done that.'

'Isn't there?' He looked confused.

She shook her head. 'No, there isn't. Not at all. You loved her. It's not like you left her or anything. And, well …' She paused, trying to find the right words to express something she felt so keenly. 'You'll probably think I'm daft for saying so, but I want to feel she's with us. That's she's happy for you – for *us*. That we have her blessing.'

She felt a blush creep up her cheeks even as she said it, she felt so silly. But at the same time not, because if there was one thing she'd hated after her mam had died, it was how her dad wasn't supposed to ever speak of her again. As if she'd been extinguished from his heart as well as this life. Could Terry understand that? She suspected so. She'd never forgotten something her dad had said, way before this. Way before *them*. A few months after, when Terry, who'd moved to this house around the corner had become a regular – the young widower everyone felt so sorry for. 'They were a grand couple,' her dad had said. 'Made a lovely pair the two of them – 't isn't right.' And he would know all about that,

Kathleen remembered thinking. Know the tragedy of suddenly losing someone you loved. Someone so young and vibrant, with their whole lives ahead of them.

A small silence stretched between them, Terry just gazing at her with his greeny-grey eyes. And he didn't laugh at her, or make light of it. He just pulled her close and kissed her hair. 'You're one in a million, you are,' he said. 'You know that?'

Chapter 17

Though he usually worked all hours, having no family to take care of, Terry had taken a whole week off work to spend time with Kathleen and help prepare for Christmas. He'd be off on another European job soon, which would see him away right up to Christmas Eve, but for now they could exist in a world of their own making, and, dizzy with the love that he'd now also shown her physically, Kathleen had to mentally pinch herself, and regularly – to remind herself, given her inclination to feel undeserving, that she deserved such happiness not a jot less than anyone else.

Still, slipping in here and there between the walls of her ivory palace was the ever-present worry about her dad. Yes, it was true that since Irene had moved in with Monica and Darren, Christmas had become less and less a day for celebration and, given that it mostly involved lots of extra grafting in the pub, more and more just another busy day.

But it was her dad that had made what he could of it. Irene had never been much of a cook, so it had been him that had made the effort; popping a chicken in the oven before they went down to open up at Christmas lunchtime, and popping up every so often to baste it and check all was well. And then it would be Kathleen's turn, since no one ever suggested she might prefer to do otherwise, to spend much of the time when everyone was laughing and singing downstairs, peeling the potatoes, the sprouts and carrots, getting the table laid and so on – the regular skivvy, she'd been standing sentry over Christmas lunch for years.

Not so now, however. Now she was managing her own festivities, and who would help her dad with his Christmas chicken dinner? Would they even have one? Somehow, with Darren gone, she doubted it. Yet she couldn't bring it up; she went in to clean every morning, at seven, and she couldn't quite bring herself to broach the subject of his Christmas for fear that it might break the barrier she'd erected, have her cave in, offer to help. Offer to go round and eat it with them, or – another thought that had wormed its way into her mind – suggest they came and had their lunch with her and Terry.

In fact, it had been Terry who had put the idea in her mind. There they were, with everything they wanted right in front of them – from the twinkling tree, set on an upturned crate in the front window, to the tinsel that adorned every mirror and picture – Iris's included – and the plastic holly that now graced the mantelpiece. And it had been Terry who'd remarked that, as she'd done such a brilliant job, it seemed almost wrong that there was no one with whom to share it.

He'd also, just the previous day, taken her out shopping. 'You fill the basket, love,' he'd told her. 'Get everything you think we'll need. And a much bigger Christmas pudding than you think we need, an' all. I could eat my bodyweight in Christmas pudding, me.'

And she realised how much this Christmas mattered to Terry, too. An only child, with his mam and dad living so far away, he'd had a couple of pretty lonely Christmases under his belt. And as they edged their way round the Co-op, in a crocodile of shuffling shoppers, she'd known what he was going to say before he said it.

'Are you sure you're happy, love – with it just being the two of us, at ours? Because I'll understand if you'd rather we went to your mam and dad's. It must be hard for you, being apart from your dad and that.' He paused. 'Hard for him, too.'

She loved how he said 'ours' and she loved him even more for understanding her father's feelings. But her mind was set, however much she felt for her father. To go back there – to sit down at that kitchen table with Irene ... To go back to her role – or, more than that, to *allow* herself to do so ... She shook her head. 'Course not,' she told him. 'I want to be with you. Yes, I'll miss my dad, and I'm sure he'll miss me, too, but I'll see him. I'll see him at some point, course I will. But I really want it just to be you and me.'

Terry had kissed her then. Right in the middle of the biscuits and confectionery. 'And your Christmas present,' he reminded her. 'Don't forget that.'

'Which is *what?*' she asked. She'd been asking him for days now, but he wouldn't tell her, any more than she was going to divulge the gift she'd got for him, about which she was even more excited, if that were possible. After speaking to Sally, and Sally speaking to Ronnie, she'd struck gold. Terry loved his dominoes, and she'd spent her few precious savings on a really posh set for him from Brown Muff, the department store in town. They were in an ornate wooden box, the likes of which she'd never seen in the pub before, and they were currently stashed in the bottom drawer of the bedroom dressing table.

He winked at her, then shook his head. 'Not a chance,' he said. 'I *told* you – it's a *surprise*. So you're not winkling it out of me, by either fair means or foul.'

'Not even a clue?' she said, snaking both her arms around his middle. She'd been asking for him to give her a clue for days now as well. It had become something of a game with her.

He shook his head. 'No clues. Not even trying to get round me with your womanly wiles. All you need to know is that it's the perfect present for you.'

Which was no clue at all, but then, she didn't really want one. It was gift enough to know that he was going to surprise her as well. That he'd thought what to get her and *wanted* to surprise her. Because he loved her. That was the best present of all.

Kathleen could, had she wanted, have given up work – Terry had said so. He earned really good money as a long-distance driver, and she knew he could easily support them both. But she hadn't wanted that. Though she was glad to give up the bar work, so she could spend that bit more time with him, she was anxious to keep up her morning cleaning schedule, both so she could earn her own money and see something of her dad – and at a time when she wouldn't have to see her stepmother.

And today, Christmas Eve, was no exception. The weather had turned bitter again after being wet and mild the previous week, and as she made her way from the house to the back wall of the pub – her usual route now – she found herself mentally crossing her fingers, hoping for snow. Well, as long as it didn't start till Terry was safely home, anyway.

She'd been in her element over the few days while he'd been away. Yes, she'd missed him, and it had felt a little strange to be in the house all by herself, but she'd also been revelling in the housework, and in washing and ironing all the bedding, so that everything would be nice and fresh for when he came home later that afternoon.

She climbed over the back wall and went inside, expecting to find the pub empty, but a draught snaking round her ankles made her wonder if someone was

194

around. Expecting it to be Monica – in her usual mad dash to leave on time for work – she followed the cold and found the front doors of the pub open – and her dad, fully dressed, outside, smoking a fag.

'Bloody hell, Dad!' she greeted him. 'You'll freeze to death out here. What are you even doing up at this time?'

Her father ground out his cigarette with his heel and held the door open for Kathleen. 'Just getting a bit o' fresh air, lass, that's all. Come on up. The fire's already lit and the kettle's on for a quick cuppa.'

'Blimey, it must be Christmas or something,' Kathleen joked as she closed the door behind her. But something was up. Her dad looked drawn. And why *was* he already up and dressed?

'Are you alright, Dad?' she asked, thinking about the time of year and Darren. All too easy to forget that her dad missed him, too. And Irene would be in a right state, with the day almost upon them.

Her dad confirmed it. 'Oh, it's just this time of year, love,' he said. He then lowered his voice. 'You know, remembering your mum, and that. Your *real* mum. And with your mam – Irene – struggling … You know, with Darren and that.' He paused to mash the tea. 'I don't know, love. It just seems neverending, that's all.'

And now her gone, too. There was a price to pay for her happiness – she was looking at it now. 'Oh, Dad,' she said. 'I'm so sorry …'

'You've nothing to be sorry for, lass. Here,' he said, pouring a tea and shunting the cup and saucer in her direction. 'Warm you up. Reckon we might see some snow tomorrow, don't you?'

She nodded, and pushed her nose into the cup. It warmed it. 'Where you off to, Dad? All dressed up like that.' She nodded towards his clothing. Good trousers. Shirt and tie under his diamond-patterned sweater.

'Up the cemetery, love,' he told her. 'I was hoping you might come with me. I've already made a start on the taproom,' he added, reading her very thoughts about what Irene might have to say about her not having got everything done in time. As ever, she was struck by the injustice of it all. Why – just for once – couldn't *she* help with the cleaning? What was her dad doing, running around before the dawn, in his own pub? Just so he wouldn't get on the wrong side of her.

But it was what it was. She nodded. 'I'd love to do that, Dad,' she told him. 'Maybe we could even see if we can pick up some holly for Mam's grave on the way.'

Her dad nodded towards the door. 'Thought it best. Get it done before your mam and Monica wake up. I don't want them to know about it.'

'Monica's not in work?'

'Not today. Off till the day after Boxing Day. So it was a bit of a late night downstairs last night, between the two of them. Any luck, they'll both sleep till noon.'

Much as it sickened Kathleen that her dad was too scared to even visit his dead wife's grave except in secret, she said nothing, because what was the point? Instead she worked double speed to get the pub cleaned alongside him, and by nine they were driving along the road to the cemetery, having stopped at the newsagent's on Southfield Lane for one of the small holly wreaths they had outside.

Kathleen's mother had been buried at the Scholemoor Lane end of the cemetery, beneath a white marble stone, now getting weathered in places, which was carved with the inscription: *Linda Adamson, loving wife to John and devoted mother to Kathleen. Sadly missed and forever with the angels. RIP*, followed by dates that bracketed her short life on Earth.

Kathleen could recite those exact words in her sleep – and more than that, she could bring the image of the gravestone to mind at any time. Since that day when she'd first clapped eyes on it as a small bewildered child, that stone – along with the bed of cream-coloured stone chips that sat underneath it – was, she thought, the saddest thing she'd ever seen. She remembered that image even more clearly than her poor dead mother's face, and it made her glad she'd had Terry put Iris's picture back.

Her dad was already crying when they reached the graveside. Not noisily. Far from it. The only sounds were the distant hum of rush-hour traffic and the clop of their feet on the footpaths. He just shed tears as he walked; an unbroken stream of them, sliding down his pale cheeks unchecked, perhaps even unnoticed.

Kathleen felt the tears spring in her own eyes, as they always did when she came here. Tears not just for herself, but for her father and the pain she couldn't make better for him, and for the mother who'd never see how happy she now felt, and who'd never be around to be the wonderful grandmother Kathleen had always known intuitively that she'd have been, to any children her only child might one day bear.

It was something she didn't think she'd much thought about till now; another mark, she decided, of the woman she was turning into; capable of thinking beyond her own gaping loss, to the losses that would stack up down the line.

She stepped closer to her dad and slipped a hand into his cold one, bending with him as he bent to place the wreath against the headstone.

They stood for a long time, maybe ten minutes or more, her father's cold hand growing less so in her warm one. Then, finally, he turned his gaze away and looked at Kathleen. 'She'd have been so happy for you. You know that, don't you, lass? That smile you've had plastered on your face these past couple of weeks.'

She nodded. 'I know,' she said. 'And are *you* happy for me, Dad?'

He paused. But it seemed only to draw breath from the frosty air. 'Oh, I reckon so,' he said. 'Come on. Time we headed back.'

Though no snow had yet arrived – and wasn't forecast to till tomorrow or maybe Boxing Day, by 7 p.m. Kathleen was glued to the little black-and-white telly, hoping to hear about snow that might have fallen else-where – hopefully in places that wouldn't hinder Terry's onward journey home.

He wasn't exactly late, but she'd learned that it wasn't a precise business; ferries could be missed, acci-dents could happen, roads could be choked with traffic – all manner of happenings could affect such a journey, so she was silly to even decide when to expect him – best to keep busy and accept that she'd see him when she saw him.

And she'd certainly been busy; she'd prepared all the veg for the following day's dinner, cleaned the house – yet again – and even made some sausage rolls. She'd also wrapped and arranged his presents under the tree, along with the ones Sally had sent for them and the gifts Mary had given her. Her presents from her father (and Irene?) she would open when they went there, which they must, but that would not be till after Boxing Day now, when the pub would be less busy.

Because Terry's car was still off the road, he was being dropped off by Ronnie, but though she kept an ear out, she didn't hear the car pull up. It was only the creak of the front door that alerted her that he was home.

She leapt up and rushed into the little hallway to greet him, thrilled, as she always was, by the way her stomach flipped at the sight of him; what a gift in itself to have something going on inside you that was so nice and that you had absolutely no control over.

She threw her arms around him. 'Oh, I've missed you so much,' she told him.

'I've missed you too,' he said, clearly anxious to press the point home by dropping his holdall and kissing her all over her face.

He then let her go. 'And I've bought your present. Just a tick. Best we don't leave it out in the cold, eh?'

'Ooh, gi's it here, then. I can pop it under the tree with yours.'

He shook his head, and then turned to pick up a box on the doorstep. A plain cardboard box, about the size of a milk crate, which he picked up and passed her, before shutting the door. 'Go on,' he said, 'take it into the sitting room. Open it.'

'Open it?' she asked, as he followed her in. 'What, now?'

'Yes, now,' he said. 'Can't leave this one till the morning. Go on,' he said, grinning at her. 'Put it down. Open up the flaps.'

Kathleen did so, and just at the moment when they parted, heard a noise – albeit a quiet one – that was unmistakable. She peered in to see a pair of huge blue eyes looking anxiously up at her.

'Oh my God!' she cried, reaching in to pick up the ball of trembling tortoiseshell fur. 'A kitten! Oh, my! You've bought me a kitten!'

'I told you I had the purr-fect present for you, didn't I?' he said, laughing. 'Something to keep you company when I'm working away. What d'you reckon? Isn't she lovely? She's a she, by the way. Seven weeks old. So the timing's pretty purr-fect as well. All you have to do now is name her.'

Kathleen cradled the frightened animal in her hand, close to her chest. She could feel the steady beat of its tiny racing heart. 'Shhh,' she told the kitten. 'Shhh … you're home now, my little darling. Nothing to be afraid of here, except being smothered with love. Oh, Terry,' she began. 'She's just adorable. What a poppet!' What a –' But her exclamations were arrested by a sudden feeling of warmth. Warmth that pooled in her hand and began to run down her arm.

'So what do you reckon for a name?' Terry wanted to know. 'Tinsel, perhaps? Holly?'

Kathleen lifted the little kitten, who was now fairly dripping. She laughed. 'I reckon we'll have to call her Tiddles.'

Chapter 18

Kathleen smiled weakly as Terry appeared in the bedroom doorway, holding a steaming cup of tea.

'You feeling a bit better today, chick?' he asked, sitting down on the bed. She'd been ill for over a week now, and his voice was filled with concern. A horrible sore-throat bug had struck her down just after New Year, and she just couldn't seem to shake it off.

'A little bit,' she said as she pulled herself up on the pillows, though more to reassure him than because she actually did. In truth, though her throat no longer felt it was being scoured by razor blades, the fever that had come with it was still making her giddy, and she felt weak – as if she'd been hit by a truck and then dragged along behind it along the length of Little Horton Lane. She shivered as Terry put the tea down on the bedside table and felt her forehead. She really ought to try to eat something, too.

'You still seem to have a bit of a temperature,' he said. 'I could take today off work to look after you, if you like. It's only local jobs I've got. Sure Ronnie could sort it.'

Kathleen heard a mewl, and caught side of Tiddles attempting to jump onto the bed. But it was a lost cause. She'd be far too small to jump so high for a while yet, and could only manage to get her front claws into the bedspread, before promptly falling off again, squealing furiously as she fell.

Kathleen sat up properly, and reached down to scoop up the kitten. 'No, Tez,' she said, 'I don't want you getting into trouble. I'll be fine, honest. I'm going to get up today. I promised Dad I'd be back to work today, didn't I?'

'But you mustn't. He'll understand. You look pale as a ghost. And I'll stay here. I don't like to think of you ill here all on your own.'

'Tez, go to *work*, love. I'm feeling better, honest.' She opened her mouth wide. 'See, look at my throat.' Then she shut it again. 'On second thoughts, don't come too close. Don't want you going down with this as well. Go on. Get off, or you'll be late. Scoot.' She waved a hand to dismiss him.

'Well, if you're sure … But I'm stopping by the pub to let your dad know you won't be in. Oh yes I *am*,' he added firmly as she raised her hand again to protest. 'And I'll get the fire going and make you some porridge for your breakfast. You've hardly eaten anything in three days.'

Kathleen nodded and smiled, as she sank back against the pillows. The joys of Christmas already felt so long ago, yet it was only the second week in January. But that was what January was best at: making you forget that Christmas had just happened, however magical it had been, too busy reminding you that spring was still a long way away. It was pitch black now – it was only a little after six in the morning, but even once the dawn had broken, these last couple of days, it never really got properly light – the sun, hidden from view, and probably feeling unwanted, slinking back behind the horizon all too quickly again.

Terry went back downstairs, and while she listened to the reassuring thumps and bangs that meant he was busy in their little kitchen, she held the kitten in front of her face and kissed her nose. 'I don't know what you're shivering for,' she said. 'You've got a bloody fur coat on. Let's get downstairs and help Daddy, and get you a saucer of warm milk, eh? Before he goes.'

As was becoming the norm lately, she felt a moment of dizziness as she stood up, and resolved that, today, she would force down the bowl of porridge Terry was making her, even if it did make her gag. That was the trouble with not eating, she decided – it had that way of making you feel even less like eating. She'd lost weight, she knew. She felt hollowed out as she put on her dressing gown, her cheeks sunken as she glimpsed her reflection in the mirror. Still, the dressing gown cheered her up at least; it had been her Christmas present from Sally and Ronnie. Pale pink satin, and glamorously floor length, it made her feel like a film star. Well, *had* done. She grimaced. Not quite so much today.

She made her way downstairs, Tiddles tucked into the crook of her elbow, and accepted the steaming bowl of oats Terry had made for her. Despite feeling so groggy she still hadn't quite adjusted to the luxury of having a cosy room to sit in, with a fire someone else had already lit, a radio blaring cheerfully and, best of all – better than anything – the loving eyes of her very own man to gaze into. Not eighteen yet, and yet she had everything she wanted. Everything she could ever imagine wanting.

Well, apart from not feeling quite so sick.

'I've put loads of treacle in, just how you like it,' Terry told her. 'Now, promise me you'll eat that up? I'm going to have to set off.'

'Ta, love,' Kathleen said, smiling, as he leaned to kiss her cheek. 'It smells absolutely lovely,' she added, which was a lie. 'And, look, don't go see Dad. I'll be fine once I've had this. I'll get into work, even if I can't manage to do the full clean this morning. Dad'll understand. And you know he'll send me home if I'm not up to it, so don't worry. And if nothing else, I need some exercise and fresh air.'

Grudgingly, he finally agreed, though now his car was fixed he told her that if she needed him she'd only to call the office at the depot – he'd pop back there at lunchtime, too, just in case she'd been in touch. And then, finally, *finally*, he was out of the front door, and Kathleen breathed a massive sigh of relief. She'd held on as long as she could – if she hadn't, he'd have refused to go at all, and she couldn't have that, her as some fragile moaning Minnie he had to nurse. That wasn't her. She didn't *get* ill. She'd hardly been off school or work ever. But right now the familiar clamminess was already coming over her. And she felt her gorge rise as she placed the porridge bowl down on the coffee table. Felt the unstoppable surge as she sidestepped the kitten to yank open the back door, and though the blast of freezing air was a balm against the flushed skin of her face, there was no stopping the force that was building inside her. She'd barely pulled open the toilet door and lifted the lid of the loo before out it all came, the tears streaming unbidden down her face as her body heaved.

She sank down then, spent and panting, against the cool of the concrete floor, grateful for the breeze that was blowing across her from the yard, and the ice she could feel against her legs. But the respite was only brief; no sooner had she started breathing normally than up came the surge again – how could she possibly have anything left inside her *to* vomit? – and once again she hung over the toilet bowl retching, feeling as if she was being turned inside out.

She stayed there an age. A good twenty minutes, she reckoned. But after a third bout, she felt confident the episode was over, and after spitting out the last of the disgusting yellow bile, she sat back against the rough painted brick wall of the outhouse and rubbed her now sore stomach gingerly.

There was no way she could face her porridge now; just the thought of it made her feel sick again, and although she knew she ought to try to eat something, she decided she wouldn't risk it. Instead she'd wash and dress and try to get herself off to work. She'd obviously picked up some gastric flu thing – that had been going around, too, hadn't it? But she felt better now, not least because Terry had already fed Tiddles and she didn't have to face the stench of a tin of cat food. The warm milk, she decided, could wait as well.

Once back upstairs she realised she felt markedly better. Perhaps the reason she'd been so sick was because she'd been brewing it all night. She only hoped she hadn't passed it on to Terry.

Ten minutes later, Kathleen was walking along Louis Avenue in the dark, head down against the bitterly cold air. Despite her determination to go into work today, she wasn't looking forward to it one bit, and checking her new watch – Terry's other present, which he'd told her was rolled gold – she decided she'd make a quick detour to the phone box. This was generally a good time to catch up with Sally – like Kathleen she was a lark, and would be up getting organised before getting the children off to school.

Kathleen so wished her aunt lived a bit nearer. Especially now she was with Terry and happy herself. Which had felt odd at first, but she realised it was *because* she was happy, and in her aunt she had someone she could share that happiness with. She also missed all the gossip that had come with working in the bar. All that time when she'd dreamed of a better life away from it, she now knew she wasn't cut out for spending lots of time alone – something that, of necessity, she was now having to do, and even with her little Tiddles, who was an absolute darling, she badly missed the regular human interaction. She'd been out for a milkshake with one of her old school friends, but it was mostly the bustle that she missed, and she'd already decided her New Year's resolution was going to be to get herself some work in *another* bar. It never hurt to have that bit more money coming in, after all.

She also missed her dad, who she'd not seen properly since Christmas. Just for a few minutes here and there, if he came down into the pub early, on those mornings when he had deliveries or needed to clean the pumps. He'd not been round. Despite giving them his blessing, he'd not been over, and it was a source of sadness – not to mention anger – to know precisely why that was. Just as Irene had barred Terry from the pub, so she'd probably barred her husband from going to her and Terry's. She might not have a bug, but was there no end to the bile she produced?

Sally answered at the second ring and it was good to hear her voice. 'Hello, love,' she said. 'You're an early bird today. Thought you'd still be sleeping yourself better. How are you feeling now? Any improvement?'

Sally knew all about Kathleen's illness via Ronnie, of course. And, in this case, there was no point in being economical with the truth about the sickness. Sally might even be able to suggest something she could take for it.

'I'm not too bad now,' she said. 'My throat's way better. So's my head. It's just that it's left me with this bloody awful sickness. I can't face eating, which makes me more nauseous, which means I *really* can't face eating. But it makes no difference. I've been throwing up for three days now. Though don't tell Terry,' she added quickly. 'He keeps wanting to stay at home and look after me. And I can't have that. I just thought …'

'For three days? What, in the mornings?'

'Yes, mostly. Though I've been feeling icky on and off all the time. But yes. I was just sick fit to bursting, half an hour back, and –'

'Kathleen, my love, you've been vomiting in the mornings?'

'Yes, I told you …'

'Any other symptoms? Tummy troubles? Other end?'

'No, I –'

'Fever?'

'No, that's gone now – though I keep breaking out in sweats …'

'Oh, my giddy aunt!' Sally said and then, to Kathleen's astonishment, she burst out laughing.

'Sally?' she asked. 'Sally?'

'Oh, my love, I'm sorry. I couldn't help it.'

'Help what?'

'Help but laugh. Oh, you daft mare,' she spluttered. 'Shall I tell you what I think's wrong with you? I mean, I could be wrong, obviously. But pound to a penny you've a bun in the oven, girl.'

'A what?' Kathleen asked, the term not quite sinking in yet.

'You're *pregnant*! Like I said, a pound to a penny. You need to get to the doctor's, love, and ask him to examine you.'

Kathleen stood stock still in the phone box, trying to assimilate what was being said to her. The sky was just beginning to lighten, the black turning to a deep charcoal grey. *Pregnant*? The idea had not occurred to her. Not once. She'd been so *careful*. Checked the dates when she was safe, just like she'd read you had to do. And Terry had been, well, careful too. How on earth could that have happened? Yes, maybe there was the odd slip, but surely not? Could it really be that *easy*? Hadn't someone told her once that there were only three days in a month when it was possible? Could they have *really* been so unlucky?

'Course, it *could* be something else,' Sally was saying. 'But if I were you, I'd get down to the doctor's. Love? You still there?'

'Yes, I'm still here,' Kathleen answered. 'I just can't believe …'

'Oh, believe it,' her aunt said, her voice jolly. 'Ronnie only had to so much as *glance* at me and I'd be up the duff – same thing with both of them … And, well, you and Terry, young love and all that …'

She didn't elucidate further. She didn't need to.

After the pips went – for which Kathleen was grateful, as she'd been stunned into silence – she hung up the phone, pulled her collar up and braced herself to go back out into the bitter cold. And then stood there, on the street, simply staring at the phone box, thinking how odd it suddenly looked against the grey of the streets and sky – so bright, and red and shiny, so – that was the word – cheery. So out of place in the half-light of the colourless January morning. So clean and fresh, in a way she'd never noticed before.

She hugged her belly, trying to fathom how she felt – how she *should* feel. Like the phone box, she felt suddenly out of place as well. But in a good way or a bad way? Her mind couldn't unscramble enough to decide. Not quite yet. But one thing *was* clear. She no longer felt ill.

Chapter 19

Having had no real mother in her formative years with whom she could discuss such things, Kathleen knew almost nothing about pregnancy. She knew a little, though; enough to feel a welling of certainty that her Aunt Sally was spot on in her diagnosis.

Now she thought about it rationally it all made perfect sense. However much time she'd spent poring over the calendar, and that comforting 'only three days a month' thing stuck in her mind, other facts now struck her as well. Such as the fact that you could get pregnant without even 'doing' it. Hadn't she been told that back in school, too? When that lady had come in and shown that film to them? Such as the fact that her last period had been not quite as expected. Hardly anything even – and another thought hit her. Hadn't her friend Sandra said you could have a period even when you were pregnant?

God, what an idiot she'd been! 'Yes, Terry,' she'd say, every time he'd asked her if it was safe. 'Yes, it's fine,' she'd say blithely, 'I've worked it out.' Such an *idiot*! An idiot wrapped up in a big bow of ignorance – of thinking everything was fine because of some half-baked optimism; that things like that didn't happen if you were 'careful'. She almost laughed as she set off to walk the long way to the pub. Being 'careful' doing something where she'd never felt so carefree, or passionate, or abandoned. Well, now she was paying the price, and she *still* didn't know how to feel. Only enough to know that perhaps clambering over walls wasn't the best thing to be doing.

For the first time she could remember, she was actually hoping *not* to see her dad. She even crossed her fingers as she let herself into the pub – as quietly as possible – and continued to do so mentally as she set about the cleaning, moving around the various rooms like a burglar. God forbid she'd see him; something would show on her face, she didn't doubt that. And the last thing she wanted was for him to get any sort of inkling; not before she'd been to the doctor's and confirmed it – if that were even possible? How would the doctor be able to tell? And definitely not before breaking the news to Terry.

Heart in mouth. That was the expression for what she was feeling, she thought distractedly, as she hurried round the taproom and the bar area and cleaned. For all that Sally's diagnosis had made her head spin, and it had, grim reality was beginning to creep in – in the form of questions she couldn't answer. An unmarried mother at her age. What would people *think*? And what if Terry

hated the idea? Was cross with her, even? Or worse –
the idea came to her in a cold draught of anxiety – what
if he didn't accept the truth of it? That she'd simply
been stupid and naïve and dozy. What if he thought she
was trying to trap him into marriage? For the first time,
Irene's situation with Darren and Monica's father hit
her hard. What if Terry *was* furious? What if he threw
her out?

The little bubble of unreality suddenly popped.

Kathleen returned home after finishing at the pub,
thankfully having seen no one. Not even Monica, who
she'd heard leave while on her hands and knees behind
the bar. And once home, she'd stayed home, for a long,
thoughtful hour, drinking tea and dithering about going
to the doctor's on Park Avenue where she'd be bound to
see someone she knew. The morning surgery finished at
eleven, and she knew she'd probably have a wait; they
did a first-come-first-served thing and if you weren't
there when the surgery doors opened, you could have a
dozen or more patients in the queue in front of you,
especially at this time of year, with everyone suffering
from coughs and colds.

Which was what decided her. She might feel shame-
ful and silly turning up with her questions about possible pregnancy, but she could legitimately go because
she'd been ill with an infection, too. She poured the last
of her tea down the sink and berated herself for being so

daft anyway; no one would know anything – consultations with doctors were confidential. So, having given Tiddles the milk she'd promised earlier, she set off down Louis Avenue and across to Park Avenue. Impossible to deal with something when you didn't even know what it was you were dealing with, after all.

Once in the surgery, Kathleen looked around and was struck once again by how it seemed as if there must be some evidence of her condition in her face. She was the youngest there by decades, bar a frazzled-looking mother with a toddler whose nose was streaming thick yellow mucus and who was fidgeting and grizzling at her constantly. Everyone else was elderly and gave the pair a wide berth.

And everyone – *everyone* – looked at her. Quite without any compunction or subtlety either, a couple of elderly ladies not even moving their legs out of the way as she passed them. She carefully stepped over them, conscious of all the eyes following her progress, all of them wondering, no doubt, why a young girl like her was here, taking up the precious time *they* might be allocated. She had always hated going to the doctor's anyway, having a healthy fear of illness and death, and had not been inside the place since she was thirteen or fourteen when Irene had taken her because of a rash. It had turned out to be German measles and she remembered it well. Being stuck in the stuffy bedroom for days, banished in case of contagion, crying like a baby, wanting her mum.

The surgery looked exactly the same now; a tiny, too-hot room, with ragged posters on the wall that flapped in greeting as the outer door was opened, and a hole in the wall at the end that opened into a back office, at which the greeting was invariably more hostile. Between the two, the room was given over to high-backed bench seating – one row of it taking up the length of the remaining walls, and two benches, back to back, down the middle.

She gave her name and took the last remaining seat available, thankfully in the corner, and buried her nose in one of the magazines that was piled just beside it, reading an article about a man who made mosaics out of old plates, and hoping no one would try to engage her in conversation.

A good twenty minutes passed, and, in that time, the room emptied, and before long, with more leaving than were now shuffling in, there were just four patients left in the room. None looked ill, any more than she realised she must look pregnant, and she was just biding her time wondering what might be wrong with them when the receptionist in the office beyond called her name.

Kathleen took her notes from her – though woe betide you if you ever dared to look at them – and made her way into the corridor to Dr Jackson's door. The name was familiar, though she couldn't remember having ever seen him herself, and when she entered the room she was dismayed to find a grizzled man, swivelling in a swivel chair, with hairs sprouting from his nose. She flushed from head to foot. He looked about a hundred. Where on earth would she begin?

'Take a seat, young lady,' said the doctor, taking the envelope of notes she proffered, but, before so much as glancing at them, he sat back and considered her over a pair of tortoiseshell glasses that sat at the end of his nose. Then he sat forward suddenly, startling her, and said, 'So, what seems to be the trouble?'

Now she was here there seemed little point in beating around the bush, so she told him she'd been feeling sick and thought that she might be pregnant, which unleashed a torrent of questions that came one after another, each more embarrassing than the last. When was her last period? Had she frequency? A desire to go for a wee more often than usual? Had she any breast tenderness? Giddiness? Any aversion to smells or food? And, almost as an afterthought, and which made her blush to her hair roots, a question about something that he seemed to have only just thought about: 'I take it you *are* having regular sexual relations?'

Kathleen didn't know where to look, let alone how to begin to answer, but her blush did the job for her instead. The doctor smiled then, and pulled her notes out, perhaps noticing her discomfort. Looking down at them and picking up a pen, he made a short note. 'Well, yes,

Kathleen,' he said, glancing at the top of the envelope to get her name right. 'Given what you've told me, and in the absence of other factors that might preclude it, I rather suspect that pregnant is *precisely* what you are.'

The doctor had made no comment nor asked a question about her marital status, for which Kathleen was extremely grateful. He must have known, though. No wedding ring. And he also knew her age, of course. So he knew. But he didn't judge her. Or if he did, he didn't seem to. She felt comforted by that, and felt a warmth for the kindly GP. A welcome warmth. The world at large would no doubt view it more coldly. The world at large and her father, no doubt. *And* her hated stepmother.

It was dark once again by the time Terry's car pulled up outside, while Kathleen was pacing the little sitting room, at sixes and sevens about what to say and do. That she was pregnant was no longer in question. She'd gone back and worked out how long it had been since her last period and had also realised what she suspected might have been her downfall; that the light bleeding she'd experienced in December had *not been* a period. That was all so obvious now – how stupid had she been to think so? So she'd blithely reassured him of her dates … She cursed herself anew.

And now she'd been enlightened as to what the symptoms of pregnancy might be, it was all too obvious that she had the full set. Again and again, she'd considered running back to the phone box to speak to Sally, but again and again she decided against going out, as it was freezing, and there seemed little point. It would keep.

She knew what she knew – that she was almost certainly expecting a baby, that an appointment would be sent to her so she could attend the local hospital, and that once she had it, she should attend her first antenatal visit – that was, of course, assuming she didn't have a period in the meantime (or any other worrying symptoms that might mean it was something else), in which case she should hurry back to the doctor's, and the appointment at the hospital would be cancelled.

It all seemed so matter of fact, so calm and calculated, so clinical, that such excitement as she'd dared to feel (and now she could finally admit it to herself – she'd been excited above all things) had been swept away with all the efficiency of the family-planning lady who'd come to the school and whose lecture now came so readily to mind. Her with her dire pronouncements about the perils of 'letting boys have their way with you', and about the terrible, mortal shame of being an unmarried mother, which would see her shunned and reviled everywhere she went, and about the agonies of childbirth.

And as the minutes ticked by, she found she could *only* concentrate on such negatives. They'd been together less than half a year, they'd been living together barely a month, and she realised she didn't know if Terry even *wanted* children. Surely if he had, he and Iris would have already had some? She just couldn't imagine he'd be happy about it, not becoming a first-time father at his age. Now he really *would* have to support her, despite her claims to independence – at least when the baby was little. And not just her either. A baby he probably didn't want as well.

She heard Terry's key in the front door, and the sound of it swinging open and then shutting, before getting up to go into the hall and welcome him home. And as she passed Iris's picture she gazed into the other woman's eyes, feeling a sudden connection to the girl who'd once loved the man *she* loved – and an unspoken question formed on her lips. *Will it be alright? Do you think so?*

She went into the hallway and watched as he hung his coat up on the row of hooks, the cold air from outside eddying around as he did so. He turned to greet her.

'Hello, sweetheart,' he said. 'How you doing now? Any better?'

'Sort of …' she began, but then, overcome with emotion, turned back towards the sitting room. He followed her in there.

'Love, what's *up*?' he said, placing a hand on her shoulder. 'What's the matter?'

She turned to face him and he immediately put his arms around her. 'I knew I shouldn't have gone to work today! Look at you! You're shivering! Come on. Sit down. Take the weight off. *Damn*. I shouldn't have left you. You didn't go into work, did you?' he wanted to know, urging her towards the settee.

Kathleen sat down, even though sitting down was that last thing she wanted to do. She felt like a coiled spring in a jack-in-the-box, ready to explode at any moment. *Just tell him*, she ordered herself. *Just get it over with!*

'Terry, I'm not ill any more. Well, *sort* of not. No, no. That's wrong. I'm not ill. I'm *fine*. But I'm …'

'*What?*' His eyes bored into hers, his hands gripped her own.

She dropped her gaze. 'Oh God, I don't even know how to tell you …'

Terry's frown deepened, the concern written all over his face. 'Don't scare me, love,' he said, letting go of her hands to hold her face up to look at him. 'What *is* it, Kathy? You can tell me *anything*. Have you been to the doctor's? I knew it …'

'Terry, I *told* you. I'm fine. It's just …'

He gripped her hands again. 'Now you're *really* scaring me … What's happened? Is it something *I've* done? Is that it?'

Kathleen shook her head. He was getting all the wrong ideas and she needed to toughen up and just tell him. 'God, no! Terry, *no*. Nothing like that! There's nothing wrong with us. *Or* me ...' She dredged a shy smile from somewhere. 'Well, unless you count being pregnant as an illness.'

Terry's mouth gaped open, and he let go of her hands once again. Then, finally, he spoke. 'You're *pregnant*?'

She nodded.

'You mean we're going to have a young 'un? But you said ...'

'I did my sums wrong.'

He cupped her face in his hands again. 'Oh my God, Kathy! Oh, my God! We *are*, aren't we? We're going to have a kid! You're actually *pregnant*!'

She placed her hands over his. They were still cold. She would warm them up for him. 'You're not cross, then?'

'Cross? Why ever would I be cross?'

'Because I'm seventeen ... because it's so soon ... because we're not ...' No. She couldn't even *think* of saying the other thing. And didn't need to say any more anyway, because, whooping with joy, he had hauled her back up onto her feet, and was spinning her around and around the centre of the sitting room, like her dad used to do when she was little. Which made her giddy. Almost faint. But she no longer cared.

Chapter 20

It was a night like no other; as if she'd been whisked to a parallel universe, where the cares of the world no longer existed for either of them. They'd talked long into the night about the past, present and future, about getting married – Terry aghast – 'I can't believe you thought I wouldn't want to marry you!' – and much later, with Tiddles banished from the bedroom – a rare sanction, about which she was most indignant – they made love, keeping the world further at bay.

But with the morning – another alarm-shrill in the blackness of the bedroom – came the inevitable reality that the world *wouldn't* go away. Was very much present, in fact, in the shape of the fact that Kathleen must now go and tell her father.

'Well, you're not doing *that* on your own,' Terry said as he sat and ate his porridge. Once again, she was pole-axed by the intensity of her nausea, but now she knew the cause she felt better able to deal with it. It would be gone in a bit and, in the meantime, she'd ride it … well, as best she could. Smelling his breakfast was already making her retch.

'I wasn't planning on it,' she told him. 'I want you there right beside me.'

'As I should be. As I aim to be. Let's go round there tonight.'

Kathleen nodded. 'I was thinking the same. I want to catch him on his own. I don't think I can face her ...'

'I'll bloody well face her.'

'I know, love, but I think it's best if we leave Dad to tell her, don't you?'

He frowned. 'Much as it's even her business, love.'

'It is, Terry. I'm still her stepdaughter.'

'And doesn't she let you know it! But, no, if that's the way you want to play it, then that's fine by me. More than happy to knock the witch off her bloody broomstick!'

It was a Thursday. Which was good, because it was games night at the pub, and she knew her dad would be down half an hour before opening to brush the billiard table and polish the balls before the match.

She'd gone to clean as usual, first thing, and, happily, seen nothing of her father, and had been buoyed all day – well, once the sickness went – by the joy she was feeling. Terry was a gem, and she kept going over and over everything; unlike her father, he would not have a word said against her by Irene, and, though she was fearful about the inevitable confrontation, she cared less. Why should she care? Irene's opinion no longer mattered. Only Terry's, and Terry loved her, and would not let her down.

They walked round to the pub for six-thirty, almost as soon as Terry had got in from work. He'd be away for a few days from tomorrow, on another European job, so it was important they do it as a matter of urgency – Kathleen knew she wouldn't be able to keep it from her dad for very long, and she needed Terry by her side when he was told.

They knocked on the front door and waited, it not escaping their notice that Terry was still officially barred from the Dog and Duck. He'd not set foot over the threshold in over two months now, and cared not at all. Well, Kathleen mused, wondering still what had passed between the two men, except for the time when he'd had the conversation with her father which could so easily have meant she was still slaving away on the other side of this very door. It still made her shudder to think that, if he hadn't passed her in his lorry that day, she might never have seen him again.

Her dad looked confused as he slid the bolts to unlock the doors.

'What's up?' he asked, looking from one to the other as he let them in. 'I'm guessing you're not here for the tournament.'

Kathleen stepped forward and hugged her father, who smelled exactly as he always did of the woody aftershave he'd used for as long as she could remember. He returned her hug tightly, then let her go and stepped back, his face, seeing their expressions, now becoming anxious.

'You on your own, Dad?' Kathleen asked. Then, 'It's okay, there's nothing wrong. We just have something important to talk to you about, that's all.'

'No, he's not on his own!'

Kathleen felt her heart plummet. It was Irene's voice. She appeared at the back of the bar just as they stepped into the taproom. 'So if you've sneaked in here asking for money,' she said, lifting the counter and coming around it, 'you've no bleeding chance. We're completely skint.'

Kathleen glanced in dismay at Terry, who was eyeing Irene with cold distaste. And then beyond Irene, she felt further dismayed, as Monica had appeared too. Seemed the routines had changed somewhat since she'd stopped doing all the donkey work. But no, it looked like Monica had just come in from work. She certainly didn't look as if she'd been on her hands and knees scrubbing any toilets.

Kathleen's stepsister gave her a long slow appraisal – head to foot and back up again. What little bond they'd shared seemed to have vanished completely, and Kathleen supposed it was probably for much the same reason; that her underling wasn't there to be bossed about any more. 'Oh look,' Monica said sarcastically, 'it's Kathleen and her old man. *Literally*.' She then grinned smugly at her own joke, threw down the tea towel she'd been holding and got herself a glass so she could pour herself a drink.

John glared at her, but he still looked as uncomfortable as Kathleen was feeling. And once again, seemed unable to speak up himself. 'You alright, Terry?' he asked instead, touching the younger man's forearm. 'Why don't you sit down, the pair of you, and you can tell me what's up.'

'There's nothing up,' Kathleen responded, looking pointedly at Irene, who had now crossed the room and stood behind John, hands on hips.

Neither sat. 'Kathy?' Terry said, gently, squeezing her hand. 'Do you want to tell them, love?'

In for a penny, Kathleen thought, taking a breath and holding it for a moment. She'd rehearsed this. And also a mantra to keep in her head. *It doesn't matter what they think. This is my life. They can't hurt me. Be brave.*

'It's just as well you're all here anyway,' she started. 'Because we've come round to let you know that we're going to have a baby. I'm pregnant. We don't know how far yet, but a good few weeks I think. Anyway, that's it. That's our news.' She paused and held her father's astonished gaze. 'And we're both really happy about it,' she finished.

She felt the pressure of Terry's hand holding hers and was grateful for it, too, as now she'd made her speech she felt lightheaded.

Low blood pressure, she remembered, from her visit to the doctor's. Perhaps she should sit down. But she didn't. In a situation like this, her height mattered to her.

Irene and Monica were both staring at each other, open-mouthed. Which was gratifying. An image she liked to think she would remember. But it was her father's reaction that she cared about the most. After Terry, he was the person she most wanted to be pleased for them. Not to condemn, not to judge, just to be thrilled. Stupid society could go to hell, she thought. And she willed him to think that too. And little by little, as the news seemed to settle into his brain, she saw the ghost of a smile, then an actual smile, light his drawn features.

Is he thinking what I'm thinking? she wondered, returning his smile. *That Mum's grandchild is going to come into the world?*

And then she was in her father's arms, and he was shaking Terry's hand and congratulating him, and there was a smiling exchange about Terry promising to 'make an honest woman' of her and for a moment it was as if Irene and Monica didn't exist. And, of course, they were not having that.

'Congratu-*fucking*-lations?' Irene yelled at him, 'is that all you have to say?'

She marched up to John, her face red and angry. 'This little *slut* calmly tells you she's going to be an unmarried mother, and you pat her – *and* him – on the pissing *back*? Oh this is going to be the final nail in our coffin, is this!' She threw her hands up in the air, as if beseeching some deity. 'Can you imagine it? Oh the *shame*. We'll be the talk of frigging Canterbury, yet *again*!'

'Not an unmarried mother, Irene,' Terry quickly corrected her. 'As I just told John, we'll get wed just as soon as we can afford a proper do.'

'Oh, and you think that'll make any difference? People can *count*, you know!'

'I dare say they can, and they will, but you really think we care about the sleazy opinions of folk who have nothing better to do than will ill on other folk and spread gossip?'

'Er, excuse *me*! *You're* calling folk sleazy? *You*? You, carrying on with that little dolt who's half your age?'

Terry automatically put a protective arm around Kathleen and pulled her towards him. There was a little tic working in his jaw and Kathleen feared he might lose his cool completely. But his voice was level as he spoke. 'Irene, it doesn't matter what *anyone* else thinks, so long as we're happy about it. My *fiancée* and I. That's all that counts.'

Irene flinched at the term. '*Happy* about it?' Irene spluttered before turning to Monica. 'Have you heard this? Aah, how sweet. They're *happy* about it.'

Monica's lip curled, and Kathleen wondered what she'd ever done to deserve the cruelty and derision she routinely got from her stepsister. And wondered again how one woman's corrosive influence could be so strong that Monica could be so full of spite. She vowed instantly that she would be a better mother to her own child, and her hand went reflexively to her belly. 'They don't look right happy to me,' Monica said to Irene. 'And no wonder. Tongues'll be wagging all over Bradford about this.'

Kathleen caught her dad moving out of the corner of her eye. Not much. Just standing up that little bit taller. 'Irene,' he said, addressing his wife for the first time, 'she isn't the first and she won't be the last. She's having a baby, my first *grandchild*,' he glanced over at Kathleen. 'And *bugger* what anyone else thinks!'

That seemed to be the spark that lit the flame. To Terry's shock and Kathleen's horror, her stepmother launched herself, fists flying, at her poor dad.

'You horrible bastard!' she screamed as she punched anywhere she could find a target. 'Her! Having a baby! *Her?*' She seemed apoplectic at the thought. 'Up the duff, *her?*' she seemed to be directing this now mostly at Monica, as if her daughter had failed her in not being pregnant first. In not having a man. In not coming up with the goods. And Monica's expression said it all – that she was finally in accord with Kathleen, that their mam had *really* lost it, and that she was perplexed about why any of her vitriol should be aimed at her.

Terry bent and brushed his lips against Kathleen's ear. 'Come on, love,' he whispered, 'let's get out of here. This is just sick.'

Irene turned on him. Her hearing was still fully functional, evidently. 'Oh, sick is it? Sick? I'll tell you what's sick, mate. An old bleeding man like you, preying on a young 'un who's a bit backwards. That's what's sick, and you're a fool if you think folk won't let you know it. And I'll make sure everyone knows it an' all,' she added, catching her husband with a whack around the face with the flat of her hand, before Terry, darting forward, could stop her.

It was her father's slight lurch, before correcting himself, that did it for Kathleen. And the way he had to rearrange his glasses back on his nose.

'Stop it!' she yelled, tears flooding her eyes. 'All of you! Just stop it. Stop it now!' She turned to her dad, willing him to be half the man Terry was. To stand up for her. 'Dad, I love you,' she sobbed, 'and I want you to be happy for me. For *both* of us,' she added, clutching once again at Terry's hand. 'But I promise you this,' she said, 'I won't have it a part of this bloody war zone. Dad, I *mean* it.' She then pointed at Irene. 'Sort her out, because I won't be bringing my baby here, *ever*, unless you do.'

Kathleen tugged on Terry's hand and pulled him with her to leave. But Irene hadn't finished. 'Yes, piss off!' she yelled. 'Bugger off. That'll suit us all just fine. You and your old man *and* your bleeding bastard sprog.

231

You're fired *and* you're barred, so just piss off, the pair of you,' she finished, flecks of spittle flying from her mouth.

'Irene, pack it in!' John barked, wiping his own mouth from where she'd caught him. 'Leave the lass alone, will you!'

'You know where I live, Dad,' Kathleen said, feeling lighter and braver now she'd done what she'd come to do, and because *finally* her dad had defended her. Well, to an extent. 'Call round anytime you like.'

'You'll be welcome,' added Terry.

'Ooh, he'll be *welcome*!' sang out Irene.

Terry's gaze shifted. 'Unlike *you*,' he said, 'who won't. Not till you can learn to treat *decent* folk with a modicum of respect, at any rate.'

'D'you *hear* that?' she bellowed at John.

'Mam, *leave* it!' shouted Monica.

Kathleen's dad's expression was fraught. 'Just *go*, love,' he told her, looking anxiously at his watch. 'Opening time any minute. Leave me to deal with this, okay? Go on, lad,' he said to Terry, gesturing towards the door again. 'Get her home.'

'"A modicum of respect",' Kathleen said, as they headed back down Louis Avenue. 'You don't half talk posh sometimes, Terry Harris.'

'Hidden depths,' he said, chuckling. 'That's me. Lots of hidden depths. Seriously, love, it'll be fine. You do know that, don't you?'

She felt strangely content now – very strange, given all unpleasantness and shouting. Not to mention the small matter of losing her job. But she couldn't help it. Now the deed was done, she felt free, and also determined. She didn't ever need to lay eyes on her stepmother again, and, in her current frame of mind, that felt good. And she knew Terry felt the same way, too. She could tell by the spring in his step and how he swung the arm that hers was attached to.

'And you're really set on making an honest woman of me, are you, Terry Harris?'

'I'm not so sure now,' he said. 'I quite like you as a fallen one, to be honest. As a wanton one …' He grinned as he patted her stomach.

'Well, you've certainly *made* a woman of me,' she replied, smiling coyly.

'Takes a man to do that, that does,' he said, pulling her against him.

'Stop it!' she hissed, as he leaned down to kiss her. 'You'll have those tongues start up wagg—'

He silenced her. 'Let them.'

It was only hours later, unable to sleep, that Terry's words had come back to her. Why couldn't her dad properly take her part like Terry had – fight her corner, be a man for her? Perhaps he would. Perhaps he yet would.

Chapter 21

Kathleen couldn't help but smile as she lifted her night-gown. She turned this way and that, marvelling at the way her body had begun changing. Not hugely, not yet, but enough to reassure her that the life inside her was growing, and growing fast.

It was the third week in March now, and you could definitely tell she was pregnant. Well, *she* could, even if, when she was dressed, there wasn't a gnat's chance that anyone else would notice. And pregnant by some thirteen or fourteen weeks now, given what they'd told her when she'd been to the hospital. She and Terry would have their baby by the middle of August. Which felt perfect. A summer baby. And on the anniversary of the month she'd fallen in love. Well, sort of, she thought to herself. She knew she'd half-loved him long before he'd even noticed her. Her smiled widened. She wasn't giving him the satisfaction of knowing that.

'Bloody gorgeous,' Terry said as he appeared behind her reflection, around the bedroom door. She dropped her nightie.

'Terry!'

He strode in, looking entirely unabashed. 'Cup of tea,' he said passing a mug to her. 'And you're going to have to stop doing that.'

'No, *you're* going to have to stop doing that!' Kathleen scolded. 'Sneaking up on a girl when she thinks she's on her own. And you know how I hate you to look at my belly.'

'Nonsense,' he said, planting a kiss on her forehead. 'Anyway, get your skates on. Sal'll be here any time, won't she? Or were you planning to give her a show of it as well?'

Terry dodged the slap he'd asked for, but he was right. She was doing way too much mooning around. Which she had no business to be doing while he was working all hours, despite him constantly telling her she must rest and that they could manage. Pregnancy wasn't an illness, after all. It was a natural part of life. But still the bit to make the most of, before the busy bit arrived – which it would all too soon, as her aunt had pointed out the last time she'd been to visit. 'So make the most of it,' she'd counselled. 'And that's an order!'

Kathleen had seen her dad only three times in all since the row. It had been several weeks now, and she kept hoping she'd see more of him, see him properly, but each time he'd come round he'd had an anxious look about him, stayed only a short time, checking if she was okay, having a quick cuppa, and then was gone almost as soon as he'd arrived.

'You know how it is, love,' he'd explained. 'We need to let the dust settle, don't we? You know how sensitive your mam is about folk gossiping and speaking ill of us.'

Kathleen had been bold then. 'Dad,' she'd said, 'has it ever occurred to you that it takes one to know one?'

Her dad had blinked at her, as if confused. So she spelled it out. 'That if you run around hating people you end up so bitter and mean-spirited that you think everyone else thinks just like you.' She'd gone further. 'Dad,' she'd said, 'is this how it's going to be now? Even when the baby's born? That we're going to be your dirty little secret?'

He'd no answer to that bar the one he always gave her. That it was complicated. That Irene would come round eventually. That in the meantime, it just took a bit of getting used to. Give it time, give it time, give it time.

But she had one regular visitor who made no bones about her excitement. Since the day Kathleen had called her to confirm what she'd expected, Sally had been round to visit every single week – making the long bus journey, sometimes with the kids, sometimes without, but always with advice, support and invariably a few groceries, including something specially baked for them, like a pie or some buns.

She'd made no secret of her feelings about the situation with her sister, either. Though Kathleen had only given her a potted account of how things stood between her and her dad and Irene, Sally's first port of call had been to the Dog and Duck.

'What, to have it out with Irene?' Kathleen had squeaked, fearing the possible repercussions. Her dad had been over to see her once at that time, and Kathleen still felt a bit raw.

'Oh, no, love. Wouldn't waste my breath on that – though she was definitely there. Hiding away upstairs, she was. Couldn't face me, I don't doubt. No, I went round to speak to your father.'

'Dad? Oh God, Auntie Sally, what did you say to him? What did you do?'

'Humph!' Sally snorted. 'There you go, see!'

'See what?'

'Your worried face! You're sticking up for him straight away, aren't you?! Listen, love,' she said, 'here's the thing. You've got to stop thinking like that. It's you letting him off the hook that means he gets away with it, doesn't it?'

'Gets away with what?' As far as Kathleen could tell, her father got away with precisely nothing. He couldn't so much as slip out for a ciggie without getting a row.

Sally sighed. 'Look, my love, I know he's your dad and you love him, but my bloody awful sister wouldn't be half as bad as she is if he'd had the bollocks to stand up to her all these years. It's like letting alcoholics loose in the drinks cabinet – I heard about it on some television programme. He *allows* her to behave badly and that just makes her worse. You'll learn all about it when you've a nipper on your hands, trust me.' She leaned forwards. 'He needs to be a bloody man, Kathleen. That's what it amounts to. You're his flesh and blood, love, his little girl. And at times like this, *you* should come first, not that miserable mare!'

Kathleen wondered quite what sort of conversation had then ensued. She couldn't imagine her father taking kindly to being told how to run his life, but then, this was Sally, and when Sally got her teeth into something …

'So what happened? What did you say?'

'I just told him some home truths. Look, I know Rene's my sister, love, and, trust me, I feel heart-sorry for her, losing her Darren the way she did, but that's not an excuse for treating *you* the way she does, any more than anything else is. And you know what they say, don't you? Familiarity breeds contempt. She's been too damned used to your dad running around after, letting her do what she likes, so perhaps she needs to wake up and realise what she could lose! So here's hoping that one day – pray it be soon – your dad will frigging wake up and see her for what she is. I'm sorry, but her and that niece of mine are nasty pieces of work. Anyway, let's just hope I set him on the road a bit quicker than he might otherwise have got there – as much as for his own sake as anything. You're with Terry now, life of your own. Flown the nest and so on. What's life going to be like for him when it's just the two of them rattling around?'

Since then, Kathleen had seen her dad again twice more, which was nice, but though both times she'd been glad of it – even if she felt it was really Sally that had prompted it – she'd felt needled that he still had this inability to do what *he* wanted. Go where he liked. See whom *he* chose. The backbone to 'sort Irene out', as Kathleen had told him he must. To make her see that he wasn't going to tolerate her vileness and nonsense, that Kathleen and Terry were welcome in *his* home. To stand up for her. Why was that so bloody hard?

As for the goings-on at the pub, she had to rely on the one thing at the centre of it all – the all-inclusive nature of the local gossip. Be it in the Co-op or the post office, there was always some snippet – she knew the price of the beer had gone up, that Monica had had her hair permed and that Irene had taken an unhealthy liking to Sid the butcher. 'She'll be after his pork sausage,' Sandra Collins had said loudly, while queuing at the till with her friend, knowing full well that Kathleen was in front of her. She heard the laughing and spluttering behind her, but didn't give them the satisfaction of turning around, and instead just smiled politely after paying for her bread and milk.

Let them gossip about me too, she thought. Because she honestly didn't care. To be pregnant out of wedlock might be a cardinal sin, but Kathleen found she really couldn't find it in herself to worry. She'd leave the judgements to God and the rest could go hang. She'd be marrying Terry soon enough, so who *cared*? One day – and she felt this with as much conviction as she felt anything – people would come to realise it wasn't a sin to make a baby with someone you loved. The sin was in the making them, giving birth to them and then doing wrong by them – no bloody ring made a blind bit of difference to *that*.

She pulled her clothes on, sipping at the hot tea between garments, reminding herself that she needed to start planning. All too soon her slim frame would be replaced by a Minnie Mouse one, and the majority of her clothes wouldn't fit.

She then pulled back the curtains – best not to give the elderly neighbours too much of an eyeful – to see Terry down below her, pottering in the little front garden, knelt down and digging away contentedly with a fork and a trowel. Enjoying the first day off he'd had in almost a fortnight.

The happiness welled in her, and she hoped Sally would arrive just at this moment. So that she would know that all was well and what a fine life they were going to have. What with the sun shining and daffodils springing up, it felt like the dawn of something new and wonderful. Spring was definitely in the air, a new life was growing in her belly, and she had a man who wanted to give her the world.

She stepped back from the window and drained her tea, glancing at herself again in the dressing-table mirror, marvelling at the light in her eyes, the bounce in her hair. She'd never thought of herself as pretty; quite the opposite. The many years of slights and barbs and put-downs had all taken their toll. But now she saw something that made her re-evaluate herself – saw glimpses of what Terry saw, and told her all the time, too. That she *was* pretty. More than that. Even beautiful.

Not that she could quite believe it. Not properly. Because love was blind, wasn't it? So he might not be seeing straight. And she still wondered, often, what right she had to be this happy. It actually scared her at times, and she had to remind herself when the fear threatened her that this *was* her life now; that she'd left all the awfulness behind. It was difficult, though – after what seemed like a lifetime of fear and uncertainty, it felt alien to relax – to not have anything to worry about.

She said as much to Sally when she got there. She'd made a second pot of tea and Sally had opened a tin of homemade butterfly buns, and they were sitting on the little settee, the morning sun shining long bars of light onto the carpet. Terry was still outside gardening.

'I still wake up every morning and have to pinch myself to stop my stomach lurching, wondering if I'm late for cleaning or lighting the fire or knocking somebody up or something.'

Sally laughed her big laugh. 'You'll drive yourself mad, girl,' she said. 'Just be happy that you've got a man who does all the worrying *for* you. Enjoy it, kiddo, because when that baby comes along, you'll have a whole new set of worries, trust me. And them worries last you a lifetime.'

Kathleen winced. 'Oh God, Sally, that's another thing. I'm bloody dreading that. I mean, not the baby – I can't *wait* for a baby of my own. But I'm scared of the pain. Really scared. I keep seeing the film they showed us back in school. The woman having one was screaming like a bloody banshee! Honest to God, I'm terrified.'

Sally smiled and patted Kathleen's lap. 'I reckon they choose those films 'specially. To make impressionable young girls so bleeding scared that they never dare uncross their legs till they're safely wed.' She roared with laughter. 'And even then, in some cases, they have to be prised apart with a crowbar! The nonsense women talk about sex, eh? But take it from someone who knows, love. It's like shelling peas, honest. Yes it makes you cross-eyed for a bit there, but it's *natural*. It's what we were built for. And once you get that bundle in your arms, any pain is forgotten instantly. Trust me, you'll see. You'll be fine.'

Kathleen thought for a moment before speaking again. There was something she'd been thinking a lot about recently, but she hadn't wanted to say anything to Terry in case he thought he wasn't helping her enough. But she was absolutely sure Sally would understand.

'I've been having these dreams you know,' she told her aunt. 'Really intense they are, really real. Where I keep seeing my mum in the distance and run to her and I ask her if she'll help me … you, know, show me what to do, how to be a mum, but she never answers. I keep running towards her but she never gets any closer. And never speaks. Just smiles and watches me … it's really weird.'

'That'll be your hormones, love. And the fact that she'll be much on your mind right now. You must miss her dreadfully, knowing everything that's coming now …'

She leaned across and put an arm around Kathleen's shoulder. 'Must miss her *so* much. Having a baby of your own is bound to stir up feelings. But you know what, you will be the best mum ever, I don't doubt it. So just you stop worrying. *Just* enjoy it. And you know what, come hellfire, or flood, *I'll* be there for you.' She looked deeply into Kathleen's eyes. 'You *do* know that, don't you? Oh gawd,' she said then. 'Don't you start snivelling on me, now, for pity's sake. Honestly, you'll have me bawling in a minute.'

243

Kathleen drew the backs of her hands over her eyes, and stood up, feeling cross with herself. 'You're right, as usual. I'm going to stop all this nonsense and grow up a bit. It's silly at my age, fussing and fretting like a kid. I'm only going to have a baby, for God's sake!'

'Exactly,' said Sally, standing too. 'Piece of cake, eh? On which note, shall we be naughty? Seems a shame to leave them to go stale.'

Kathleen laughed. 'You're trying to fatten me up, you are. So. Do you fancy another cuppa? I'm going to make one for Terry.'

Sally grabbed their cups. 'You know what you need, girl?' she said, as she followed Kathleen back to the little kitchen. 'A bloody good night out. Once all this sickness finally stops anyway. Several, in fact, while you still have the chance.'

'Oh, I'd *love* a night out,' Kathleen admitted. 'If feels like ages since I've had a proper one. I miss the pub – even if I don't miss the bloody slave labour I used to do in it.'

'I'll bet you do,' Sally said. 'And I tell you what – we should try to make a bit of a night of it on a regular basis. You know, you and me, Terry and Ronnie. Have a proper old knees-up. Carefully, in your case, of course. No dancing on the tables.'

'I'd *love* that. We could go to the Bull. Have a dance. They've usually got a band there at the weekends.'

'Well, there's a plan then. We'd have to bring the kids with us, of course, but d'you think you could get a sitter for them?'

'I'm sure Mary would do it – she doesn't often work Saturday nights. Well, didn't. That might have changed now. But I'll check. I'll call her in the week, eh?'

'Grand,' Sally said. 'Ooh, I'm quite looking forward to it, poor old stop-at-home that I am.'

'You?' Kathleen laughed. 'Poor old stop-at-home? Sitting in of an evening when there's a chance to go out dancing? Yeah, and I'm a flipping monkey's uncle.'

It was a comment that would haunt her for the rest of her days.

Chapter 22

Saturday 18 June 1966

A *whale, that's what I look like*, Kathleen thought to herself, as she lay in bed and considered her bump. She had long since thrown off the covers, as it was so hot and sticky. For the last couple of weeks she'd been going to bed naked as well. Which didn't seem quite seemly, even though Terry was all in favour, and had the downside of her now being able to see the vast expanse of flesh in front of her – the naked truth of it, unkindly bathed in morning sunlight.

A *whale with nothing to wear*, she remembered, grunting as she pushed herself upright. In the last couple of weeks she seemed to have swelled alarmingly. She was at the point where getting dressed in the morning was a constant challenge, her cry of 'I've nothing to put on' completely genuine. One day this week she'd even tried on one of Terry's work boiler-suits, which, though unflattering, at least had the virtue – and it was a big one – of being substantially bigger than she was; something that could no longer be said of any of her clothes.

But it was Saturday, and tonight she and Terry were going out. And Sally, too – though not Ronnie tonight as he was working away – but Sally was coming, with Stuart and Lisa, so they could all have a night in the Bull.

They barely went anywhere near the Dog and Duck now. True to type, the bit of time her dad had insisted she give things had stretched and stretched and stretched. Yes, she saw him – he'd pop round for an hour or between the lunchtime and evening shifts – and she was always glad to see him, glad of his quiet, uncompli-cated company, but there it ended; as far as Irene was concerned she'd heaped disgrace on the family, shamed them, committed the most heinous crime imaginable – not only had she got pregnant out of wedlock, she'd not even done the decent thing and gone to those mother and baby homes, and let the nuns whisk it off for adoption – oh, no. No, she'd brazenly moved in with the father of the coming bastard – who was old enough to *be* her father! Oh, the *shame*.

Had it not been so sad, Kathleen would have found it extremely funny. And she did find it amusing to hear all the hearsay about just how far down she had fallen. And now they'd decided not to wed till she could fit into a proper wedding dress (as well as something perfect for their perfect newborn, obviously) there was no end to Irene's mortification. She had, she knew, been completely disowned.

And partly, she found she rather liked that. But at the same time, it both hurt and frustrated her to imagine bringing this little perfect child into the world and her father still having to sneak around like a thief in the night instead of showing off his grandchild to his friends, in *his* pub, involving himself fully in the young family's life.

Well, he'd made his choice. And so had she. And she was happy she'd made the right one. And it was Saturday, and she was going out, and the babysitter had been booked, and, knowing she wouldn't be able to do the twist for much longer, she was really looking forward to it.

Or, rather, had been, till yesterday, when she'd tried on the two-piece she'd hoped to wriggle into, to find she couldn't even get the skirt on, let alone do it up, even with the alterations she'd made to the elastic round the waist.

'Breakfast!' Terry's voice rang out and wafted up the stairs to her, along with the smell of frying from down in the kitchen. She reached for her dressing gown – thankfully spacious – and tried to remember her figure. If she wanted it back, she must take care not to stuff her face too much, despite her appetite – that whole 'eating for two' rule had turned out to be nonsense. However big she felt, just as Sally had pointed out more than once, she was actually only eating for 'one and a little bit'.

Even so, the egg sandwich that Terry plonked in front of her was too good to resist, and she was several bites in before she came up for air.

'I don't know what I'm going to wear tonight,' she grumbled, licking grease from her fingers. 'Nothing I've got fits me anymore.'

'What's that?' Terry asked, glancing up from his newspaper. He nodded back towards it, then ran his hand over his chin. He wasn't working today, so he'd not shaved, and it made a satisfying rasp; a noise Kathleen had always loved. 'It says here that they've sent more Yanks into Vietnam,' he said, frowning. 'Sounds like it's getting bad over there again – there's loads gone over now.'

Miles away, thinking about the manly shape of Terry's jaw, it took a moment for Kathleen to digest it. 'Terry,' she told him then, 'there's a war going on right here! A big, bloody one. Between me and my *wardrobe*.'

'What, love?' He looked up.

'I've got nothing to wear tonight. *Nothing*. Everything's too bloody small.' She took another bite of her sandwich, fully aware of the irony in doing so. Then sighed. 'I look a right fat cow, I really do.'

Terry smiled at her, and calmly folded his paper. It had long since struck her how his maturity suited her so perfectly. That and his calm, matter-of-fact personality, which was the perfect antidote to her by now raging hormones. 'Cinderella *will* go to the ball, my sweet,' he said, reaching across to pat her knee. 'Because after you've eaten that, I'll run you a lovely hot bath, then we'll go spend some of my wages on a nice new frock for you. How does that sound? Oh, and by the way, you have egg on your chin.'

'*Can* we?' Kathleen said, wiping the yolk from her face. She could never quite get used to how much Terry spoilt her and she felt guilty now for moaning. 'Are you sure? Can we afford it? What with all the baby clothes still to get and everything ...'

'If I couldn't afford to dress you, I'd be a pretty poor show of a fiancé, wouldn't I? Of course you can have something nice to wear tonight, my love.'

'Well, it won't be exactly nice,' Kathleen corrected him. 'I'll still look like a whale, whatever I find to wear. But a nice whale. An *elegant* whale. Ooh, and there's a thought. Do you think we could go to Brown Muff? They have maternity dresses, lots of them. They're bound to have something. And I've never had a dress from Brown Muff.'

Terry laughed. 'I'll go run your bath. Then Brown Muff it is. Nothing's too good for my girl, you know that.'

She blew him a kiss. '*You* are,' she told him.

* * *

By the time she could hear Sally arriving with the children downstairs, Kathleen was positively floating. It had been such a lovely day, and she'd felt like a princess, Terry having insisted that she choose absolutely anything she wanted – a gesture that had the Brown Muff ladies all dancing attendance, one even being charged with being her personal assistant, fetching and carrying clothes for her to try on in the little dressing room and twittering around her like an enthusiastic bird.

She'd even called her madam, as if she were royalty or a film star.

And she felt like a film star right now. In the end she'd chosen a navy and white two-piece, thinking she could alter the skirt later; the little white-collared jacket would continue to fit her perfectly.

She turned to look at her profile, as pleased as ever with her newly developed bust, and then wriggled into her shoes – navy courts, which Terry had insisted on her getting also – before giving her hair, piled up in a bun, a final tweak, and clipping on her white plastic earrings.

The whole effect stunned her, even though she had been the one who'd created it. It was such a far cry from the make-up-free, ponytailed teenager she'd once been, and she wondered if she bore any resemblance to the mum she so missed, and of whom she had all too few photographs. She wished, more than anything, that her dad could see her right now. See how glamorous, how smart and grown-up she looked. He'd notice it, that resemblance, and she'd see it in his eyes.

She tottered down to meet them, taking care not to waddle. 'Will I do?' she asked, doing a twirl in the front-room doorway.

She stopped, seeing four pairs of eyes staring at her in silence. 'What?' she asked. 'What's up? Is my skirt caught in my knickers?'

Little Stuart giggled. Sally spoke. 'Oh my, Kathleen! *No*. You just look so beautiful. I don't think I've ever seen you with your hair done like that, and with the make-up, and oh, that *outfit* …!'

'You look bloody *gorgeous*, love,' Terry added, looking her up and down appreciatively. 'No one will believe my luck when they cop for us tonight. She certainly scrubs up well, my Kathy, doesn't she, Sal?'

'Cheeky sod!' Kathleen laughed, before turning to the children. 'You two catching flies?' she asked, pointing at their open mouths. 'Or have you never seen me dressed up before either?'

She extended her arms, and they both ran to hug her. Since the baby, well, since Terry, really, everything had slightly shifted. She didn't feel much different, but they clearly did. Seemed to see her differently now, as a grown-up – as a mother-in-the-making? She didn't know, but she liked it. 'You look lovely,' Lisa said. 'Just like a film lady. Like a film lady with a big, ginormous tummy.'

'Lisa!' Sally admonished, but she was smiling as she said it.

'That's absolutely what she looks like,' Terry reassured her, winking. 'So, who's for a drink before we go?' he added, dodging Kathleen's attempt to clip him round the ear. 'Want to come and help me get the glasses, young Stuart?'

Kathleen had changed their bed and brought some bedding down so she and Terry could sleep downstairs. But Sally was having none of it. 'Absolutely not. You can't be sleeping on the sofa in your condition. We'll be perfectly fine down here – and besides, the kids want to sleep with Tiddles. Even if Tiddles doesn't much care for sleeping with *them*,' she finished, eyeing the children, who were chasing the poor kitten around mercilessly, trying to catch her.

But for once, Kathleen stood firm in the face of Sally's insistence. 'Oh yes I can,' she said. 'In fact, it'll suit me much better, to be honest. Down here I get the whole sofa to myself while Happy Harry –' she grinned at Terry – 'gets to snore his booze off on the floor. It'll be bliss.'

And she'd clearly made a good job of convincing Sally, because she threw her head back and laughed. 'Oh lord,' she agreed. 'I feel your pain!'

'Hey, enough of that,' Terry began, and would doubtless have admonished them further had the doorbell not rung at that moment. 'That'll be Angela,' Terry said instead. 'I'll go and let her in.'

'And us!' the children chorused. They'd grown very fond of Angela, the thirteen-year-old from two doors down who'd babysat them twice now. In the way of kids, she was their best friend in the whole world.

But it wasn't Angela. It was her mum, with an apology. 'I'm so sorry,' she told them, after Terry had shown her in. 'She's gone down with some horrible tummy bug and the last thing I'd want is for any of you to catch it. I'd offer to sit myself, but she's so poorly ... keeps being sick, bless her. Can't seem to stop. Though I could pop back for an hour or so if she improves, if you like.'

Sally shook her head. 'Absolutely no need,' she said. 'I'll stay in with the kids. It's no bother.'

'No, you can't do that!' Kathleen said, once they'd seen Angela's mum out again. 'Not now you've come all this way. We'll all stay in. We'll have fun.'

'Oh no we won't,' Sally said firmly. 'Not now you're all done up to the nines in your best bib and tucker. I won't hear of it.'

'I don't know ...' said Terry. 'Seems a bit –'

'Nonsense,' said Sally, interrupting him. 'You both need a night out. And we're happy enough, aren't we kids? Us and Tiddles'll have a fine time. And then, tomorrow, we'll all go to the park to play on the swings and eat ice cream before going home.'

Both Kathleen and Terry protested, but Sally refused to be swayed. With Ronnie away on a long-distance job, she'd be at home with the kids anyway. And as a change was as good as a rest – especially with them being able to camp out in Terry and Kathleen's big double bed with their mam – she was just as happy knowing they were out having fun. So eventually they conceded and, an hour later, were sitting in the Bull, among the Saturday-night crowd, waiting for a local band to come on.

It seemed half the estate was in there and she wondered if it was quiet in her dad's pub. There were certainly plenty of their regulars in, several of them shouting hellos at Kathleen, and she felt a jolt of pleasure knowing it would get back to Irene that they were in here and, hopefully, that she was looking good as well.

But Irene was soon out of her mind, as the effects of a half of lager hit her. She wasn't a big drinker at the best of times, and, in her current state, hardly at all, and as they'd eaten a good while back, it made her head swim a little.

'You don't think it'll hurt the baby, do you?' she asked Terry as she accepted a second.

'Don't be daft,' he said above the din. 'Couple of beers never hurt anybody. And if it's a lad, it'll do him good to start early!'

She batted him with her handbag. 'Silly sod,' she said. 'Anyway, it's a girl. I'm convinced of it.' She was, too, because Mrs Potter, who lived on the other side of the road, had told her she could tell it was from the way she was 'carrying'. She didn't know about that – she was carrying it like a sack of potatoes, just like every other woman – but she'd just had this sense, at the outset, that she was destined to have a daughter, so she could re-create the mother–daughter bond that had been snatched away from her so young. She didn't tell Terry any of this, because she imagined he'd think her silly, but since he didn't care what they had, 'well, as long as it's human, obviously', it mattered little anyway. It would be what it would be and it would be perfect and they'd cherish it.

In the meantime, however, it was making its presence felt, because, despite everyone telling her she was blooming (which put her in mind of blowsy fat chrysanthemums more than anything) by the time the band stopped for a break, she felt she needed one, too. The heat was getting to her, and her clothes chafed, and her ankles felt like they were swelling; for all that she felt so grand in her posh togs and heels, she wanted nothing more now than a sit down and a cuppa. A cuppa with Sally, who she felt bad about and wanted to get back to.

'I think I'll take a break, too,' she told Terry. 'Pop outside for a bit of fresh air.'

'You're flagging love, aren't you?' he said, instantly solicitous. 'Shall we just head home? Would you prefer that?'

She would, but he was having such a nice time that she hesitated to suggest it. Terry didn't see enough of his mates, especially since he no longer used the Dog and

Duck as his local. And once the baby came … 'No, no, love, I'm fine. Just a breath of air and I'll be back.'

'Are you *sure*?' he said. 'I don't mind. I'll sup up, say a couple of goodbyes and be out with you in a jiffy.'

'Love, I'm fine,' she said again. 'But tell you what. How about I go and you stay, eh? You stay and I'll wait up for you.' She winked at him suggestively.

'Give over!' he said immediately. 'I've had enough anyway, love. 'Specially if there's offers like that on the table. Go on out and clear your head. I'll be right behind you in a tick.'

With the balmy night, it was almost as busy outside the Bull as in it. But the cooler air was at least a relief. She sat down on the wooden bench outside the front doors, watching the traffic going up and down Little Horton Lane, and the distant glow of the lights from Brigella Mills factory, where some poor sods were working nights at the weekend.

Human and motorised – all the sounds and sights were amplified somehow, as if, in celebration of such a lovely summer Saturday evening, someone had turned the telly up. She could hear shouts and calls, peals of laughter, a siren wailing in the distance. The usual cocktail that was life in their busy corner of Bradford; the place that would soon be home to the infant curled in her belly. Baby Adamson. Who would soon after become baby Harris. And she'd have a ring on her finger and be a Harris herself.

'Penny for them, lovely lady?' She looked up to see Terry, his cuffs rolled back and his jacket slung over his shoulder.

'Just daydreaming,' she said, standing up and threading her hand through his proffered arm.

'Falling asleep, more like,' he said, as they fell into step. 'We need to get you to bed, don't we? Get you to *sleep* ...' he added, nudging her. Then, 'Hmm ... you smell that?' He sniffed the air. 'I can smell smoke. Can you?'

'I heard a siren earlier,' she said, sniffing too. 'And yes, I can. Maybe someone's started a fire. Kids up behind the youthy perhaps. You know what kids are like. While the cat's away ...' She gestured back towards the pub.

'And that's another siren,' Terry said, as they set off down Little Horton Lane. 'And it's smelling stronger now. You reckon there's a building on fire somewhere?'

Kathleen sucked in air, then she pointed. 'Look, Terry – look at that smoke over there – see? That's coming from behind the Dog and Duck isn't it? Yes, it is. That's coming from *our* way.' She gaped, transfixed now. 'It *is*, isn't it?'

Their eyes met. 'What the *hell*?' said Terry. They both broke into a run.

* * *

Kathleen emerged out of the snicket a good few yards behind Terry.

Emerged into mayhem. A terrible kaleidoscope of sights and sounds and colours; fire engines, police cars, ambulances, sirens and flashing lights. People running, people shouting, someone screaming in the distance, and at the centre of it, a giant plume of thick, billowing smoke – blacker than the night, belching up into the sky, being licked by a forest of orange flames.

She could hear Terry – 'Oh, Christ! Let me through! Let me *through* there!' – and then saw him swallowed up, the crowd closing in behind him, disappearing into nothing as she cast blindly about. It was his house! It was *their* house! A stab of terror now consumed her. Oh, God – Sally! The children! It was *their* house ablaze!

It was only when rough hands took hold of her and dragged her, stumbling, staggering, tripping across the street that she realised she was screaming.

'Terry! *Terry!*' She caught sight of him again, and tried to wriggle from the man's grasp. He might be a fireman or a policeman, she didn't know and didn't care. 'Terry!' she yelled again, but he didn't seem able to hear her. He was yelling himself, struggling to free himself from the grip of two big firemen. 'There's still kids in there! Let me *go!*' She could hear his voice above every other. 'There are kids in the house still! There are kids in there! Two of them!' Then, almost as if in slow motion, like a replay on the telly, he freed himself and ran headlong into the flames licking round the house.

'Terrrryyyyyy!' she screamed. 'Terrrryyyyy!'

'Love, they'll *get* him! They won't let him in there! They'll sort it!'

'He's *already* in there!' she shrieked at the man who had a grip on her, who she only now saw was a uniformed policeman.

'Look – there they go – see? They'll get him out again. And they'll get anyone else in there. They'll –'

'Children!' she screamed at him, 'There are two children in there!'

'They *know*,' he said firmly – even harshly. His grip was iron-like. 'Come on, come away, to where it's safer. If it's gas there might well be another explosion, and you don't want to be …' But the rest of his words melted away from her, because not five yards away what she saw took up all her attention – a mound on the street behind an ambulance. A partly covered mound, black and wet-looking, alien, impossible to get to grips with, with two policemen and an ambulance man kneeling around it. She felt the bile rise in her throat, and her legs begin to buckle.

'C'mon love.' A different voice. A man called Sonny – one of her dad's regulars. Her dad. She needed her dad. Where was her dad? But first she needed to get Terry out. She *had* to get Terry out. 'I'll look after her,' he told the policeman. She felt the grip on her arm vanish. 'I'll look after her now,' he was saying again, trying to put his own arm around her. She threw it off. Kicked off the shoes and then ran hell for leather. Blindly, across the road again, back towards the house.

'Whoah!' Another iron grip. And this time she didn't fight it. '*Terry* …' was all she could manage to get out as the man whirled her round. '*Terry!*', before she fainted and fell into her father's arms.

Chapter 23

'They're out? So they're both out of there? Jesus, imagine if … *Imagine*.'

Kathleen came around to find the world swimming, and the voice a disembodied one. But then, slowly, moving shapes began to resolve into faces. And one particular face. Her father's. His profile sharp above her. He was speaking to a fireman. A man in waterproofs. A giant of a man.

'Best you don't,' the fireman said. 'Best you don't.' Then he looked away. 'Over here, mate,' he then called, in a louder voice, to someone Kathleen couldn't see. Her dad glanced down at her. Then up again. 'She's coming round,' he said. 'She's coming to.'

The fireman peered down at her. Stuck two enormous gloved fingers up. 'How many can you see, love?'

'Two,' she tried to say, but her voice was little more than a croak. He stepped away anyway, and a young man in green took his place.

'You had a fall, love,' her dad said. 'I did my best, but I couldn't hold you. Couldn't stop you going over. What with all this water everywhere, and you barefoot. You went down like a ton of bricks, you did.' He patted the back of his skull. 'You've had a bit of a bump on the back of your head. Anyway, lie still a minute –'

'*Terry*, Dad!' she squeaked, as everything tumbled back into her consciousness.

'Terry's okay, lass. Don't you fret. He's alright. Seems he'll have to go down to the hospital. With the kids, like. In the ambulance. They've all got to be checked for smoke inhalation. But he found 'em, love. He *found* 'em. Hidden away at the bottom of your wardrobe, they were. Saved their lives, that did, they reckon ... there's the way, sit up a bit, so the man can take a proper look at you ...'

'Oh, for sure it did,' the ambulance man said. 'Bloody miracle. Got to be thankful for that. So. How far along are you, love?'

'Seven months ...' Kathleen squirmed. 'Dad, where's *Terry*?'

'Over there a ways. And he's *fine*. Like I said, he's got to go in the ambulance to the hospital.'

'Then I want to go with him.'

'Love, you can't. There's no room –'

'You might need your own ambulance,' the ambulance man told her. He was busy fixing a blood-pressure cuff around her arm.

'I'm fine,' she said. 'Honest.'

'Love, you've had a fall,' said her dad. 'Let the man see to you. There's nothing to be done anyway. Let the professionals do their jobs. Sort the kids out. And Terry. *Mad* he was. But thank God for him.' Her father squeezed her hand.

It came to her all in a rush and then gathered in her throat. 'And Auntie Sally?'

Her father shook his head. 'I'm so sorry, love,' he said. 'They did their best, but ...'

There was another voice then. A female one. She craned her head over the shoulders of the ambulance man to see. It was Angela's mum, from over the road. She looked sheet-white against all the headlamps and floodlights and torches, and was hurrying towards them, carrying something in her arms.

'Oh, my poor love,' she said. Then 'Sorry, I just wanted –' to the paramedic. 'Love, I just wanted to let you know is all.' She thrust what she was holding out in front of her. A rat, it looked like. A quivering animal. With a long piece of string looped through its collar. Kathleen stared at it, confused. Then it hit her. Its *collar*! 'We managed to catch her,' Angela's mum said. 'Soaked through she is, terrified. But I've got her, love. I just wanted to tell you that, okay? Let you know she's safe. I'll take her home for you, okay?'

'That your cat, love?' the paramedic said, now checking Kathleen's pulse. 'What's its name?'

Kathleen tried and tried, but she found that she could no longer speak. They were in the wardrobe. Where Sally must have put them, to save them. So they'd be *safe*. She'd *saved* her children. She'd managed to do that. And now she'd died.

And there was a hole – a gaping wound – where her voice used to be.

'Tiddles,' her dad supplied for her.

In a matter of minutes, Kathleen was confirmed good to go. But to where? Because she no longer had a home.

'Back with me,' her father told her, and she had no choice but to do so, Terry having been taken off to hospital in an ambulance. She was desperate to be with him. Desperate to distraction. But unless her father took her, she had no way to get there. And there was no way he was going to take her. So she had to go with him. She had no choice.

'So they've got hold of your Uncle Ronnie,' her father was saying to her, quietly, calmly, as if explaining instructions to a small child. She was dimly aware of other people walking back up the road with them. Sonny Chippendale. One of the Hudson boys. A couple of other regulars. Back to the pub, because it wasn't yet closing time even. Back for a last drink, now the show was all done. 'So he's going to drive down tonight. He's in Scotland, of all places. He'll go straight to the hospital. To the children.'

* * *

'Dad, *I* want to go to the hospital,' she repeated. How many times was she going to have to say it? She was dimly aware of young Vinnie McKellan just ahead of her, trotting along with her shoes swinging in his hand.

'And you will, love. In the morning.'

'No, now!'

'In the *morning*. Early as you like, but I'm not taking you there now. It's not visiting hours. Think of the staff, love. *Tomorrow*. When it's visiting.'

As if that was remotely relevant! They'd completed the short walk to the pub, and even as her dad reached to hold the foyer door open she saw it. That small adjustment, that bracing, as if entering some sort of lair, and not knowing where the dangerous animal might be.

She followed him in. There was nothing else to do. Where could she run to? Where would she go? And Irene was there, though she didn't quite see her at first. Just a blur of frizzy red in the midst of a small group of customers, and with her back to them, so she'd not yet even realised they'd arrived. A couple of her cronies were leaning in on either side of her. There were a couple of men she didn't recognise, too.

Her father cleared his throat, but not nearly loud enough to make impression on the wall of sound, as they all sat there – all of them talking away nine to the dozen, no doubt dissecting the gossip-worthy events of the night. *She doesn't know her sister's dead*, Kathleen thought. *She doesn't even realise*. Had no one yet told her? No, it seemed they had not – it was a piece of gossip that had not yet reached their ears.

But there was gossip enough anyway, gossip to be chewed over and spread. 'Well, that's the thing. All a bit peculiar. Isn't it?' Irene was saying. She was drunk, that was obvious. 'That's *two* house fires he'd had now. *Two* women dead.'

Kathleen gaped. So she did know. She *did* know. And was sitting there gossiping about it. She was completely inhuman.

'Certainly makes you think, doesn't it?' Irene finished, slurring slightly.

Kathleen clearly heard her father's sharp intake of breath. As did Irene. Or more likely saw the expressions on the faces of the women opposite, who could now see the storm that was slowly approaching, and whose eyes were like saucers as a result.

Kathleen didn't think. She didn't need to. She needed to act. So by the time Irene had staggered up, smoothed her skirt down and turned around, Kathleen was perfectly placed to lift her arm, pull it back, then slap her stepmother around the face. As hard and as fast as she possibly could, too. Enough to topple her right over.

For Sally.

Chapter 24

Visiting hours were strict – just an hour a day, from 2 p.m. till 3 p.m. – so when Kathleen's eyes opened the following day, she knew, without question, that was what had woken her. Her instinctive need to see if Terry was okay.

After whisking her away from her apoplectic step-mother the previous evening, her dad had taken her up to Monica's room and helped her into her bed, her old one being out of commission having become an additional clothes-flinging space in the months she'd been gone. Monica herself, her dad explained, was in Morcambe with Carol, so there was no danger of her crashing in at any point. And she'd been too trauma-tised to do anything other than lie down as instructed and try to find refuge in sleep. And she must have slept finally, though it had been almost light by the time she did. And for some time, because she turned over in bed now to find tea and a plate of toast on the bedside table. She touched the cup. Stone cold. And the toast was concave now. She had no memory of it having been brought in.

She checked the clock again, measuring out the things she had to do into minutes, then pushed back the bedcovers, swung her body around and stood up. She needed to find some clothes to wear and get to the hospital. To see Terry. To see Lisa and Stuart as well, if she was allowed to.

She opened the bedroom door as quietly as she could and peered out onto the landing. No Monica, but there was a chance Irene or her dad would be in the flat somewhere, and, not at all sure how she'd react, given the anger that still burned within her, she dreaded seeing Irene more than anything.

But all was quiet. They were both presumably downstairs, serving customers; the familiar buzz of activity floated up to her – glass on glass, the toilet doors banging, disembodied voices – so she rummaged feverishly in Monica's wardrobe for something that might fit her, and was just scouring her face and washing her hands in the bathroom when her dad suddenly appeared in the doorway.

Kathleen looked behind him, newly anxious, but he was alone. 'How are you doing, love?' he asked her, his tone gentle and solicitous. 'Thought I'd come up and check on you. Manage to sleep a bit, eh? You were out for the count earlier on. That's good.'

She felt her pulse slow a little. It had been hammering away. 'I'm going up to the hospital,' she told him, wiping her hands on the towel hanging by the basin.

He nodded. 'Course you are, love. Want me to come with you?'

Kathleen shook her head. 'No, you're busy,' she said, immediately realising this was the wrong thing to say. Because it wasn't that. She wanted to go alone.

He seemed awkward, perhaps realising. Perhaps feeling excluded. 'It's no bother. Pretty quiet down there, to be honest.'

As it would be, Kathleen thought, given what had happened the previous evening. How could people go to the pub? Many would have stayed away, surely? It was hardly seemly to be out drinking today – at least for the locals. She wondered that they'd opened up at all.

'No, you stay here,' she said gently, adding, 'I need to be on my own, Dad.' She felt claustrophobic, too. Slightly panicky. Desperate to escape. And in her dad's home. How had it come to this?

'Well, if you're sure,' her father said. He looked barely less traumatised. As smart as ever, but strangely diminished somehow. Old. She wondered distractedly what price he'd had to pay for what she'd done last night. 'Still, a bit of good news,' he added, his tone growing brighter. 'Couple of the regulars have been in … you know, locals. Seen the house, a couple of them have – and they've got it sealed up, apparently. Put a bit of a fence up, you know, to stop any nippers getting in. But apparently it's maybe not as bad as folk thought it might be. Not upstairs. I mean there'll be fire damage, and

that. Water damage, too, of course, but the upstairs …
well, it sounds like some things might be salvageable –
you know, once they've been in and that. Made it safe
again, of course.'

Kathleen came out of the bathroom, cradling her
bump, and edged past him, back towards Monica's
bedroom to get her bag. Again, it occurred to her that
this was it now – she had just that one little handbag
she'd taken out with her last night. But it would have
to do. She didn't want to rummage among her stepsister's things further. What else did she have to put in a
handbag in any case?

Her dad followed her across the landing. 'Next week,
perhaps,' he was saying. 'Know a bit more then, perhaps
…' And it struck Kathleen that this was the most ridiculous conversation to be having. Sally dead. Little
Stuart and Lisa motherless. And Ronnie … poor, poor
Ronnie … And her dad was standing there, shuffling
from foot to foot on the landing, chattering on about
whether there were going to be some salvageable sticks
of furniture. Some clothes perhaps. Stuff. It made her
reel. How could he be standing there talking about *stuff*,
for God's sake? When so many lives had imploded?

And sounding so matter-of-fact about it, too – almost
jolly, even. She despaired of him, even as she felt for
him, and, having done so, it hit her with some force
that this was exactly how it had been when her own
mother's life had ended. *Shall we see about getting you*

some of those biscuits you like, Kathleen? Ooh, it's a lovely day today – shall we go down to the park and feed the ducks? Nothing, absolutely *nothing* about pain or loss or grieving, about the fact that all she'd wanted to do was throw herself on the floor and scream.

'I'm sorry I hit Mam,' she said, the word 'mam' cloying on her tongue. 'It was an unforgiveable thing to do.'

Her father frowned and pushed his glasses a little further up his nose. 'I know, love,' he said, though she wasn't clear if she meant the action or the apology, and if the latter, he was wrong, because she wasn't sorry at *all* – not in the way he probably expected. No, she was only sorry because it lowered her in her own eyes – to slap Irene was to stoop to her level.

'But, Dad,' she added quietly, since he seemed unwilling to say more, 'it was an unforgivable thing to say.'

She let it hang there. And it did. And eventually he sighed again. Then he nodded. 'I know, love,' he said. 'And look, you know you can stay here as long as you want, don't you? Terry too, once he's out of hospital. Long as you need to. Till you're both back on your feet.'

Kathleen nodded and said she did know and thanked him politely. Though privately she doubted she knew any such thing. And forget what Irene thought – she knew for sure that it wasn't what *she* wanted.

'Could I take some of Darren's pyjamas? Or yours perhaps?' she asked him. 'Only he won't have any, and I don't know what sort of thing they'll have given him.

One of those horrible operating gowns that do up down the back, most likely. And maybe some clothes – you know, something to wear to come home … till I can get to the shops,' she added, thinking as she spoke, feeling the enormity of it all rising up again.

'Of course, love,' he said, seeming happier to be back with practicalities. 'Come on, let's sort something out for him before you go, then. Sure I've got something that'll fit him.' Which wasn't quite true – certainly in terms of trousers, because her dad was so tall. But he led the way along to his own bedroom, not Darren's.

Kathleen presented herself to the ward sister at two o'clock precisely. She'd already been told that she wouldn't be able to see Lisa and Stuart, who were up on the children's ward and were apparently doing okay. 'Not till after their dad arrives, at least,' the receptionist told her apologetically, explaining that they were also still sedated, and that she hoped Kathleen understood.

She feared for Ronnie. Feared for his long journey back from Scotland. How could you be left in charge of an articulated lorry in the midst of such a nightmare? How on earth would he find the strength to tell them what they apparently didn't yet know? She tried to imagine, and found she couldn't, so she tried to shake it from her mind instead, as she made her way to a bed at the far end of the long, half-empty, male medical ward. Most of the beds seemed to be occupied by slumbering pensioners, some of them snoring. Most of the chairs adjacent were occupied by women – their wives, presumably. Some talking in quiet tones, some knitting or crocheting.

Terry, who in his youth looked like he shouldn't even be there, saw Kathleen straight away and waved. He was sitting up in bed, his legs drawn up under a thin cellular blanket, and as she neared him he leaned across to pull the chair a little closer, though what she most wanted to do was climb up on the bed.

'C'mon, come here, love,' he said, opening his arms and then wrapping them tightly round her, saying nothing more but 'there now' as he held her.

'You know, then?' she asked him, when he eventually released her, and she'd sat down, sniffing, on the edge of the chair.

He nodded. 'Yes, I do, love. Such a shock. Such a tragedy. I don't suppose you've heard anything about what happened, have you?'

She shook her head. 'Not yet. And what about you?' she asked, taking in the sight of him, scanning his face and body, looking urgently for clues. Some of his hair was singed – a big patch of what had previously been his fringe. 'How long have they told you you'll have to stay in here?'

'Only till tomorrow, all being well,' he said. 'The doctor's just been round to see me. They need to do another X-ray, that's all. Well, that and keep me under observation. Smoke inhalation, that's all. But they've got to watch me. Make sure I don't take a downturn.'

'That's *all*? Terry, you could have been killed too!'

There were too many tears in her to keep dammed up any longer, and now they spilled over, down her cheeks, onto Monica's pink summer dress.

'But I *wasn't*,' Terry said. 'So don't you be going off down that road. I wasn't, I'm here, and the children are safe.' Then he looked past her, his face wrestling with itself, his own eyes shining. 'C'mon,' he said, grabbing her hand and tugging on it. 'Come sit up on here, sweetheart. That's the way. Sod the matron. Let's think what best to do, shall we?'

They talked the full hour, Kathleen telling him the things her dad had told her, that there may yet be things that had escaped the fire – and the putting out of it, of course. And he'd managed a laugh – albeit a short one, laced with wry understanding. He'd not *had* very much in the way of stuff to begin with, had he? That was the truth of it. But he had what he *needed*, which was her and their child safe. Which made her sob and sob all over again. And she'd told him of her dad's offer; to make his home their own for as long as they needed, and how difficult she thought she was going to find that.

'But you'll *cope*, love,' he said softly. 'We'll cope. We'll have to. Least till they can find us a new place to rent. And who knows? Perhaps out of tragedy will come some good, eh? Just a smidgin. There's nowt that'll bring Sally back, but if one *tiny* good thing comes out of all this, perhaps it'll be that her sister comes to her senses – or whatever she has in the place of senses anyway. Perhaps all that bad blood can be put behind you, eh?' He stroked her hair. 'I think Sally would have liked to see that happen, don't you?'

She knew what he was driving it. She knew he was just trying to comfort her. She knew he was saying what he probably felt he couldn't say – that silver linings were out there in ways you didn't expect them; that, perhaps, he'd experienced his own silver lining even – in that his wife had perished but in time he had moved to Louis Avenue, and started going in the Dog and Duck, and met Kathleen …

She knew all of this, and that he was right; that they must try to focus on the good things, on the future, the baby – above everything, the baby. Which was why – even if she had, and she'd already decided she wouldn't – she didn't have the heart to tell him about slapping Irene, because she knew he would want to know exactly what it was that Irene had said, and wouldn't let up till he'd winkled it out of her.

Kathleen tried again to see the children before leaving the hospital – or if not the children, at least to try to establish if Ronnie had made it back from Scotland yet. Terry had told her that someone – he didn't know who'd told him, or when – had decided it would be best not to get word to him late in the evening, lest what Kathleen had feared might become a reality and, racked with grief, he'd driven through the night and had an accident.

He hadn't yet returned, but he'd telephoned and they were expecting him in a couple of hours; his mam and dad were apparently on their way to Bradford as well. So there was nothing for it but to return to the Dog and Duck. She wished she could be anywhere else.

She left a note at the hospital for the receptionist to give to Ronnie. She was there, she said. She was around if there was anything she could do for them. Anything. Just let her know. She was there for them, always. She'd happily come and stay and help out. Then, because, without Terry, the day and night stretched so grimly into the distance, she instead went to Louis Avenue to see the house. Once there, however, she was horrified. The downstairs window and door were huge black gaping holes, the upstairs ones, no longer glassed, ringed with soot. She found she couldn't bear to look at it, and hurried instead across the road. At least she could see Tiddles, reassure her she hadn't forgotten her, but Angela and her mum were out and, with no idea how long for, she turned around and reluctantly headed back towards the pub, her feet, in their new shoes, now screaming.

It was Tiddles she was thinking about when she decided to go round the back way; no sense dragging the walk out, as her feet now *really* hurt. She was wondering how her dad would feel about Tiddles staying as well – optimistically, perhaps, since she was sure Irene would veto it, but you never knew … there seemed a new set to his jaw today, somehow.

She headed up the street planning to scramble over the same wall she'd scaled back in December, into Terry's arms, with her trust and all her worldly goods.

She'd just rounded the corner when she heard them. And moments later, saw them as well. Her dad and stepmother, both with their back to her, thankfully, standing out on the rooftop balcony outside the kitchen. It was almost four now, and, it being a Sunday, the pub would be shut till seven so they were both presumably having a break. It was a fine afternoon – as if in mockery of all that had happened – the sun beating down from an unbroken blue canopy, currently marked only by a single plane trail.

Kathleen knew eavesdroppers never heard good about themselves; it had been rammed home to her since she was small. But there was something about the way Irene was standing that drew her into the shade now, and made her inch along the wall by the dustbins, so that, unobserved, she could get close enough to hear.

Irene had been drinking. Which in itself was nothing noteworthy. Had a day passed since Darren's death when she *hadn't* had a drink? Kathleen didn't think so. And she couldn't imagine when that might change.

Both Irene and her dad were smoking cigarettes, too, her dad, ever mindful of ash and dog ends cluttering the place up, holding the circular pub ashtray that habitually sat on the makeshift beer-crate table, and proffering it to Irene after every puff.

They were arguing. That much became obvious very quickly as she edged nearer. And it struck Kathleen, catching the edge in her stepmother's voice, that perhaps her younger sister's death had hit her hard, too, despite her proclamations to the contrary, her snide reflections on the vagaries of fate. Didn't it happen like that sometimes when people died unexpectedly? That those left behind who'd let bad feeling fester were hit the hardest, having been denied the chance to make up, make friends?

But it wasn't of Sally that they were speaking. And as Irene's voice rose, it was obvious what the subject of their argument was – that John had now had an opportunity to tell her of the offer he'd made to Kathleen earlier that afternoon.

'Not for a minute!' she was saying. 'Not for a minute, John Adamson! The little bitch raised her hand to me! Knocked me over! Or had you forgot?'

Kathleen saw her father's shoulders move as he sighed. 'Not without provocation,' he pointed out. 'And, Rene, you're being ridiculous. Where on earth else are they supposed to go? They've a baby due in weeks now, and if you think I'm going to stand by and –'

'Exactly!' she screeched at him. 'And if you think' – she was stabbing him in the chest now with an index finger – 'that I'm going to have that little bastard living under my roof, you've another think coming! Haven't they brought enough shame on us already? Her and that … that bloody *cradle-snatching* Terry Harris! Old enough to be her bleeding father! Make no mistake, that girl of yours and her fancy man are the talk of the whole of Canterbury –'

'No, that's what *you'll* be, Irene!' Her father's voice had gone up a notch or two. 'Turning them out on the streets after a tragedy like this has happened –'

'Oh, for Pete's sake, John, you're as soft as you're naïve! You think anyone's sympathetic? Dirty beggars, they are, the pair of them. And her strutting about the place' – she did a kind of mime, thrusting her already substantial belly out – 'even throwing it in decent folks' faces! It's a disgrace is what it is, and you've no business telling them they're welcome here, because they're not. The very thought of the pair of them' – she sort of shivered – '*sleeping* together, in Darren's *bedroom*! It makes my blood run cold, it really does –'

'Terry doesn't need to sleep in there with Kathleen,' her father pointed out. 'He can kip on the settee –'

'Oh, like that will make a difference? Like he won't be sneaking off in there in the small hours? That a couple of *doors* are going to stop them? At it like rabbits, they'll be. You're a fool if you don't realise. How d'you think she got up the duff in the first place?'

Kathleen felt for her father, having to listen to all that. And something else – a sense of something she'd not previously realised. Something in Irene's voice. A kind of salaciousness, almost. Something unsavoury – almost wistful – in its tone. Was she jealous, even of that?

She watched her father stub out his cigarette and place the ashtray back on the beer crate, while Irene, swaying slightly, looked down at his bent back. If looks could kill, she thought wretchedly. She realised she was shaking.

And weak. She'd not eaten since they'd had their tea before Sally and the children had arrived. She must eat. She must eat. Not for two. Just for her baby.

Her father straightened, cleared his throat, and elected to say nothing as Irene flicked her cigarette above and beyond him down into the yard. He would, Kathleen knew, go and retrieve it later.

Then finally he did speak, though mostly to the top of Irene's head, as, the cigarette smoked, she now seemed more intent on keeping her balance, and had leaned down to grab the rail.

'Shame on you, Rene,' Kathleen's father said quietly. '*Shame* on you. Call yourself God-fearing? Decent? Well, you're not. Carrying on like this, and with those two little ones in hospital, and your own *sister* – your *flesh and blood* – not yet dead twenty-four hours!'

281

Irene's head flicked up. '*Sister*? She's no sister of mine, John. If you think I'm going to shed a single bleeding tear over *that* one' – again she poked him with a finger – 'you're even dafter than you look. You really think I give a tinker's cuss about her? Or that slut of a daughter of yours? Or that little bastard she's carrying?' Kathleen flinched. 'My Darren's *gone*!' The words came out almost as a howl. 'My Darren's *gone*, John! And I don't care about anything – not *anything*! You hear me? They can *all* rot in hell. And if there's any justice, they *will*!'

Under normal circumstances, Kathleen would have simply slipped inside the pub, unnoticed. After all, she knew exactly how Irene felt about her, and this wouldn't have been the first time she'd overheard her ranting in this way. She'd totted up several such overheard tirades over the years, principally because Irene seemed not to care who could hear her. No, more than that. Definitely more than that. She seemed to derive particular pleasure from ranting about people – well, certain people anyway – loud enough that she could be certain they *could* hear her. It had taken a while for Kathleen to discover this as a child, to understand that if she overheard her stepmum going on at her dad about 'that girl of yours', it wasn't accidental; wasn't something to be regretted. It was all a part of her armoury. Yes, she'd snap and bark *at* her – and this was true too of her father, who would often have his shortcomings aired in the pub, more often as not to the male clientele, even as he stood feet away along the bar. But Irene also seemed to have a kind of instinct for this particular sort of cruelty, knowing just how effective it was hearing nastiness second hand.

But these were very far from normal circumstances. Kathleen was aware of this, and of the uncharacteristic nature of her behaviour, even as she stomped into the back of the pub and climbed the stairs to the flat. She was also painfully aware of the enormity of Sally's loss; of her kindness, her wisdom, her ability to make things better – of the intuitive understanding she had of her elder sister. Of just how profoundly, perhaps irreparably damaged Irene was. How jealous she was of anyone who 'stole' attention away from her. What a terrible day it had been when she'd come into her father's pub and seen in him everything she desired.

But Sally had given her sister no quarter. She wished her brother-in-law hadn't either. *The more he's let her get away with it*, she'd said to Kathleen, *the worse she's got. Haven't you noticed? Just like a toddler. He was actually making her worse.*

Kathleen reached the kitchen just as both of them were heading back into it from out on the balcony, Irene first, stumbling, almost tripping over the doormat, her father afterwards, the shock at seeing her there registering on his face.

It was Irene who she looked at, however. She'd regained her balance, and now stood and glared at Kathleen, hands on hips. 'Oh, you're back, then, are you?' she said. Her eyes strayed to the pink dress, to the bulge of the bump. *I don't want you even so much looking at my baby*, Kathleen thought.

She nodded at Irene. 'Yes, and I just came to say I'm sorry.'

'As well you might be, you little brat!' Irene responded, true to form, shaking off her husband's hand on her arm, and clearly ready for a resumption of the previous night's hostilities.

But Kathleen wasn't. Not anymore. So often she'd fantasised about taking on her stepmother – of having the courage to defy her where her dad failed to do so – to take her on, as they said, at her own game. But it no longer seemed worth it. There was nothing to be gained by it. *She* wasn't worth it. That was the nub of it. That was what it all came down to in the end.

'Yes, and I *am* sorry,' Kathleen answered, her voice cool and level. 'More sorry than you know, Mam. I'm sorry that it wasn't *you* dead, instead of Sally.'

She left the kitchen then, left both Irene and her father open-mouthed. It was such a little thing to say but it was everything really. How she felt. What she most wished, God forgive her.

Chapter 25

It was ink-dark and viscous and Kathleen felt like she was drowning. Thrashing desperately but ineffectually, in a storm-lashed sea, dragged along by a current she couldn't seem to fight against, and struggling to come up for air.

She surfaced. Tried to breathe. Tried to calm herself. But there really *was* no air. No air or light. No noise or smell. No nothing. It was the middle of the morning. She knew it must be. A bright new midsummer morning. Yet it felt like the room was closing in on her. Darren's room now, since Monica had come back. Everything still as it had been, more or less, for all those long miserable months since his suicide. Unchanged since the day she'd moved out last December – kept like some kind of shrine. Or a crime scene.

'Where else are you going to go, love?' She kept coming back to that. The words her father had said to her when he'd first taken her back to the pub, limping and shaking, her head hammering, her mind screaming ... The same words he'd said when she'd told him she was leaving; that if need be she'd happily sleep on the street – *anything* to get away from that witch.

How long had it been now? Ten days? Eleven? She was losing count. But she knew why she'd slept late: because she'd worked right till close there the previous evening – precious money earned, much-needed, but a complicated dance all the same, with her and Irene conspiring – and succeeding – to keep out of one another's way. And in that sense, Darren's room had become both her refuge and her sanctuary, horrible, grisly and nightmare-inducing though it was to be sleeping in her dead stepbrother's bed.

And her dad had been right. Where else *was* she to go?

Everything after that Sunday afternoon seemed to happen slightly apart from her. Terry had been discharged, finally, late on the Monday, and she'd thought – well, just assumed – that his return would help mend her. That they'd be able to tackle everything together; think things through; make a plan for escape; for putting their lives back together. But no sooner had they been reunited than he was back off to work again.

It felt wrong. Like an outrage that couldn't possibly be allowed. Sally dead, her poor husband and her children in pieces, yet everyone else's life simply trundled on unimpeded. How could that be? The world should stop, surely? At least for a small while, out of respect.

But there was no choice, Terry had explained, but for him to return to work, because without Ronnie – who was obviously going to be away for a while now – they *needed* him to work. They couldn't do without him, so work he must do. And, more than ever now, he'd added gently, *they* needed the money. There was the baby to think of, after all. So he'd gone again early on the Wednesday – for five, horrible, endless days – driving off less than a day later, wearing ill-fitting clothing, cobbled, once again, from her father's wardrobe.

And, knowing what she knew, what had been said of them (which she dared not tell Terry either, not before he'd left, because she'd been too fearful of what he might do or say) she'd felt weak and unsupported and incapable, her grief and her guilt and the overwhelming sense of hopelessness and isolation all conspiring to stop her managing to do even the smallest thing.

How could a former home cease to be one so completely? Despite everything she'd ever known about Irene's feelings towards her, the place where she'd lived with her dad had still been her home, primarily because *he'd* been in it. But now she was back, she was aghast by how dramatically that had changed. How she felt like a visitor – a *deeply* unwelcome visitor, there only on sufferance. It was wretched and claustrophobic.

Sally's funeral, the previous day, had been a blur. Like Darren's, it had been a huge affair; Ronnie and his mam and dad had seen to that. Cherished by all who knew her, Sally been delivered to the next world accordingly, on a beautiful open carriage, pulled by four glossy black horses – so beautiful and stately that they took little Lisa and Stuart's breath away, making them forget, just for a time, why they were there.

Lisa and Stuart – how Kathleen's heart ached for them – had stumbled around blindly, not sure where to sit or stand, clinging to their father like a pair of frightened urchins. You could see by their faces that they just couldn't process what was going on. Where had their mother gone? Why wasn't she with them, to straighten their clothes and wipe their noses? To spit on her hankie and wipe tears from their cheeks? To pat them and fuss over them and gather them to her, chick-like? To reassure them that, actually, however terrible it must seem, it would be okay. It would *all* be okay.

But it would not be okay, and, as naturally perhaps as breathing, as the day wore on they had been drawn to Kathleen, and she, feeling so desperately isolated without Terry, was equally drawn to them, the three of them huddled and separate in their incredulity. She didn't think she had ever felt so close to them as yesterday, both seeing her own small anguished self in their stunned incomprehension, and them, in her, someone who felt just as they did – confused and lost; that this was all just some terrible mistake.

Something had been found for her to wear. Something that had come from Mary. A huge, hairy black tent of a dress – widow's weeds, didn't they call it? – which still lay across a chair back, where she'd slung it the previous evening, right at the edge of her vision. She had no idea whose it had been because she'd never seen it before. And as she'd pulled up the stockings she'd accepted from an ashen Monica – who'd returned just in time, on the eve of her aunt's funeral – and slipped her feet into those same navy courts that had travelled from her past life to this one, she'd caught a whiff of camphor, which had distressed her to a ridiculous degree. As if moths might flutter out from some fold or other at any moment, marking her out as the cursed one, the cause.

Gossip had reached her. She'd hidden well, but it had floated along and found her anyway. Some said it was a gas leak, but there had been no explosion. Others, faulty wiring, a short circuit, an electrical fault. Some conjectured that Sally must have left a cigarette unattended, but that couldn't be. Because Sally didn't smoke.

Time would tell. She knew men would be picking over the debris. Measurements made. Things inspected. Ashes stirred and considered. It mattered little what they found, or decided, or guessed at. Sally was gone. The source of the fire couldn't have mattered less.

Sally was *gone*. It had slowly seeped in, like Darren's blood had into the carpet. Gone from this earth, to be with the angels, as she'd taken pains to explain to little Lisa, who needed angels in the same way as she had herself all those years back. They must not talk about biscuits, or feed ducks, or *anything*. Not yet. Not *instead*.

They must talk about her mam, and how much she would be missed.

'She's safe, now, with the angels,' Kathleen had told Lisa as she'd hugged her, 'and with *my* lovely mum, who'll take care of her. Jesus wanted her for a sunbeam and so she will be too. You'll see. The very brightest sunbeam in the sky.'

No angels here on earth. How could there be? No angels and, it now seemed, no God. Just the same earthly round, with all its miracles and tragedies, all so cruelly and wantonly and randomly assigned. Here a blessed birth, here an untimely death. It was a lottery, the lot of it. You didn't get to *choose* any of it, that was the point. As Terry knew. Oh, poor *Terry*. She couldn't imagine how he must be feeling, and wanted so much to comfort him, to reassure him and hold him. Instead, he'd been God knew where – France somewhere? Holland? – alone in his cab, doing his deliveries, stuck with just the endless road and his thoughts. She was counting the hours – the very minutes now – till his return.

Most of all, she wanted back the things that were her own, which, as of this moment, numbered just two. She wanted her kitten, who was still safe with Angela and her mum. Apart from Terry – her whole world – Tiddles was her proverbial 'one thing to cling to'. She had lost everything else bar the clothes she'd returned in that night. And both earrings. Neither lost, despite the dramas, the traumas, the running and the falling. And the skirt and jacket that had cost Terry such a ridiculous amount of money but which she knew she would never be able to face wearing again. She wanted her kitten, to cuddle. She wanted Terry, to hold. Like a drug addict, she ached for him physically. Wanted nothing more than to curl up in his arms, warm and safe, till the horror of it all went away.

She must have dozed off again, and been left alone to do so, because she woke with a start when the bedroom door opened and sunlight from the landing streamed in.

'Only me, love,' Terry whispered. 'How are you doing?'

She rubbed the sleep from her eyes, not making sense of the sudden brightness. Then, realising, threw off the blanket with a squeal of relief, aware as she did so of the baby growing inside her doing a somersault, having been so rudely disturbed from its doze. Funny, she thought, easing her legs over the side of the bed, to think this baby will be born to a world in which its Aunt Sally (well, great-aunt Sally – it didn't matter either way) didn't exist. But she would tell it. Tell it all about the care Sally had taken of *her*. Make sure she was still a powerful presence in her child's head.

Terry plonked himself down beside her before she could get up and placed a proprietorial hand on her bump. 'And how's our nipper?'

He looked pale and exhausted. Seizing the opportunity, she moved his hand so he could feel the baby kick. 'Extremely glad you're back,' she said. 'See?'

He kissed the top of her head. 'God, I feel like a refugee,' he said, casting around at the walls of the cramped bedroom, closing in at the best of times, but even more so with them both sitting in it; with the bags of shopping – all the essentials Kathleen had managed to get in the summer sales for them – taking up what little floor space there was. And with the pile of bedding by the door that, on the two nights he'd slept there, had accompanied him into the sitting room and onto the horrible brown sofa, there to sweat against the stupid plastic covers. 'We can't go on like this, can we, love?' he said. 'Tell you what – I've an idea. Shall we just jump in the car and run away?'

Kathleen frowned. 'If it'll start,' she said.

'Which it might not,' he admitted, squeezing her hand. 'I tried to turn it over back at the depot. Dead as a dodo, it was. Had to borrow the boss's jump leads. *Again*. Battery's going. It doesn't get enough proper run outs, that's the problem,' he said. 'A decent long journey, to charge it up, it needs. Tell you what,' he said, smiling at her. '*Shall* we just up sticks and run away?'

Kathleen smiled too. For the first time in days. They had talked of running away the night before he'd gone back to work again – wove it into an oh-so-beguiling fantasy. And she'd been happy to do so, to lose herself in dreams; anything to remove them from reality, even temporarily. And *anything* to stop her blurting out the things Irene had said. Whispering in the dark like children after lights out, making plans that were a comfort but had no basis in logic.

There would be a place for them eventually, she knew that of course. Terry had spoken to someone from the council about it as soon as he was out of hospital. They'd be a priority, the man had said, because of the baby being on the way. But that wasn't now, so it couldn't suppress the urge to run, to escape everything they knew.

Which they could, in theory, because they had nothing, did they? No furniture, no clothes, no pots and pans, no sheets or blankets, *nothing*. Oh, they'd manage. But Terry was not really one for flights of fancy, and, for all that they conspired, there was work, and Ronnie and the children to think about also, and he'd been very keen to make Kathleen see reason. If they stayed with her dad and Irene, they'd at least save on rent, which would give them a little bit to set them up when they did manage to find a new place. Possibly even in Thornton? Oh, if only it could be *now*, though.

But having Terry back made everything more bearable. Kathleen felt energy suffusing her body just at the sight of him. She'd been wrong about how long she'd slept. It was still before noon. Yet he was here. 'How did you get back here so early?'

'Worked like Speedy Gonzales. Managed to catch the last crossing last night. Then drove all night, like a raving maniac –'

She grabbed his arm. 'Please don't tell me that. I don't want to know.'

'Couldn't stop myself.'

'But you should have.'

'With my fiancée here, and my baby, and everything that's happened? You need your head testing, woman. Anyway,' he added, getting up and stretching before peeling off the sweater – her dad's – he must by now be sweltering in. 'I have some news that I think you'll be glad to hear.'

Kathleen stood up, too, and took the jumper from him. Began pulling the sleeves the right way out. 'What?'

'Well, it's just that before I left I asked at work – you know, to see if anyone might know of anywhere we could stay temporarily …'

'And?'

'And when I came back today one of the other drivers collared me. Top bloke, he is. He said we can move into his flat while he's away if we want to.' He reached into his pocket. 'Ta da! And here's the keys,' he said, dangling them in front of her. 'I mean, it's up to you. It's a bit of a distance. Over in Fairweather Green.'

'But that's near Thornton!'

Blood Ties

Terry smiled at her. 'That's what I thought. So I said I'd check with the missus – *obviously* – but that I had a hunch we just might.' He handed her the bunch of keys.

'What, as in *now*?'

'He left today, love. That's why I've got them. And, yes, before you ask, he's happy for us to take the cat with us, too. And, well,' he looked around him again, at the dim, stuffy bedroom, so full of ghosts, 'it's got to be better than … well, than *this*.'

'Yes, but as in *now*?'

'As in any time you like, my darling girl. And yes, now would suit me a great deal more than another bloody night on that wretched sofa.'

295

Chapter 26

Because Kathleen had told her dad she was happy to work that lunchtime and evening, she was expecting, and already braced for, another row. And, as Irene was apparently not in the flat, according to Terry, she assumed they'd find both her and John downstairs.

'But, you know,' Terry said, once she'd washed and dressed, and he'd changed, 'you could still do the lunchtime shift, if you want to. I could drive over, see what's what, get some milk, bread and whatnot, then come back ready for three – that way, you wouldn't have to let your dad down.'

Bless him, she thought, *for understanding so well*. For though there was no way on earth she would still be in the pub by that evening, she didn't want to let her dad down today. Mary was off, after all, and she knew it would give him some leeway to catch up with all his jobs around the place.

Not only that, it mattered greatly that she bring in some money. They were on the back foot now, despite Terry bringing in such good wages. And though she knew they couldn't soon replace everything they'd lost, she was determined to replace the things they'd bought for the baby.

'I like the sound of whatnot,' she said, as they descended the stairs. 'A home's not a home unless there's a good supply of whatnot. But get the good stuff. Nothing cheap from down the market.'

They kissed on the stairs then, and, amid the fuel smell that clung to his hair still, she caught a whiff of something else. It was hope.

'I'm pleased, lass,' her dad said, when they explained what was happening. 'Pleased for the both of you. That's good news, that is.'

It was almost opening time, and Irene was nowhere to be seen. She'd apparently gone to town to meet up with Monica on her lunchbreak; she'd been invited to a party by a local boy she'd met in Morecambe and, in a rare moment of closeness – perhaps stunned by Sally's death? – had asked her mam to come along and help her choose something to wear.

So the avoidance dance between Kathleen and Irene continued, and she felt a profound sense of relief that it would just be her and her dad behind the bar.

'Well, it'll be good to be out of your hair, John,' Terry said. 'Been weighing heavy on me, that has. Us imposing on you like we have.'

'Not at all,' Kathleen's father said. 'Besides, we've hardly seen you, Terry. Good trip this time, was it? You must be shattered.'

Terry told him that, yes, he was, but that a bit of kip would soon see him sorted, and her dad said 'Perhaps better for *not* being on that sofa!' and all three of them had found that so funny. And for a moment, Kathleen thought she could just glimpse the future – *a* future, at any rate, the one she had planned. She'd thought long and hard about it, night after night, whiling the hours away, sleepless in Darren's bed. There were many futures open to her – several different from what they'd planned now, but there was just one she was prepared to accept.

Her dad put his arm around her. 'And as for this one, well, she knows I've loved having her here. Terrible circumstances, of course,' he said, pushing his glasses up his nose a bit. 'But, well, how would I not?' he finished, his eyes glinting behind the lenses. 'She is my daughter, after all. And this here' – he pointed to her belly – 'is my little grandkid.'

It was that comment, more than anything, that broke the spell. Just a little, but enough to harden Kathleen's heart a touch, remembering all that had been said – could she really rely on that already doting granddad to fight her baby's corner against Irene? And she was glad that the pub became busy very quickly, so that she wasn't tempted, once Terry had left – laden with bags full of stuff to take to the flat – to say anything about all the things left *unsaid*.

It was such a great weight of things, now, as well. They'd not spoken, her and her father, about what she'd said to Irene up in the kitchen, and Kathleen supposed that her father had 'made allowances'. That's how he would have put it to Irene, Kathleen was sure – that she was under strain and that Irene must make allowances. It would have been the same as it always had been, down the long pugnacious years, when his wife had been hateful to his daughter for this thing or that; that there was always something that Kathleen must 'understand' when it came to Irene. Some reason why she must make allowances.

But, in truth, there were none – not in Kathleen's case, not now. In fact, she baulked at the thought of her dad asking Irene to let her off for what she'd said to her, because she'd meant what she said, and she still felt the same. No, she wouldn't actively wish death on anyone – even her monster of a stepmother – but, if fate had decreed that *someone* was to die that night, oh, how much better it would have been if lovely, caring Sally had been spared. How much more *right* if it had been Irene who had been taken.

So, no, she didn't want excuses to be made on her behalf, and though she was grateful for whatever change her father had effected, and had led to Irene being so keen to keep out of her way, she could not un-remember the things she had heard her say, particularly about her and Terry's baby. A *little bastard*, she'd called it. *Their bleeding bastard child*.

Kathleen had long outgrown fairy tales – real life had seen to that – but one that stuck in her mind now was the story of Sleeping Beauty, and how the snubbed fairy godmother, excluded from the christening, was so enraged that she cast her wicked, murderous spell upon the child. So there was no way on *earth*, not if Kathleen could help it, that her own wicked stepmother was going anywhere near her baby.

Not that she thought Irene would want to – not for a single naïve minute. But it would mean that this place – this pub, this home she'd once lived in – would no longer be a place she intended to go to. Not when her baby was with her, at any rate. She didn't once want to even bring it over the threshold; she just *wouldn't*. In case it became infected by the evil thoughts within.

No, she was done here. And if that made life difficult for her dad, then so be it. He might make excuses to Irene for *her* behaviour, but from now on she was done. She was no longer going to make excuses for him.

Perhaps logically, though it felt like the worst kind of coincidence, Terry and Irene both returned to the pub at almost exactly the same time, just as Kathleen was about to slide the bolts on the front door.

Irene came in first; Terry was still busy locking the car, perhaps waiting a few seconds to let the queen re-enter her castle – or more, accurately, thought Kathleen as Irene looked her up and down, the wicked witch re-enter her lair.

'Is that Monica's dress?' she asked Kathleen as she swept past her, bags in hand, the cloying scent of the intense musky perfume she preferred filling both the foyer and Kathleen's prickling nostrils. She was long past the business of morning sickness now, but she didn't think she'd ever like perfume again. As with cat food, the association was too strong.

She turned back to Terry, who was coming in behind her, and smiled, then said, 'Yes, it is'.

'And does she know you've got it on?'

'Of course she does, Mam,' Kathleen said, struggling to mask her irritation. 'She gave me several,' she added, trying hard to resist saying it but failing. 'To *keep*. Ones that don't fit her anymore.'

She regretted the barb as soon as it left her lips. Yet another incidence of stooping to a level she didn't mean to. And it *was* a barb; she was seven and a half months pregnant, after all, as Irene could hardly fail to notice.

'Did she get anything for the party?' Kathleen asked quickly, nicely.

But Irene ignored her, just marched straight behind the bar, threw her bags down, plucked a glass from the drainer and jammed it up under an optic.

Terry looked from John to Irene and then opened his palms, looking at Kathleen. 'Well, all's well at the flat, love. Are you done here?'

'Aye, she is, lad,' John said, also nodding towards Kathleen. 'Want to run up and get your stuff, love?' Now Irene did finally take notice.

'What flat?' she asked Terry, following the question with a gulp of spirit.

'My mate's flat,' said Terry mildly. 'He's away working, so he's let us borrow it. Just for a couple of weeks, like, but I'm hoping we'll have found somewhere by then …'

'Though if they haven't –' John began.

Irene skewered with him with a glare. And then Kathleen. 'Thank God for that,' she said. 'About *bleeding* time, and all.'

After Irene stomped off upstairs, and Terry followed – at a distance – to grab the last of their things, Kathleen spent a couple of minutes reassuring her father that, really, she was done with it. It no longer mattered. There was nothing Irene could say to her that could hurt her anymore, and then, feeling a sudden need to communicate with him properly, told him she'd thought long and hard and she truly understood.

'It's only because you love me,' she told him, wondering quite how he'd take it. 'Sally made me see that, isn't that funny? She can't help it. It's because she's jealous that she'll never have what we have. Our memories. Mum. Each other.' She paused, then stroked her bump. '*This*.'

Terry rattled back down at that point, another couple of carrier bags in his hand. 'You want to check if there's anything I've missed, love?' he asked her. God, how she loved him. And when she turned back to her dad, she thought he was going to cry.

She grabbed his hands between her own. 'Right, Dad, we're off, then. Just got to pick up Tiddles, then we're away. And I'll call you tonight, yes? Maybe you can come over and visit?' She painted on a smile – no, not painted. It was a real smile, she realised. 'You know what, it almost feels like I'm going on holiday! Anyway, see you soon, yes?' She kissed his cheek. Squeezed his hands. Allowed him to release himself and crush her to him.

'Soon, yes. I'll come soon, lass.' He could hardly get the words out.

Angela made a mock show of not letting Tiddles go. 'Oh, I can hardly bear to part with her!' she wailed. 'Please don't make me! She's such a poppet. Mum, why can't *I* have a kitten? It's not *fair*!'

Kathleen took the ball of fluff Angela was holding out for her to take, and Kathleen was surprised at how much heavier she felt. They grew so fast, did kittens. Faster than babies did, for sure. 'How long have you got now, love?' Angela's mum wanted to know.

Kathleen told her, to the day. 'Though, knowing my luck, it'll come late,' she said. 'Dad tells me I was almost two weeks behind my due date when I was born. But that's fine. If it's really late, it might even come on my birthday. Which would be nice.'

'It would indeed, love,' Angela's mum said. 'It'd be grand. And we'll see you again soon, yes? I hope you'll be back?'

She nodded towards the house, which was currently bathed in strong, midsummer sunshine. It had hardly rained since Sally'd died. Hardly once. And Kathleen took comfort from that. For the children. Even if she wasn't quite sure why. Perhaps because it just felt as if Sally had arranged it.

And that was that. Terry carried the box to the car – the box he'd had the foresight to bring back with him – and once Tiddles was safely stashed on the back seat of the Cortina, he did a three-point turn and they set off down the road. But not for long.

'Is that your dad?' Terry asked, seeing a figure waving in the distance.

Kathleen peered out too, squinting and having to shield her eyes from the sun. 'It is,' she said. 'He obviously wants to talk to us. Or we've forgotten something. Pull in, and I'll see what he wants.'

Terry had already done so. And as her father approached, and Kathleen began opening the passenger door, he waved her back, then stepped past her and climbed in beside Tiddles, in the back.

'Alright, John?' asked Terry, twisting round in his seat to look at him. 'You coming with us, then?'

Kathleen's father caught his breath and shook his head. 'If I'd an ounce of sense, I could have left this till tomorrow or something. I'm too old for all this dashing around.'

'What's up?' Kathleen said. As he was sitting behind her, she'd had to swivel her whole body to see him. He had a sheen of sweat on his face. 'What on earth have you been doing, Dad?' she asked him.

'Up and down too many stairs and hurrying to catch up with you,' he said ruefully, winking at her as he began ferreting in his trouser pocket. Beside him, in the box, Tiddles mewled.

'To give you this,' he said, pulling out whatever it was that he'd been looking for. He held it out in the space between the front seats of the car. Kathleen gaped. It was a huge wad of notes.

'What on earth?' Terry began.

'Go on, take it, lass. Take it, the pair of you. It's for the both of you. And for your nipper. Help get you set. Help get you back on your feet.' He flapped his hand, once Kathleen had taken it from him. 'Well, do what you like with it. Whatever you like. That's not down to me.'

'But it's a fortune, Dad!' Kathleen said. Even rolled, she could see that. She'd enough money pass through her hands working in the pub for her to know.

'Five hundred pounds,' her dad told her.

She gasped again. 'Five hundred *pounds*? But that's a fortune! Where did you *get* it?'

Kathleen's dad leaned forwards slightly, then twisted his head round to scan the street. 'Our Darren,' he said.

'Darren?' Terry said. 'This money's *Darren's*?'

'In a way of speaking,' John said. 'It's winnings he didn't collect.'

'From the horses?' John nodded. 'But why ever didn't he collect it?'

'Not sure we'll ever know that, lad. Been thinking it through for months, I have, but I'm no nearer knowing. Maybe he didn't realise – but that doesn't make a lot of sense, does it? Not with Darren. Maybe didn't think it was worth it –' He eyed the notes again. 'Much as it is, it's a drop in the ocean compared to what he owed. Or maybe – and this is my best guess – he knew he'd won but lost the ticket. Remember that day, love?' he said, turning to Kathleen. 'That day we went to sort his things out?'

'So *that* was what you found!' Kathleen said, remembering. Then found herself suddenly full of questions. Principal of which being – why did her dad still have it? And why was he giving it to them? Why now? Irene surely didn't know. Couldn't. That much was clear.

Irene knew nothing of this, or it wouldn't even be here.

'I wasn't sure they'd pay up,' her father went on. 'You know what they're like. They'd find some reason. But a bet's a bet, and they did, and then I had to decide, didn't I? Hand it over? Share it out? Help towards some of Darren's debts?'

'But you didn't …' Kathleen mused, trailing off. That much was self-evident.

Her dad shook his head. 'I could've, but I didn't. I thought, "You know what? They don't deserve it." You know as well as I do, love – the sort of people he was getting in with. For what it's worth, I reckon he did have that gun to do a job for someone. Way of paying back what he couldn't find in cash. And a betting slip's anonymous, isn't it? So I cashed it and I brought it home. And then I sat on it …' he finished. ''Till I could think what best to do with it. And now I have. It's yours. Yours and that grandkiddy of mine's.'

Kathleen looked at Terry, smiled a wobbly smile. 'Am I dreaming?'

Her father reached over the seat back and squeezed her shoulder. 'I don't know about you, lass, but I reckon I've just woken up. And' – he glanced around him once again – 'I'd also better go.'

'But, Dad,' she began. She still had so many questions. 'If this was Darren's … you know … what about

Mam?' The word still rankled. 'What if she finds out about it? What if …'

Her dad touched his nose. 'I'm hoping I can rely on you two to keep mum.'

'Oh, but *Dad*,' Kathleen started, now completely overcome. With so much to say, so much to communicate, but so unable to find the words. 'But she'll find out somehow, she's bound to, and all the *secrets* … the whole horribleness of it all …' She waved a hand in front of her. 'I know. Horribleness isn't even a word, is it? But just, *Dad*, can we go on like this, really? You know, the baby, and everything, and you having to sneak around to see us. That's not what I want, Dad! I know it's not for me to make you choose, and I never would. It's just I love you – *we* love you – and I can't do it any more, Dad … She just *can't* –'

She was aware of Terry's hand on her arm. 'Shh a minute. Listen up to your dad, love …'

'You're right,' Kathleen's dad said. 'She can't.' Kathleen was confused now. 'And I don't care if she does find out either. I doubt she will, but I don't care. Well, long as you keep it to yourselves for two weeks.'

'Two weeks?' Terry now seemed as confused as Kathleen. Tiddles mewled again.

'Well, all things considered, our Monica's not a bad 'un. Not really, is she? Hard working. Honest. So I thought two weeks would be fair. Can't just pitch them out on to the street, after all.'

'You mean you're throwing them *out?*' Kathleen said, aghast. She felt Terry's hand back on her arm again.

Her father chuckled. The most glorious sound she'd heard from him in *years*. 'Like I said –' He grinned at Terry. 'That's not *quite* the word I'd choose to use, love. More asking them to "move on". More like that.'

Kathleen looked at him wide-eyed, this father she'd almost forgotten she had. 'But –'

But her father was already clambering back out of the back door. 'We'll speak tonight,' he said, slapping the roof of the car with the back of his hand. 'And I'll see you tomorrow perhaps. Safe journey, all of you.'

And then he was off back up the road.

Acknowledgements

I would like to thank, as always, my fantastic team at HarperCollins, and a big shout out for the return of super editor Vicky – even if it is only for a while! Forever grateful to the wonderful Andrew Lownie and his never-ending support and belief, and last but by no means least, my partner in crime, the very fabulous Lynne Barrett-Lee, who helps me to see the light on the darkest days, and transforms my stories into something amazing.